# "Who the devil are you?"

In no way discomposed, she answered, "My name is Caroline Twinning. And, if you really are the Duke of Twyford, then I'm very much afraid that I'm your ward."

Her announcement was received in perfect silence. A long pause ensued, during which Max sat unmoving, his sharp blue gaze fixed unwaveringly on his visitor. She bore this scrutiny for some minutes, before letting her brows rise in polite and still amused enquiry.

Max closed his eyes and groaned. "Oh, God!"

# FOUR
## IN
# HAND

## STEPHANIE LAURENS

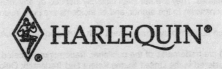

# HARLEQUIN®

TORONTO • NEW YORK • LONDON
AMSTERDAM • PARIS • SYDNEY • HAMBURG
STOCKHOLM • ATHENS • TOKYO • MILAN • MADRID
PRAGUE • WARSAW • BUDAPEST • AUCKLAND

ISBN 0-373-30334-3

FOUR IN HAND

First North American Publication 1999

Copyright © 1993 by Stephanie Laurens

This edition published by arrangement with Harlequin Books S.A.

® and TM are trademarks of the publisher. Trademarks indicated with ® are registered in the United States Patent and Trademark Office, the Canadian Trade Marks Office and in other countries.

Visit us at www.romance.net

Printed in U.S.A.

## STEPHANIE LAURENS

Born in Sri Lanka, Stephanie Laurens has lived mostly in Australia. After qualifying as a scientist, she traveled with her husband extensively through the Far and Middle East, as well as throughout Europe and England. Four years in London gave her the settings for her Regency romances. Now settled once more in Australia, she lives in a comfortable suburban house with her husband, two young children, a mindless but lovable dog and a cat with a crooked leg.

# Chapter One

The rattle of the curtain rings sounded like thunder. The head of the huge four-poster bed remained wreathed in shadow yet Max was aware that for some mysterious reason Masterton was trying to wake him. Surely it couldn't be noon already?

Lying prone amid his warm sheets, his stubbled cheek cushioned in softest down, Max contemplated faking slumber. But Masterton knew he was awake. And knew that he knew, so to speak. Sometimes, the damned man seemed to know his thoughts before he did. And he certainly wouldn't go away before Max capitulated and acknowledged him.

Raising his head, Max opened one very blue eye. His terrifyingly correct valet was standing, entirely immobile, plumb in his line of vision. Masterton's face was impassive. Max frowned.

In response to this sign of approaching wrath, Masterton made haste to state his business. Not that it was *his* business, exactly. Only the combined vote of the rest of the senior staff of Delmere House had induced him to disturb His Grace's rest at the unheard-of hour of nine o'clock. He had every reason to know just how dangerous such an undertaking could be. He had been in the service of Max Rotherbridge, Viscount Delmere, for nine years. It was highly unlikely his master's recent elevation to the estate of His Grace the Duke of Twyford had in any way altered his temper. In fact, from what Masterton had seen, his master had had more to try his temper in dealing with his unexpected inheritance than in all the rest of his thirty-four years.

"Hillshaw wished me to inform you that there's a young lady to see you, Your Grace."

It was still a surprise to Max to hear his new title on his servants' lips. He had to curb an automatic reaction to look about him for whomever they were addressing. A lady. His frown deepened. "No." He dropped his head back into the soft pillows and closed his eyes.

"*No*, Your Grace?"

The bewilderment in his valet's voice was unmistakable. Max's head ached. He had been up until dawn. The evening had started badly, when he had felt constrained to attend a ball given by his maternal aunt, Lady Maxwell. He rarely attended such functions. They were too tame for his liking; the languishing sighs his appearance provoked among all the sweet young things were enough to throw even the most hardened reprobate entirely off his stride. And while he had every claim to that title, seducing débutantes was no longer his style. Not at thirty-four.

He had left the ball as soon as he could and repaired to the discreet villa wherein resided his latest mistress. But the beautiful Carmelita had been in a petulant mood. Why were such women invariably so grasping? And why did they imagine he was so besotted that he'd stand for it? They had had an almighty row, which had ended with him giving the luscious ladybird her congé in no uncertain terms.

From there, he had gone to White's, then Boodles. At that discreet establishment, he had found a group of his cronies and together they had managed to while the night away. And most of the morning, too. He had neither won nor lost. But his head reminded him that he had certainly drunk a lot.

He groaned and raised himself on his elbows, the better to fix Masterton with a gaze which, despite his condition, was remarkably lucid. Speaking in the voice of one instructing a dimwit, he explained. "If there's a woman to see me, she can't be a lady. No lady would call here."

Max thought he was stating the obvious but his henchman stared woodenly at the bedpost. The frown, which had temporarily left his master's handsome face, returned.

Silence.

Max sighed and dropped his head on to his hands. "Have you seen her, Masterton?"

"I did manage to get a glimpse of the young lady when Hillshaw showed her into the library, Your Grace."

Max screwed his eyes tightly shut. Masterton's insistence on using the term "young lady" spoke volumes. All of Max's servants were experienced in telling the difference between ladies and the sort of female who might be expected to call at a bachelor's residence. And if both Masterton and Hillshaw insisted the woman downstairs was a young lady, then a young lady she must be. But it was inconceivable that any young lady would pay a nine o'clock call on the most notorious rake in London.

Taking his master's silence as a sign of commitment to the day, Masterton crossed the large chamber to the wardrobe. "Hillshaw mentioned that the young lady, a Miss Twinning, Your Grace, was under the impression she had an appointment with you."

Max had the sudden conviction that this was a nightmare. He rarely made appointments with anyone and certainly not with young ladies for nine o'clock in the morning. And particularly not with unmarried young ladies. "Miss Twinning?" The name rang no bells. Not even a rattle.

"Yes, Your Grace." Masterton returned to the bed, various garments draped on his arm, a deep blue coat lovingly displayed for approval. "The Bath superfine would, I think, be most appropriate?"

Yielding to the inevitable with a groan, Max sat up.

One floor below, Caroline Twinning sat calmly reading His Grace of Twyford's morning paper in an armchair by his library hearth. If she felt any qualms over the propriety of her present position, she hid them well. Her charmingly candid countenance was free of all nervousness and, as she scanned a frankly libellous account of a garden party enlivened by the scandalous propensities of the ageing Duke of Cumberland, an engaging smile curved her generous lips. In truth, she was looking forward to her meeting with the Duke. She and her sisters had spent a most enjoyable eighteen months, the wine of freedom a heady tonic after their previously monastic existence. But it was time and more for them to embark on the serious business of securing their futures. To do that, they needs must enter the *ton*, that glittering arena thus far denied them. And, for them, the Duke of Twyford undeniably held the key to that particular door.

Hearing the tread of a masculine stride approach the library door, Caroline raised her head, then smiled confidently. Thank heavens the Duke was so easy to manage.

By the time he reached the ground floor, Max had exhausted every possible excuse for the existence of the mysterious Miss Twinning. He had taken little time to dress, having no need to employ extravagant embellishments to distract attention from his long and powerful frame. His broad shoulders and muscular thighs perfectly suited the prevailing fashion. His superbly cut coats looked as though they had been moulded on to him and his buckskin breeches showed not a crease. The understated waistcoat, perfectly tied cravat and shining top-boots which completed the picture were the envy of many an aspiring exquisite. His hair, black as night, was neatly cropped to frame a dark face on which the years had left nothing more than a trace of worldly cynicism. Disdaining the ornamentation common to the times, His Grace of Twyford wore no ring other than a gold signet on his left hand and displayed no fobs or seals. In spite of this, no one setting eyes on him could imagine he was other than he was—one of the most fashionable and wealthy men in the *ton*.

He entered his library, a slight frown in the depths of his midnight-blue eyes. His attention was drawn by a flash of movement as the young lady who had been calmly reading his copy of the morning *Gazette* in his favourite armchair by the hearth folded the paper and laid it aside, before rising to face him. Max halted, blue eyes suddenly intent, all trace of displeasure vanishing as he surveyed his unexpected visitor. His nightmare had transmogrified into a dream. The vision before him was unquestionably a houri. For a number of moments he remained frozen in rapturous contemplation. Then, his rational mind reasserted itself. Not a houri. Houris did not read the *Gazette*. At least, not in his library at nine o'clock in the morning. From the unruly copper curls clustering around her face to the tips of her tiny slippers, showing tantalisingly from under the simply cut and outrageously fashionable gown, there was nothing with which he could find fault. She was built on generous lines, a tall Junoesque figure, deep-bosomed and wide-hipped, but all in the most perfect proportions. Her apricot silk gown did justice to her ample charms, clinging suggestively to a figure of Grecian delight. When his eyes returned to her face, he had time to take in the straight nose and full lips and the dimple that peeked irrepressibly from one cheek before his gaze was drawn to the finely arched brows and long lashes which framed her large eyes. It was only when he looked into the cool grey-green orbs that he saw the twinkle of amusement lurking there. Unused to provoking such a response, he frowned.

"Who, exactly, are you?" His voice, he was pleased to find, was even and his diction clear.

The smile which had been hovering at the corners of those inviting lips finally came into being, disclosing a row of small pearly teeth. But instead of answering his question, the vision replied, "I was waiting for the Duke of Twyford."

Her voice was low and musical. Mentally engaged in considering how to most rapidly dispense with the formalities, Max answered automatically. "I am the Duke."

"You?" For one long moment, utter bewilderment was writ large across her delightful countenance.

For the life of her, Caroline could not hide her surprise. How could this man, of all men, be the Duke? Aside from the fact he was far too young to have been a crony of her father's, the gentleman before her was unquestionably a rake. And a rake of the first order, to boot. Whether the dark-browed, harsh-featured face with its aquiline nose and firm mouth and chin or the lazy assurance with which he had entered the room had contributed to her reading of his character, she could not have said. But the calmly arrogant way his intensely blue eyes had roved from the top of her curls all the way down to her feet, and then just as calmly returned by the same route, as if to make sure he had missed nothing, left her in little doubt of what sort of man she now faced. Secure in the knowledge of being under her guardian's roof, she had allowed the amusement she felt on seeing such decided appreciation glow in the deep blue eyes to show. Now, with those same blue eyes still on her, piercingly perceptive, she felt as if the rug had been pulled from beneath her feet.

Max could hardly miss her stunned look. "For my sins," he added in confirmation.

With a growing sense of unease, he waved his visitor to a seat opposite the huge mahogany desk while he moved to take the chair behind it. As he did so, he mentally shook his head to try to clear it of the thoroughly unhelpful thoughts that kept crowding in. Damn Carmelita!

Caroline, rapidly trying to gauge where this latest disconcerting news left her, came forward to sink into the chair indicated.

Outwardly calm, Max watched the unconsciously graceful glide of her walk, the seductive swing of her hips as she sat down. He would have to find a replacement for Carmelita. His gaze rested speculatively on the beauty before him. Hillshaw had been right. She was unquestionably a lady. Still, that had never stopped him before. And, now he came to look more closely, she was not, he thought, that young. Even better. No rings, which was odd. Another twinge of pain from behind his eyes lent a harshness to his voice. "Who the devil are you?"

The dimple peeped out again. In no way discomposed, she answered, "My name is Caroline Twinning. And, if you really are the Duke of Twyford, then I'm very much afraid I'm your ward."

Her announcement was received in perfect silence. A long pause ensued, during which Max sat unmoving, his sharp blue gaze fixed unwaveringly on his visitor. She bore this scrutiny for some minutes, before letting her brows rise in polite and still amused enquiry.

Max closed his eyes and groaned. "Oh, God."

It had only taken a moment to work it out. The only woman he could not seduce was his own ward. And he had already decided he very definitely wanted to seduce Caroline Twinning. With an effort, he dragged his mind back to the matter at hand. He opened his eyes. Hopefully, she would put his reaction down to natural disbelief. Encountering the grey-green eyes, now even more amused, he was not so sure. "Explain, if you please. Simple language only. I'm not up to unravelling mysteries at the moment."

Caroline could not help grinning. She had noticed twinges of what she guessed to be pain passing spasmodically through the blue eyes. "If your head hurts that much, why don't you try an ice-pack? I assure you I won't mind."

Max threw her a look of loathing. His head felt as if it was splitting, but how dared she be so lost to all propriety as to notice, let alone mention it? Still, she was perfectly right. An ice-pack was exactly what he needed. With a darkling look, he reached for the bell pull.

Hillshaw came in answer to his summons and received the order for an ice-pack without noticeable perturbation. "Now, Your Grace?"

"Of course now! What use will it be later?" Max winced at the sound of his own voice.

"As Your Grace wishes." The sepulchral tones left Max in no doubt of his butler's deep disapproval.

As the door closed behind Hillshaw, Max lay back in the chair, his fingers at his temples, and fixed Caroline with an unwavering stare. "You may commence."

She smiled, entirely at her ease once more. "My father was Sir Thomas Twinning. He was an old friend of the Duke of Twyford—the previous Duke, I imagine."

Max nodded. "My uncle. I inherited the title from him. He was killed unexpectedly three months ago, together with his two sons. I never expected to inherit the estate, so am unfamiliar with whatever arrangements your parent may have made with the last Duke."

Caroline nodded and waited until Hillshaw, delivering the requested ice-pack on a silver salver to his master, withdrew. "I see. When my father died eighteen months ago, my sisters and I were informed that he had left us to the guardianship of the Duke of Twyford."

"Eighteen months ago? What have you been doing since then?"

"We stayed on the estate for a time. It passed to a distant cousin and he was prepared to let us remain. But it seemed senseless to stay buried there forever. The Duke wanted us to join his household immediately, but we were in mourning. I persuaded him to let us go to my late stepmother's family in New York. They'd always wanted us to visit and it seemed the perfect opportunity. I wrote to him when we were in

New York, telling him we would call on him when we returned to England and giving him the date of our expected arrival. He replied and suggested I call on him today. And so, here I am.''

Max saw it all now. Caroline Twinning was yet another part of his damnably awkward inheritance. Having led a life of unfettered hedonism from his earliest days, a rakehell ever since he came on the town, Max had soon understood that his lifestyle required capital to support it. So he had ensured his estates were all run efficiently and well. The Delmere estates he had inherited from his father were a model of modern estate management. But his uncle Henry had never had much real interest in his far larger holdings. After the tragic boating accident which had unexpectedly foisted on to him the responsibilities of the dukedom of Twyford, Max had found a complete overhaul of all his uncle's numerous estates was essential if they were not to sap the strength from his more prosperous Delmere holdings. The last three months had been spent in constant upheaval, with the old Twyford retainers trying to come to grips with the new Duke and his very different style. For Max, they had been three months of unending work. Only this week, he had finally thought that the end of the worst was in sight. He had packed his long-suffering secretary, Joshua Cummings, off home for a much needed rest. And now, quite clearly, the next chapter in the saga of his Twyford inheritance was about to start.

"You mentioned sisters. How many?"

"My half-sisters, really. There are four of us, altogether."

The lightness of the answer made Max instantly suspicious. "How old?"

There was a noticeable hesitation before Caroline answered, "Twenty, nineteen and eighteen."

The effect on Max was electric. "Good Lord! They didn't accompany you here, did they?"

Bewildered, Caroline replied, "No. I left them at the hotel."

"Thank God for that," said Max. Encountering Caroline's enquiring gaze, he smiled. "If anyone had seen them entering here, it would have been around town in a flash that I was setting up a harem."

The smile made Caroline blink. At his words, her grey eyes widened slightly. She could hardly pretend not to understand. Noticing the peculiar light in the blue eyes as they rested on her, it seemed a very good thing she was the Duke's ward. From her admittedly small understanding of the morals of his type, she suspected her position would keep her safe as little else might.

Unbeknown to her, Max was thinking precisely the same thing. And resolving to divest himself of his latest inherited responsibility with all possible speed. Aside from having no wish whatever to figure as the guardian of four young ladies of marriageable age, he needed to clear the obstacles from his path to Caroline Twinning. It occurred to him that her explanation of her life history had been curiously glib and decidedly short on detail. "Start at the beginning. Who was your mother and when did she die?"

Caroline had come unprepared to recite her history, imagining the Duke to be cognizant of the facts. Still, in the circumstances, she could hardly refuse. "My mother was Caroline Farningham, of the Staffordshire Farninghams."

Max nodded. An ancient family, well-known and well-connected.

Caroline's gaze had wandered to the rows of books lining the shelves behind the Duke. "She died shortly after I was born. I never knew her. After some years, my father married again, this time to the daughter of a local family who were about to leave for the colonies. Eleanor was very good to me and she looked after all of us comfortably, until she died six years ago. Of course, my father was disappointed that he never had a son and he rarely paid any attention to the four of us, so it was all left up to Eleanor."

The more he heard of him, the more Max was convinced that Sir Thomas Twinning had had a screw loose. He had clearly been a most unnatural parent. Still, the others were only Miss Twinning's half-sisters. Presumably they were not all as ravishing as she. It occurred to him that he should ask for clarification on this point but, before he could properly phrase the question, another and equally intriguing matter came to mind.

"Why was it none of you was presented before? If your father was sufficiently concerned to organize a guardian for you, surely the easiest solution would have been to have handed you into the care of husbands?"

Caroline saw no reason not to satisfy what was,

after all, an entirely understandable curiosity. "We were never presented because my father disapproved of such…oh, frippery pastimes! To be perfectly honest, I sometimes thought he disapproved of women in general."

Max blinked.

Caroline continued, "As for marriage, he had organized that after a fashion. I was supposed to have married Edgar Mulhall, our neighbour." Involuntarily, her face assumed an expression of distaste.

Max was amused. "Wouldn't he do?"

Caroline's gaze returned to the saturnine face. "You haven't met him or you wouldn't need to ask. He's…" She wrinkled her nose as she sought for an adequate description. "Righteous," she finally pronounced.

At that, Max laughed. "Clearly out of the question."

Caroline ignored the provocation in the blue eyes. "Papa had similar plans for my sisters, only, as he never noticed they were of marriageable age and I never chose to bring it to his attention, nothing came of them either."

Perceiving Miss Twinning's evident satisfaction, Max made a mental note to beware of her manipulative tendencies. "Very well. So much for the past. Now to the future. What was your arrangement with my uncle?"

The grey-green gaze was entirely innocent as it rested on his face. Max did not know whether to believe it or not.

"Well, it was really his idea, but it seemed a perfectly sensible one to me. He suggested we should be presented to the *ton*. I suspect he intended to find us suitable husbands and so bring his guardianship to an end." She paused, thinking. "I'm not aware of the terms of my father's will, but I assume such arrangements terminate should we marry?"

"Very likely," agreed Max. The throbbing in his head had eased considerably. His uncle's plan had much to recommend it, but, personally, he would much prefer not to have any wards at all. And he would be damned if he would have Miss Twinning as his ward—that would cramp his style far too much. There were a few things even reprobates such as he held sacred and guardianship was one.

He knew she was watching him but made no further comment, his eyes fixed frowningly on his blotter as he considered his next move. At last, looking up at her, he said, "I've heard nothing of this until now. I'll have to get my solicitors to sort it out. Which firm handles your affairs?"

"Whitney and White. In Chancery Lane."

"Well, at least that simplifies matters. They handle the Twyford estates as well as my others." He laid the ice-pack down and looked at Caroline, a slight frown in his blue eyes. "Where are you staying?"

"Grillon's. We arrived yesterday."

Another thought occurred to Max. "On what have you been living for the last eighteen months?"

"Oh, we all had money left us by our mothers. We arranged to draw on that and leave our patrimony untouched."

Max nodded slowly. "But who had you in charge?

You can't have travelled halfway around the world alone."

For the first time during this strange interview, Max saw Miss Twinning blush, ever so slightly. "Our maid and coachman, who acted as our courier, stayed with us."

The airiness of the reply did not deceive Max. "Allow me to comment, Miss Twinning, as your potential guardian, that such an arrangement will not do. Regardless of what may have been acceptable overseas, such a situation will not pass muster in London." He paused, considering the proprieties for what was surely the first time in his life. "At least you're at Grillon's for the moment. That's safe enough."

After another pause, during which his gaze did not leave Caroline's face, he said, "I'll see Whitney this morning and settle the matter. I'll call on you at two to let you know how things have fallen out." A vision of himself meeting a beautiful young lady and attempting to converse with her within the portals of fashionable Grillon's, under the fascinated gaze of all the other patrons, flashed before his eyes. "On second thoughts, I'll take you for a drive in the Park. That way," he continued in reply to the question in her grey-green eyes, "we might actually get a chance to talk."

He tugged the bell pull and Hillshaw appeared. "Have the carriage brought around. Miss Twinning is returning to Grillon's."

"Yes, Your Grace."

"Oh, no! I couldn't put you to so much trouble," said Caroline.

"My dear child," drawled Max, "my wards would certainly not go about London in hacks. See to it, Hillshaw."

"Yes, Your Grace." Hillshaw withdrew, for once in perfect agreement with his master.

Caroline found the blue eyes, which had quizzed her throughout this exchange, still regarding her, a gently mocking light in their depths. But she was a lady of no little courage and smiled back serenely, unknowingly sealing her fate.

Never, thought Max, had he met a woman so attractive. One way or another, he would break the ties of guardianship. A short silence fell, punctuated by the steady ticking of the long case clock in the corner. Max took the opportunity afforded by Miss Twinning's apparent fascination with the rows of leather-bound tomes at his back to study her face once more. A fresh face, full of lively humour and a brand of calm self-possession which, in his experience, was rarely found in young women. Undoubtedly a woman of character.

His sharp ears caught the sound of carriage wheels in the street. He rose and Caroline perforce rose, too. "Come, Miss Twinning. Your carriage awaits."

Max led her to the front door but forbore to go any further, bowing over her hand gracefully before allowing Hillshaw to escort her to the waiting carriage. The less chance there was for anyone to see him with her the better. At least until he had solved this guardianship tangle.

As soon as the carriage door was shut by the majestic Hillshaw, the horses moved forward at a trot.

Caroline lay back against the squabs, her gaze fixed unseeingly on the near-side window as the carriage traversed fashionable London. Bemused, she tried to gauge the effect of the unexpected turn their futures had taken. Imagine having a guardian like that!

Although surprised at being redirected from Twyford House to Delmere House, she had still expected to meet the vague and amenable gentleman who had so readily acquiesced, albeit by correspondence, to all her previous suggestions. Her mental picture of His Grace of Twyford had been of a man in late middle age, bewigged as many of her father's generation were, distinctly past his prime and with no real interest in dealing with four lively young women. She spared a small smile as she jettisoned her preconceived image. Instead of a comfortable, fatherly figure, she would now have to deal with a man who, if first impressions were anything to go by, was intelligent, quick-witted and far too perceptive for her liking. To imagine the new Duke would not know to a nicety how to manage four young women was patently absurd. If she had been forced to express an opinion, Caroline would have said that, with the present Duke of Twyford, managing women was a speciality. Furthermore, given his undoubted experience, she strongly suspected he would be highly resistant to feminine cajoling in any form. A frown clouded her grey-green eyes. She was not entirely sure she approved of the twist their fates had taken. Thinking back over the recent interview, she smiled. He had not seemed too pleased with the idea himself.

For a moment, she considered the possibility of coming to some agreement with the Duke, essentially breaking the guardianship clause of her father's will. But only for a moment. It was true she had never been presented to the *ton* but she had cut her social eyeteeth long ago. While the idea of unlimited freedom to do as they pleased might sound tempting, there was the undeniable fact that she and her half-sisters were heiresses of sorts. Her father, having an extremely repressive notion of the degree of knowledge which could be allowed mere females, had never been particularly forthcoming regarding their eventual state. Yet there had never been any shortage of funds in all the years Caroline could remember. She rather thought they would at least be comfortably dowered. Such being the case, the traps and pitfalls of society, without the protection of a guardian, such as the Duke of Twyford, were not experiences to which she would willingly expose her sisters.

As the memory of a certain glint in His grace of Twyford's eye and the distinctly determined set of his jaw drifted past her mind's eye, the unwelcome possibility that he might repudiate them, for whatever reasons, hove into view. Undoubtedly, if there was any way to overset their guardianship, His Grace would find it. Unaccountably, she was filled with an inexplicable sense of disappointment.

Still, she told herself, straightening in a purposeful way, it was unlikely there was anything he could do about it. And she rather thought they would be perfectly safe with the new Duke of Twyford, as long as they *were* his wards. She allowed her mind to dwell on the question of whether she really wanted to be safe from the Duke of Twyford for several minutes before giving herself a mental shake. Great heavens! She had only just met the man and here she was, mooning over him like a green girl! She tried to frown but the action dissolved into a sheepish grin at her own susceptibility. Settling more comfortably in the corner of the luxurious carriage, she fell to rehearsing her description of what had occurred in anticipation of her sisters' eager questions.

Within minutes of Caroline Twinning's departure from Delmere House, Max had issued a succession of orders, one of which caused Mr. Hubert Whitney, son of Mr. Josiah Whitney, the patriarch of the firm Whitney and White, Solicitors, of Chancery Lane, to present himself at Delmere House just before eleven. Mr. Whitney was a dry, desiccated man of uncertain age, very correctly attired in dusty black. He was his father's son in every way and, now that his sire was no longer able to leave his bed, he attended to all his father's wealthier clients. As Hillshaw showed him into the well-appointed library, he breathed a sigh of relief, not for the first time, that it was Max Rotherbridge who had inherited the difficult Twyford estates. Unknown to Max, Mr. Whitney held him in particular esteem, frequently wishing that others among his clients could be equally straightforward and decisive. It really made life so much easier.

Coming face-to-face with his favourite client, Mr. Whitney was immediately informed that His Grace, the Duke of Twyford, was in no way amused to find he was apparently the guardian of four marriageable young ladies. Mr. Whitney was momentarily at a loss. Luckily, he had brought with him all the current Twyford papers and the Twinning documents were among these. Finding that his employer did not intend to upbraid him for not having informed him of a circumstance which, he was only too well aware, he should have brought forward long ago, he applied himself to assessing the terms of the late Sir Thomas Twinning's will. Having refreshed his memory on its details, he then turned to the late Duke's will.

Max stood by the fire, idly watching. He liked Whitney. He did not fluster and he knew his business.

Finally, Mr. Whitney pulled the gold pince-nez from his face and glanced at his client. "Sir Thomas Twinning predeceased your uncle, and, under the terms of your uncle's will, it's quite clear you inherit all his responsibilities."

Max's black brows had lowered. "So I'm stuck with this guardianship?"

Mr. Whitney pursed his lips. "I wouldn't go so far as to say that. The guardianship could be broken, I fancy, as it's quite clear Sir Thomas did not intend you, personally, to be his daughters' guardian." He gazed at the fire and solemnly shook his head. "No one, I'm sure, could doubt that."

Max smiled wryly.

"However," Mr. Whitney continued, "should you succeed in dissolving the guardianship clause, then the young ladies will be left with no protector. Did I understand you correctly in thinking they are presently in London and plan to remain for the Season?"

It did not need a great deal of intelligence to see where Mr. Whitney's discourse was heading. Exasperated at having his usually comfortably latent conscience pricked into life, Max stalked to the window and stood looking out at the courtyard beyond, hands clasped behind his straight back. "Good God, man! You can hardly think I'm a suitable guardian for four sweet young things!"

Mr. Whitney, thinking the Duke could manage very well if he chose to do so, persevered. "There remains the question of who, in your stead, would act for them."

The certain knowledge of what would occur if he abandoned four inexperienced, gently reared girls to the London scene, to the mercies of well-bred wolves who roamed its streets, crystallised in Max's unwilling mind. This was closely followed by the uncomfortable thought that he was considered the leader of one such pack, generally held to be the most dangerous. He could hardly refuse to be Caroline Twinning's guardian, only to set her up as his mistress. No. There was a limit to what even he could face down. Resolutely thrusting aside the memory, still vivid, of a pair of grey-green eyes, he turned to Mr. Whitney and growled, "All right, dammit! What do I need to know?"

Mr. Whitney smiled benignly and started to fill him in on the Twinning family history, much as Caroline had told it. Max interrupted him. "Yes, I know all that! Just tell me in round figures—how much is each of them worth?"

Mr. Whitney named a figure and Max's brows rose.

For a moment, the Duke was entirely bereft of speech. He moved towards his desk and seated himself again.

"Each?"

Mr. Whitney merely inclined his head in assent. When the Duke remained lost in thought, he continued, "Sir Thomas was a very shrewd businessman, Your Grace."

"So it would appear. So each of these girls is an heiress in her own right?"

This time, Mr. Whitney nodded decisively.

Max was frowning.

"Of course," Mr. Whitney went on, consulting the documents on his knee, "you would only be responsible for the three younger girls."

Instantly he had his client's attention, the blue eyes oddly piercing. "Oh? Why is that?"

"Under the terms of their father's will, the Misses Twinning were given into the care of the Duke of Twyford until they attained the age of twenty-five or married. According to my records, I believe Miss Twinning to be nearing her twenty-sixth birthday. So she could, should she wish, assume responsibility for herself."

Max's relief was palpable. But hard on its heels came another consideration. Caroline Twinning had recognised his interest in her—hardly surprising as he had taken no pains to hide it. If she knew he was not her guardian, she would keep him at arm's length. Well, try to, at least. But Caroline Twinning was not a green girl. The aura of quiet self-assurance which clung to her suggested she would not be an easy conquest. Obviously, it would be preferable if she continued to believe she was protected from him by his guardianship. That way, he would have no difficulty in approaching her, his reputation notwithstanding. In fact, the more he thought of it, the more merits he could see in the situation. Perhaps, in this case, he could have his cake and eat it too? He eyed Mr. Whitney. "Miss Twinning knows nothing of the terms of her father's will. At present, she believes herself to be my ward, along with her half-sisters. Is there any pressing need to inform her of her change in status?"

Mr. Whitney blinked owlishly, a considering look suffusing his face as he attempted to unravel the Duke's motives for wanting Miss Twinning to remain as his ward. Particularly after wanting to dissolve the guardianship altogether. Max Rotherbridge did not normally vacillate.

Max, perfectly sensible of Mr. Whitney's thoughts, put forward the most acceptable excuses he could think of. "For a start, whether she's twenty-four or twenty-six, she's just as much in need of protection as her sisters. Then, too, there's the question of propriety. If it was generally known she was not my ward, it would be exceedingly difficult for her to be seen in my company. And as I'll still be guardian to her sisters, and as they'll be residing in one of my establishments, the situation could become a trifle delicate, don't you think?"

It was not necessary for him to elaborate. Mr. Whitney saw the difficulty clearly enough. It was his turn to frown. "What you say is quite true." Hubert Whitney had no opinion whatever in the ability of the young ladies to manage their affairs. "At present, there is nothing I can think of that requires Miss Twinning's agreement. I expect it can do no harm to leave her in ignorance of her status until she weds.''

The mention of marriage brought a sudden check to Max's racing mind but he resolutely put the disturbing notion aside for later examination. He had too much to do today.

Mr. Whitney was continuing, ''How do you plan to handle the matter, if I may make so bold as to ask?''

Max had already given the thorny problem of how four young ladies could be presented to the *ton* under his protection, without raising a storm, some thought. ''I propose to open up Twyford House immediately. They can stay there. I intend to ask my aunt, Lady Benborough, to stand as the girls' sponsor. I'm sure she'll be only too thrilled. It'll keep her amused for the Season.''

Mr. Whitney was acquainted with Lady Benborough. He rather thought it would. A smile curved his thin lips.

The Duke stood, bringing the interview to a close.

Mr. Whitney rose. ''That seems most suitable. If there's anything further in which we can assist Your Grace, we'll be only too delighted.''

Max nodded in response to this formal statement. As Mr. Whitney bowed, prepared to depart, Max, a past master of social intrigue, saw one last hole in the wall and moved to block it. ''If there's any matter you wish to discuss with Miss Twinning, I suggest you do it through me, as if I was, in truth, her guardian. As you handle both our estates, there can really be no impropriety in keeping up appearances. For Miss Twinning's sake.''

Mr. Whitney bowed again. ''I foresee no problems, Your Grace.''

# Chapter Two

After Mr. Whitney left, Max issued a set of rapid and comprehensive orders to his majordomo Wilson. In response, his servants flew to various corners of London, some to Twyford House, others to certain agencies specializing in the hire of household staff to the élite of the *ton*. One footman was despatched with a note from the Duke to an address in Half Moon Street, requesting the favour of a private interview with his paternal aunt, Lady Benborough.

As Max had intended, his politely worded missive intrigued his aunt. Wondering what had prompted such a strange request from her reprehensible nephew, she immediately granted it and settled down to await his coming with an air of pleasurable anticipation.

Max arrived at the small house shortly after noon. He found his aunt attired in a very becoming gown of purple sarsenet with a new and unquestionably modish wig perched atop her commanding visage. Max, bowing elegantly before her, eyed the wig askance.

Augusta Benborough sighed. "Well, I suppose I'll

have to send it back, if that's the way you feel about it!''

Max grinned and bent to kiss the proffered cheek. "Definitely not one of your better efforts, Aunt."

She snorted. "Unfortunately, I can hardly claim you know nothing about it. It's the very latest fashion, I'll have you know." Max raised one laconic brow. "Yes, well," continued his aunt, "I dare say you're right. Not quite my style."

As she waited while he disposed his long limbs in a chair opposite the corner of the chaise where she sat, propped up by a pile of colourful cushions, she passed a critical glance over her nephew's elegant figure. How he contrived to look so precise when she knew he cared very little how he appeared was more than she could tell. She had heard it said that his man was a genius. Personally, she was of the opinion it was Max's magnificent physique and dark good looks that carried the day.

"I hope you're going to satisfy my curiosity without a great deal of roundaboutation."

"My dear aunt, when have I ever been other than direct?"

She looked at him shrewdly. "Want a favour, do you? Can't imagine what it is but you'd better be quick about asking. Miriam will be back by one and I gather you'd rather not have her listening." Miriam Alford was a faded spinster cousin of Lady Benborough's who lived with her, filling the post of companion to the fashionable old lady. "I sent her to Hatchard's when I got your note," she added in explanation.

Max smiled. Of all his numerous relatives, his Aunt Benborough, his father's youngest sister, was his favourite. While the rest of them, his mother included, constantly tried to reform him by ringing peals over him, appealing to his sense of what was acceptable, something he steadfastly denied any knowledge of, Augusta Benborough rarely made any comment on his lifestyle or the numerous scandals this provoked. When he had first come on the town, it had rapidly been made plain to his startled family that in Max they beheld a reincarnation of the second Viscount Delmere. If even half the tales were true, Max's great-grandfather had been a thoroughly unprincipled character, entirely devoid of morals. Lady Benborough, recently widowed, had asked Max to tea and had taken the opportunity to inform him in no uncertain terms of her opinion of his behaviour. She had then proceeded to outline all his faults, in detail. However, as she had concluded by saying that she fully expected her tirade to have no effect whatsoever on his subsequent conduct, nor could she imagine how anyone in their right mind could think it would, Max had borne the ordeal with an equanimity which would have stunned his friends. She had eventually dismissed him with the words, "Having at least had the politeness to hear me out, you may now depart and continue to go to hell in your own fashion and with my good will."

Now a widow of many years' standing, she was still a force to be reckoned with. She remained fully absorbed in the affairs of the *ton* and continued to be seen at all the crushes and every gala event. Max knew she was as shrewd as she could hold together and, above all, had an excellent sense of humour. All in all, she was just what he needed.

"I've come to inform you that, along with all the other encumbrances I inherited from Uncle Henry, I seem to have acquired four wards."

"*You?*" Lady Benborough's rendering of the word was rather more forceful than Miss Twinning's had been.

Max nodded. "Me. Four young ladies, one, the only one I've so far set eyes on, as lovely a creature as any other likely to be presented this Season."

"Good God! Who was so besotted as to leave four young girls in your care?" If anything, her ladyship was outraged at the very idea. Then, the full impact of the situation struck her. Her eyes widened. "Oh, good lord!" She collapsed against her cushions, laughing uncontrollably.

Knowing this was an attitude he was going to meet increasingly in the next few weeks, Max sighed. In an even tone suggestive of long suffering, he pointed out the obvious. "They weren't left to me but to my esteemed and now departed uncle's care. Mind you, I can't see that he'd have been much use to 'em either."

Wiping the tears from her eyes, Lady Benborough considered this view. "Can't see it myself," she admitted. "Henry always was a slow-top. Who are they?"

"The Misses Twinning. From Hertfordshire." Max proceeded to give her a brief résumé of the life history of the Twinnings, ending with the information that it transpired all four girls were heiresses.

Augusta Benborough was taken aback. "And you say they're beautiful to boot?"

"The one I've seen, Caroline, the eldest, most definitely is."

"Well, if anyone should know it's you!" replied her ladyship testily. Max acknowledged the comment with the slightest inclination of his head.

Lady Benborough's mind was racing. "So, what do you want with me?"

"What I would *like,* dearest Aunt," said Max, with his sweetest smile, "is for you to act as chaperon to the girls and present them to the *ton.*" Max paused. His aunt said nothing, sitting quite still with her sharp blue eyes, very like his own, fixed firmly on his face. He continued. "I'm opening up Twyford House. It'll be ready for them tomorrow. I'll stand the nonsense— all of it." Still she said nothing. "Will you do it?"

Augusta Benborough thought she would like nothing better than to be part of the hurly-burly of the marriage game again. But four? All at once? Still, there was Max's backing, and that would count for a good deal. Despite his giving the distinct impression of total uninterest in anything other than his own pleasure, she knew from experience that, should he feel inclined, Max could and would perform feats impossible for those with lesser clout in the fashionable world. Years after the event, she had learned that, when her youngest son had embroiled himself in a scrape so hideous that even now she shuddered to think of it, it had been Max who had rescued him.

And apparently for no better reason than it had been bothering her. She still owed him for that.

But there were problems. Her own jointure was not particularly large and, while she had never asked Max for relief, turning herself out in the style he would expect of his wards' chaperon was presently beyond her slender means. Hesitantly, she said, "My own wardrobe…"

"Naturally you'll charge all costs you incur in this business to me," drawled Max, his voice bored as he examined through his quizzing glass a china cat presently residing on his aunt's mantelpiece. He knew perfectly well his aunt managed on a very slim purse but was too wise to offer direct assistance which would, he knew, be resented, not only by the lady herself but also by her pompous elder son.

"Can I take Miriam with me to Twyford House?"

With a shrug, Max assented. "Aside from anything else, she might come in handy with four charges."

"When can I meet them?"

"They're staying at Grillon's. I'm taking Miss Twinning for a drive this afternoon to tell her what I've decided. I'll arrange for them to move to Twyford House tomorrow afternoon. I'll send Wilson to help you and Mrs. Alford in transferring to Mount Street. It would be best, I suppose, if you could make the move in the morning. You'll want to familiarize yourself with the staff and so on." Bethinking himself that it would be wise to have one of his own well-trained staff on hand, he added, "I suppose I can let you have Wilson for a week or two, until you settle in. I suggest you and I meet the Misses Twinning when they arrive—shall we say at three?''

Lady Benborough was entranced by the way her nephew seemed to dismiss complications like opening and staffing a mansion overnight. Still, with the efficient and reliable Wilson on the job, presumably it would be done. Feeling a sudden and unexpected surge of excitement at the prospect of embarking on the Season with a definite purpose in life, she drew a deep breath. ''Very well. I'll do it!''

''Good!'' Max stood. ''I'll send Wilson to call on you this afternoon.''

His aunt, already engrossed in the matter of finding husbands for the Twinning chits, looked up. ''Have you seen the other three girls?''

Max shook his head. Imagining the likely scene should they be on hand this afternoon when he called for Miss Twinning, he closed his eyes in horror. He could just hear the *on-dits*. ''And I hope to God I don't see them in Grillon's foyer either!''

Augusta Benborough laughed.

When he called at Grillon's promptly at two, Max was relieved to find Miss Twinning alone in the foyer, seated on a chaise opposite the door, her bonnet beside her. He was not to know that Caroline had had to exert every last particle of persuasion to achieve this end. And she had been quite unable to prevent her three sisters from keeping watch from the windows of their bedchambers.

As she had expected, she had had to describe His Grace of Twyford in detail for her sisters. Looking up at the figure striding across the foyer towards her, she did not think she had done too badly. What had been hardest to convey was the indefinable air that hung about him—compelling, exciting, it immediately brought to mind a whole range of emotions well-bred young ladies were not supposed to comprehend, let alone feel. As he took her hand for an instant in his own, and smiled down at her in an oddly lazy way, she decided she had altogether underestimated the attractiveness of that sleepy smile. It was really quite devastating.

Within a minute, Caroline found herself on the box seat of a fashionable curricle drawn by a pair of beautiful but restive bays. She resisted the temptation to glance up at the first-floor windows where she knew the other three would be stationed. Max mounted to the driving seat and the diminutive tiger, who had been holding the horses' heads, swung up behind. Then they were off, tacking through the traffic towards Hyde Park.

Caroline resigned herself to silence until the safer precincts of the Park were reached. However, it seemed the Duke was quite capable of conversing intelligently while negotiating the chaos of the London streets.

"I trust Grillon's has met with your approval thus far?"

"Oh, yes. They've been most helpful," returned Caroline. "Were you able to clarify the matter of our guardianship?"

Max was unable to suppress a smile at her directness. He nodded, his attention temporarily claimed by the off-side horse which had decided to take exception to a monkey dancing on the pavement, accompanied by an accordion player.

"Mr. Whitney has assured me that, as I am the Duke of Twyford, I must therefore be your guardian." He had allowed his reluctance to find expression in his tone. As the words left his lips, he realised that the unconventional woman beside him might well ask why he found the role of protector to herself and her sisters so distasteful. He immediately went on the attack. "And, in that capacity, I should like to know how you have endeavoured to come by Parisian fashions?"

His sharp eyes missed little and his considerable knowledge of feminine attire told him Miss Twinning's elegant pelisse owed much to the French. But France was at war with England and Paris no longer the playground of the rich.

Initially stunned that he should know enough to come so close to the truth, Caroline quickly realised the source of his knowledge. A spark of amusement danced in her eyes. She smiled and answered readily, "I assure you we did not run away to Brussels instead of New York."

"Oh, I wasn't afraid of that!" retorted Max, perfectly willing to indulge in plain speaking. "If you'd been in Brussels, I'd have heard of it."

"Oh?" Caroline turned a fascinated gaze on him. Max smiled down at her.

Praying she was not blushing, Caroline strove to get the conversation back on a more conventional course. "Actually, you're quite right about the clothes, they are Parisian. But not from the Continent. There were two *couturières* from Paris on the boat going to New York. They asked if they could dress us, needing the business to become known in America. It was really most fortunate. We took the opportunity to get quite a lot made up before we returned— we'd been in greys for so long that none of us had anything suitable to wear.''

"How did you find American society?"

Caroline reminded herself to watch her tongue. She did not delude herself that just because the Duke was engaged in handling a team of high-couraged cattle through the busy streets of London he was likely to miss any slip she made. She was rapidly learning to respect the intelligence of this fashionable rake. "Quite frankly, we found much to entertain us. Of course, our relatives were pleased to see us and organised a great many outings and entertainments.'' No need to tell him they had had a riotous time.

"Did the tone of the society meet with your approval?"

He had already told her he would have known if they had been in Europe. Did he have connections in New York? How much could he know of their junketing? Caroline gave herself a mental shake. How absurd! He had not known of their existence until this morning. "Well, to be sure, it wasn't the same as here. Many more cits and half-pay officers about. And, of course, nothing like the *ton*.''

Unknowingly, her answer brought some measure of relief to Max. Far from imagining his new-found wards had been indulging in high living abroad, he had been wondering whether they had any social experience at all. Miss Twinning's reply told him that she, at least, knew enough to distinguish the less acceptable among society's hordes.

They had reached the gates of the Park and turned into the carriage drive. Soon, the curricle was bowling along at a steady pace under the trees, still devoid of any but the earliest leaves. A light breeze lifted the ends of the ribbons on Caroline's hat and playfully danced along the horses' dark manes.

Max watched as Caroline gazed about her with interest. "I'm afraid you'll not see many notables at this hour. Mostly nursemaids and their charges. Later, between three and five, it'll be crowded. The Season's not yet begun in earnest, but by now most people will have returned to town. And the Park is the place to be seen. All the old biddies come here to exchange the latest *on-dits* and all the young ladies promenade along the walks with their beaux."

"I see." Caroline smiled to herself, a secret smile as she imagined how she and her sisters would fit into this scene.

Max saw the smile and was puzzled. Caroline Twinning was decidedly more intelligent than the women with whom he normally consorted. He could not guess her thoughts and was secretly surprised at wanting to know them. Then, he remembered one piece of vital information he had yet to discover. "Apropos of my uncle's plan to marry you all off, satisfy my curiosity, Miss Twinning. What do your sisters look like?"

This was the question she had been dreading. Caroline hesitated, searching for precisely the right words with which to get over the difficult ground. "Well, they've always been commonly held to be well to pass."

Max noted the hesitation. He interpreted her careful phrasing to mean that the other three girls were no more than average. He nodded, having suspected as much, and allowed the subject to drop.

They rounded the lake and he slowed his team to a gentle trot. "As your guardian, I've made certain arrangements for your immediate future." He noticed the grey eyes had flown to his face. "Firstly, I've opened Twyford House. Secondly, I've arranged for my aunt, Lady Benborough, to act as your chaperon for the Season. She's very well-connected and will know exactly how everything should be managed. You may place complete confidence in her advice. You will remove from Grillon's tomorrow. I'll send my man, Wilson, to assist you in the move to Twyford House. He'll call for you at two tomorrow. I presume that gives you enough time to pack?"

Caroline assumed the question to be rhetorical. She was stunned. He had not known they existed at nine this morning. How could he have organised all that since ten?

Thinking he may as well clear all the looming fences while he was about it, Max added, "As for funds, I presume your earlier arrangements still apply. However, should you need any further advances, as I now hold the purse-strings of your patrimonies, you may apply directly to me."

His last statement succeeded in convincing Caroline that it would not be wise to underestimate this Duke. Despite having only since this morning to think about it, he had missed very little. And, as he held the purse-strings, he could call the tune. As she had foreseen, life as the wards of a man as masterful and domineering as the present Duke of Twyford was rapidly proving to be was definitely not going to be as unfettered as they had imagined would be the case with his vague and easily led uncle. There were, however, certain advantages in the changed circumstances and she, for one, could not find it in her to repine.

More people were appearing in the Park, strolling about the lawns sloping down to the river and gathering in small groups by the carriageway, laughing and chatting.

A man of slight stature, mincing along beside the carriage drive, looked up in startled recognition as they passed. He was attired in a bottle-green coat with the most amazing amount of frogging Caroline had ever seen. In place of a cravat, he seemed to be wearing a very large floppy bow around his neck. "Who on earth was that quiz?" she asked.

"That quiz, my dear ward, is none other than Walter Millington, one of the fops. In spite of his absurd clothes, he's unexceptionable enough but he has a sharp tongue so it's wise for young ladies to stay on his right side. Don't laugh at him."

Two old ladies in an ancient landau were staring at them with an intensity which in lesser persons would be considered rude.

Max did not wait to be asked. "And those are the Misses Berry. They're as old as bedamned and know absolutely everyone. Kind souls. One's entirely vague and the other's sharp as needles.''

Caroline smiled. His potted histories were entertaining.

A few minutes later, the gates came into view and Max headed his team in that direction. Caroline saw a horseman pulled up by the carriage drive a little way ahead. His face clearly registered recognition of the Duke's curricle and the figure driving it. Then his eyes passed to her and stopped. At five and twenty, Caroline had long grown used to the effect she had on men, particularly certain sorts of men. As they drew nearer, she saw that the gentleman was impeccably attired and had the same rakish air as the Duke. The rider held up a hand in greeting and she expected to feel the curricle slow. Instead, it flashed on, the Duke merely raising a hand in an answering salute.

Amused, Caroline asked, ''And who, pray tell, was that?''

Max was thinking that keeping his friends in ignorance of Miss Twinning was going to prove impossible. Clearly, he would be well-advised to spend some time planning the details of this curious seduction, or he might find himself with rather more competition than he would wish. ''That was Lord Ramsleigh.''

''A friend of yours?''

''Precisely.''

Caroline laughed at the repressive tone. The husky sound ran tingling along Max's nerves. It flashed into his mind that Caroline Twinning seemed to understand a great deal more than one might expect from a woman with such a decidedly restricted past. He was prevented from studying her face by the demands of successfully negotiating their exit from the Park.

They were just swinging out into the traffic when an elegant barouche pulled up momentarily beside them, heading into the Park. The thin, middle-aged woman, with a severe, almost horsy countenance, who had been languidly lying against the silken cushions, took one look at the curricle and sat bolt upright. In her face, astonishment mingled freely with rampant curiosity. "Twyford!"

Max glanced down as both carriages started to move again. "My lady." He nodded and then they were swallowed up in the traffic.

Glancing back, Caroline saw the elegant lady remonstrating with her coachman. She giggled. "Who was she?"

"That, my ward, was Sally, Lady Jersey. A name to remember. She is the most inveterate gossip in London. Hence her nickname of Silence. Despite that, she's kind-hearted enough. She's one of the seven patronesses of Almack's. You'll have to get vouchers to attend but I doubt that will be a problem."

They continued in companionable silence, threading their way through the busy streets. Max was occupied with imagining the consternation Lady Jersey's sighting of them was going to cause. And there was Ramsleigh, too. A wicked smile hovered on his lips. He rather thought he was going to spend a decidedly amusing evening. It would be some days before news of his guardianship got around. Until then, he would enjoy the speculation. He was certain he would not enjoy the mirth of his friends when they discovered the truth.

"Oooh, Caro! Isn't he magnificent?" Arabella's round eyes, brilliant and bright, greeted Caroline as she entered their parlour.

"Did he agree to be our guardian?" asked the phlegmatic Sarah.

And, "Is he nice?" from the youngest, Lizzie.

All the important questions, thought Caroline with an affectionate smile, as she threw her bonnet aside and subsided into an armchair with a whisper of her stylish skirts. Her three half-sisters gathered around eagerly. She eyed them fondly. It would be hard to find three more attractive young ladies, even though she did say so herself. Twenty-year-old Sarah, with her dark brown hair and dramatically pale face, settling herself on one arm of her chair. Arabella on her other side, chestnut curls rioting around her heart-shaped and decidedly mischievous countenance, and Lizzie, the youngest and quietest of them all, curling up at her feet, her grey-brown eyes shining with the intentness of youth, the light dusting of freckles on the bridge of her nose persisting despite the ruthless application of Denmark lotion, crushed strawberries and every other remedy ever invented.

"*Commonly held to be well to pass.*" Caroline's own words echoed in her ears. Her smile grew. "Well, my loves, it seems we are, incontrovertibly and without doubt, the Duke of Twyford's wards."

"When does he want to meet us?" asked Sarah, ever practical.

"Tomorrow afternoon. He's opening up Twyford House and we're to move in then. He resides at Delmere House, where I went this morning, so the properties will thus be preserved. His aunt, Lady Benborough, is to act as our chaperon—she's apparently well-connected and willing to sponsor us. She'll be there tomorrow."

A stunned silence greeted her news. Then Arabella voiced the awe of all three. "Since ten this morning?"

Caroline's eyes danced. She nodded.

Arabella drew a deep breath. "Is he...masterful?"

"Very!" replied Caroline. "But you'll be caught out, my love, if you think to sharpen your claws on our guardian. He's a deal too shrewd, and experienced besides." Studying the pensive faces around her, she added. "Any flirtation between any of us and Max Rotherbridge would be doomed to failure. As his wards, we're out of court, and he won't stand any nonsense, I warn you."

"Hmm." Sarah stood and wandered to the windows before turning to face her. "So it's as you suspected? He won't be easy to manage?"

Caroline smiled at the thought and shook her head decisively. "I'm afraid, my dears, that any notions we may have had of setting the town alight while in the care of a complaisant guardian have died along with the last Duke." One slim forefinger tapped her full lower lip thoughtfully. "However," she continued, "provided we adhere to society's rules and cause him no trouble, I doubt our new guardian will throw any rub in our way. We did come to London to find husbands, after all. And that,'' she said forcefully, gazing at the three faces fixed on hers, ''is, unless I miss my guess, precisely what His Grace intends us to do.''

''So he's agreed to present us so we can find husbands?'' asked Lizzie.

Again Caroline nodded. ''I think it bothers him, to have four wards.'' She smiled in reminiscence, then added, ''And from what I've seen of the *ton* thus far, I suspect the present Duke as our protector may well be a distinct improvement over the previous incumbent. I doubt we'll have to fight off the fortune-hunters.''

Some minutes ticked by in silence as they considered their new guardian. Then Caroline stood and shook out her skirts. She took a few steps into the room before turning to address her sisters.

''Tomorrow we'll be collected at two and conveyed to Twyford House, which is in Mount Street.'' She paused to let the implication of her phrasing sink in. ''As you love me, you'll dress demurely and behave with all due reticence. No playing off your tricks on the Duke.'' She looked pointedly at Arabella, who grinned roguishly back. ''Exactly so! I think, in the circumstances, we should make life as easy as possible for our new guardian. I feel sure he could have broken the guardianship if he had wished and can only be thankful he chose instead to honour his uncle's obligations. But we shouldn't try him too far.'' She ended her motherly admonitions with a stern air, deceiving her sisters not at all.

As the other three heads came together, Caroline

turned to gaze unseeingly out of the window. A be-witching smile curved her generous lips and a twinkle lit her grey-green eyes. Softly, she murmured to her-self, ''For I've a definite suspicion he's going to find us very trying indeed!''

Thup, thup, thup. The tip of Lady Benborough's thin cane beat a slow tattoo, muffled by the pile of the Aubusson carpet. She was pleasantly impatient, waiting with definite anticipation to see her new charges. Her sharp blue gaze had already taken in the state of the room, the perfectly organised furniture, everything tidy and in readiness. If she had not known it for fact, she would never have believed that, yes-terday morn, Twyford House had been shut up, the knocker off the door, every piece of furniture shrouded in Holland covers. Wilson was priceless. There was even a bowl of early crocus on the side-table between the long windows. These stood open, giving access to the neat courtyard, flanked by flow-erbeds bursting into colourful life. A marble fountain stood at its centre, a Grecian maiden pouring water never-endingly from an urn.

Her contemplation of the scene was interrupted by a peremptory knock on the street door. A moment later, she heard the deep tones of men's voices and relaxed. Max. She would never get used to thinking of him as Twyford—she had barely become accus-tomed to him being Viscount Delmere. Max was es-sentially Max—he needed no title to distinguish him.

The object of her vagaries strode into the room. As always, his garments were faultless, his boots beyond compare. He bowed with effortless grace over her hand, his blue eyes, deeper in shade than her own but alive with the same intelligence, quizzing her. "A vast improvement, Aunt."

It took a moment to realise he was referring to her latest wig, a newer version of the same style she had favoured for the past ten years. She was not sure whether she was pleased or insulted. She compromised and snorted. "Trying to turn me up pretty, heh?"

"I would never insult your intelligence so, ma'am," he drawled, eyes wickedly laughing.

Lady Benborough suppressed an involuntary smile in response. The trouble with Max was that he was such a thorough-going rake that the techniques had flowed into all spheres of his life. He would undoubtedly flirt outrageously with his old nurse! Augusta Benborough snorted again. "Wilson's left to get the girls. He should be back any minute. Provided they're ready, that is."

She watched as her nephew ran a cursory eye over the room before selecting a Hepplewhite chair and elegantly disposing his long length in it.

"I trust everything meets with your approval?"

She waved her hand to indicate the room. "Wilson's been marvellous. I don't know how he does it."

"Neither do I," admitted Wilson's employer. "And the rest of the house?"

"The same," she assured him, then continued, "I've been considering the matter of husbands for the chits. With that sort of money, I doubt we'll have trouble even if they have spots and squint."

Max merely inclined his head. "You may leave the fortune-hunters to me."

Augusta nodded. It was one of the things she particularly appreciated about Max—one never needed to spell things out. The fact that the Twinning girls were his wards would certainly see them safe from the attentions of the less desirable elements. The new Duke of Twyford was a noted Corinthian and a crack shot.

"Provided they're immediately presentable, I thought I might give a small party next week, to start the ball rolling. But if their wardrobes need attention, or they can't dance, we'll have to postpone it."

Remembering Caroline Twinning's stylish dress and her words on the matter, Max reassured her. "And I'd bet a monkey they can dance, too." For some reason, he felt quite sure Caroline Twinning waltzed. It was the only dance he ever indulged in; he was firmly convinced that she waltzed.

Augusta was quite prepared to take Max's word on such matters. If nothing else, his notorious career through the bedrooms and bordellos of England had left him with an unerring eye for all things feminine. "Next week, then," she said. "Just a few of the more useful people and a smattering of the younger crowd."

She looked up to find Max's eye on her.

"I sincerely hope you don't expect to see *me* at this event?"

"Good Lord, no! I want all attention on your wards, not on their guardian!"

Max smiled his lazy smile.

"If the girls are at all attractive, I see no problems at all in getting them settled. Who knows? One of them might snare Wolverton's boy."

"That milksop?" Max's mind rebelled at the vision of the engaging Miss Twinning on the arm of the future Earl of Wolverton. Then he shrugged. After all, he had yet to meet the three younger girls. "Who knows?"

"Do you want me to keep a firm hand on the reins, give them a push if necessary or let them wander where they will?"

Max pondered the question, searching for the right words to frame his reply. "Keep your eye on the three younger girls. They're likely to need some guidance. I haven't sighted them yet, so they may need more than that. But, despite her advanced years, I doubt Miss Twinning will need any help at all."

His aunt interpreted this reply to mean that Miss Twinning's beauty, together with her sizeable fortune, would be sufficient to overcome the stigma of her years. The assessment was reassuring, coming as it did from her reprehensible nephew, whose knowledge was extensive in such matters. As her gaze rested on the powerful figure, negligently at ease in his chair, she reflected that it really was unfair he had inherited only the best from both his parents. The combination of virility, good looks and power of both mind and body was overwhelming; throw the titles in for good measure and it was no wonder Max Rotherbridge had been the target of so many matchmaking mamas throughout his adult life. But he had shown no sign whatever of succumbing to the demure attractions of any débutante. His preference was, always had been, for women of far more voluptuous charms. The litany of his past mistresses attested to his devotion to his ideal. They had all, every last one, been well-endowed. Hardly surprising, she mused. Max was tall, powerful and vigorous. She could not readily imagine any of the delicate debs satisfying his appetites. Her wandering mind dwelt on the subject of his latest *affaire*, aside, of course, from his current *chère amie*, an opera singer, so she had been told. Emma, Lady Mortland, was a widow of barely a year's standing but she had returned to town determined, it seemed, to make up for time lost through her marriage to an ageing peer. If the *on-dits* were true, she had fallen rather heavily in Max's lap. Looking at the strikingly handsome face of her nephew, Augusta grinned. Undoubtedly, Lady Mortland had set her cap at a Duchess's tiara. Deluded woman! Max, for all his air of unconcern, was born to his position. There was no chance he would offer marriage to Emma or any of her ilk. He would certainly avail himself of their proffered charms. Then when he tired of them, he would dismiss them, generously rewarding those who had the sense to play the game with suitable grace, callously ignoring those who did not.

The sounds of arrival gradually filtered into the drawing-room. Max raised his head. A spurt of feminine chatter drifted clearly to their ears. Almost immediately, silence was restored. Then, the door opened and Millwade, the new butler, entered to announce, "Miss Twinning."

Caroline walked through the door and advanced

into the room, her sunny confidence cloaking her like bright sunshine. Max, who had risen, blinked and then strolled forward to take her hand. He bowed over it, smiling with conscious charm into her large eyes.

Caroline returned the smile, thoroughly conversant with its promise. While he was their guardian, she could afford to play his games. His strong fingers retained their clasp on her hand as he drew her forward to meet his aunt.

Augusta Benborough's mouth had fallen open at first sight of her eldest charge. But by the time Caroline faced her, she had recovered her composure. No wonder Max had said she would need no help. Great heavens! The girl was…well, no sense in beating about the bush—she was devilishly attractive. Sensually so. Responding automatically to the introduction, Augusta recognised the amused comprehension in the large and friendly grey eyes. Imperceptibly, she relaxed.

"Your sisters?" asked Max.

"I left them in the hall. I thought perhaps…" Caroline's words died on her lips as Max moved to the bell pull. Before she could gather her wits, Millwade was in the room, receiving his instructions. Bowing to the inevitable, Caroline closed her lips on her unspoken excuses. As she turned to Lady Benborough, her ladyship's brows rose in mute question. Caroline smiled and, with a swish of her delicate skirts, sat beside Lady Benborough. "Just watch," she whispered, her eyes dancing.

Augusta Benborough regarded her thoughtfully, then turned her attention to the door. As she did so, it opened again. First Sarah, then Arabella, then Lizzie Twinning entered the room.

A curious hiatus ensued as both Max Rotherbridge and his aunt, with more than fifty years of town bronze between them, started in patent disbelief at their charges. The three girls stood unselfconsciously, poised and confident, and then swept curtsies, first to Max, then to her ladyship.

Caroline beckoned and they moved forward to be presented, to a speechless Max, who had not moved from his position beside his chair, and then to a flabbergasted Lady Benborough.

As they moved past him to make their curtsy to his aunt, Max recovered the use of his faculties. He closed his eyes. But when he opened them again, they were still there. He was not hallucinating. There they were: three of the loveliest lovelies he had ever set eyes on—four if you counted Miss Twinning. They were scene-stealers, every one—the sort of young women whose appearance suspended conversations, whose passage engendered rampant curiosity, aside from other, less nameable emotions, and whose departure left onlookers wondering what on earth they had been talking about before. All from the same stable, all under one roof. Nominally his. Incredible. And then the enormity, the mind-numbing, all-encompassing reality of his inheritance struck him. One glance into Miss Twinning's grey eyes, brimming with mirth, told him she understood more than enough. His voice, lacking its customary strength and in a very odd register, came to his ears. "Impossible!"

His aunt Augusta collapsed laughing.

# *Chapter Three*

"**No!**" Max shook his head stubbornly, a frown of quite dramatic proportions darkening his handsome face.

Lady Benborough sighed mightily and frowned back. On recovering her wits, she had sternly repressed her mirth and sent the three younger Twinnings into the courtyard. But after ten minutes of carefully reasoned argument, Max remained adamant. However, she was quite determined her scapegrace nephew would not succeed in dodging his responsibilities. Aside from anything else, the situation seemed set to afford her hours of entertainment and, at her age, such opportunities could not be lightly passed by. Her lips compressed into a thin line and a martial light appeared in her blue eyes.

Max, recognising the signs, got in first. "It's impossible! Just *think* of the talk!"

Augusta's eyes widened to their fullest extent. "Why should you care?" she asked. "Your career to date would hardly lead one to suppose you fought shy of scandal." She fixed Max with a penetrating stare.

"Besides, while there'll no doubt be talk, none of it will harm anyone. Quite the opposite. It'll get these girls into the limelight!"

The black frown on Max's face did not lighten.

Caroline wisely refrained from interfering between the two principal protagonists, but sat beside Augusta, looking as innocent as she could. Max's gaze swept over her and stopped on her face. His eyes narrowed. Caroline calmly returned his scrutiny.

There was little doubt in Max's mind that Caroline Twinning had deliberately concealed from him the truth about her sisters until he had gone too far in establishing himself as their guardian to pull back. He felt sure some retribution was owing to one who had so manipulated him but, staring into her large grey-green eyes, was unable to decide which of the numerous and varied punishments his fertile imagination supplied would be the most suitable. Instead, he said, in the tones of one goaded beyond endurance, "'Commonly held to be well to pass', indeed!"

Caroline smiled.

Augusta intervened. "Whatever you're thinking of, Max, it won't do! You're the girls' guardian—you told me so yourself. You cannot simply wash your hands of them. I can see it'll be a trifle awkward for you," her eyes glazed as she thought of Lady Mortland, "but if you don't concern yourself with them, who will?"

Despite his violent response to his first sight of all four Twinning sisters, perfectly understandable in the circumstances, Max had not seriously considered giving up his guardianship of them. His behaviour over the past ten minutes had been more in the nature of an emotional rearguard action in an attempt, which his rational brain acknowledged as futile, to resist the tide of change he could see rising up to swamp his hitherto well-ordered existence. He fired his last shot. "Do you seriously imagine that someone with my reputation will be considered a suitable guardian for four...?" He paused, his eyes on Caroline, any number of highly apt descriptions revolving in his head. "Excessively attractive virgins?" he concluded savagely.

Caroline's eyes widened and her dimple appeared.

"On the contrary!" Augusta answered. "Who better than you to act as their guardian? Odds are you know every ploy ever invented and a few more besides. And if you can't keep the wolves at bay, then no one can. I really don't know why you're creating all this fuss."

Max did not know either. After a moment of silence, he turned abruptly and crossed to the windows giving on to the courtyard. He had known from the outset that this was one battle he was destined to lose. Yet some part of his mind kept suggesting in panic-stricken accents that there must be some other way. He watched as the three younger girls—his wards, heaven forbid!—examined the fountain, prodding and poking in an effort to find the lever to turn it on. They were a breathtaking sight, the varied hues of their shining hair vying with the flowers, their husky laughter and the unconsciously seductive way their supple figures swayed this way and that causing him to groan inwardly. Up to the point when he had first sighted them, the three younger Twinnings had figured in his plans as largely irrelevant entities, easily swept into the background and of no possible consequence to his plans for their elder sister. One glimpse had been enough to scuttle that scenario. He was trapped—a guardian in very truth. And with what the Twinning girls had to offer he would have no choice but to play the role to the hilt. Every man in London with eyes would be after them!

Lady Benborough eyed Max's unyielding back with a frown. Then she turned to the woman beside her. She had already formed a high opinion of Miss Twinning. What was even more to the point, being considerably more than seven, Augusta had also perceived that her reprehensible nephew was far from indifferent to the luscious beauty. Meeting the grey-green eyes, her ladyship raised her brows. Caroline nodded and rose.

Max turned as Caroline laid her hand on his arm. She was watching her sisters, not him. Her voice, when she spoke, was tactfully low. "If it would truly bother you to stand as our guardian, I'm sure we could make some other arrangement." As she finished speaking, she raised her eyes to his.

Accustomed to every feminine wile known to woman, Max nevertheless could see nothing in the lucent grey eyes to tell him whether the offer was a bluff or not. But it only took a moment to realise that if he won this particular argument, if he succeeded in withdrawing as guardian to the Twinning sisters, Caroline Twinning would be largely removed from his orbit. Which would certainly make his seduction of her more difficult, if not impossible. Faced with those large grey-green eyes, Max did what none of the habitués of Gentleman Jackson's boxing salon had yet seen him do. He threw in the towel.

Having resigned himself to the inevitable, Max departed, leaving the ladies to become better acquainted. As the street door closed behind him, Lady Benborough turned a speculative glance on Caroline. Her lips twitched. "Very well done, my dear. Clearly you need no lessons in how to manage a man."

Caroline's smile widened. "I've had some experience, I'll admit."

"Well, you'll need it all if you're going to tackle my nephew." Augusta grinned in anticipation. From where she sat, her world looked rosy indeed. Not only did she have four rich beauties to fire off, and unlimited funds to do it with, but, glory of glories, for the first time since he had emerged from short coats her reprehensible nephew was behaving in a less than predictable fashion. She allowed herself a full minute to revel in the wildest of imaginings, before settling down to extract all the pertinent details of their backgrounds and personalities from the Twinning sisters. The younger girls returned when the tea-tray arrived. By the time it was removed, Lady Benborough had satisfied herself on all points of interest and the conversation moved on to their introduction to the *ton*.

"I wonder whether news of your existence has leaked out yet," mused her ladyship. "Someone may have seen you at Grillon's."

"Lady Jersey saw me yesterday with Max in his curricle," said Caroline.

"Did she?" Augusta sat up straighter. "In that case, there's no benefit in dragging our heels. If Silence already has the story, the sooner you make your appearance, the better. We'll go for a drive in the Park tomorrow." She ran a knowledgeable eye over the sisters' dresses. "I must say, your dresses are very attractive. Are they all like that?"

Reassured on their wardrobes, she nodded. "So there's nothing to stop us wading into the fray immediately. Good!" She let her eyes wander over the four faces in front of her, all beautiful yet each with its own allure. Her gaze rested on Lizzie. "You— Lizzie, isn't it? You're eighteen?"

Lizzie nodded. "Yes, ma'am."

"If that's so, then there's no reason for us to be missish," returned her ladyship. "I assume you all wish to find husbands?"

They all nodded decisively.

"Good! At least we're all in agreement over the objective. Now for the strategy. Although your sudden appearance all together is going to cause a riot. I rather think that's going to be the best way to begin. At the very least, we'll be noticed."

"Oh, we're *always* noticed!" returned Arabella, hazel eyes twinkling.

Augusta laughed. "I dare say." From any other young lady, the comment would have earned a reproof. However, it was impossible to deny the Twinning sisters were rather more than just beautiful, and as they were all more than green girls it was pointless to pretend they did not fully comprehend the effect they had on the opposite sex. To her ladyship's mind, it was a relief not to have to hedge around the subject.

"Aside from anything else," she continued thoughtfully, "your public appearance as the Duke of Twyford's wards will make it impossible for Max to renege on his decision." Quite why she was so very firmly set on Max fulfilling his obligations she could not have said. But his guardianship would keep him in contact with Miss Twinning. And that, she had a shrewd suspicion, would be a very good thing.

Their drive in the Park the next afternoon was engineered by the experienced Lady Benborough to be tantalisingly brief. As predicted, the sight of four ravishing females in the Twyford barouche caused an immediate impact. As the carriage sedately bowled along the avenues, heads rapidly came together in the carriages they passed. Conversations between knots of elegant gentlemen and the more dashing of ladies who had descended from their carriages to stroll about the well-tended lawns halted in midsentence as all eyes turned to follow the Twyford barouche.

Augusta, happily aware of the stir they were causing, sat on the maroon leather seat and struggled to keep the grin from her face. Her charges were attired in a spectrum of delicate colours, for all the world like a posy of gorgeous blooms. The subtle peach of Caroline's round gown gave way to the soft turquoise tints of Sarah's. Arabella had favoured a gown of the most delicate rose muslin while Lizzie sat, like a quiet bluebell, nodding happily amid her sisters. In the soft spring sunshine, they looked like refugees from the fairy kingdom, too exquisite to be flesh and blood. Augusta lost her struggle and grinned widely at her fanciful thoughts. Then her eyes alighted on a landau drawn up to the side of the carriageway. She raised her parasol and tapped her coachman on the shoulder. "Pull up over there."

Thus it happened that Emily, Lady Cowper and Maria, Lady Sefton, enjoying a comfortable cose in the afternoon sunshine, were the first to meet the Twinning sisters. As the Twyford carriage drew up, the eyes of both experienced matrons grew round.

Augusta noted their response with satisfaction. She seized the opportunity to perform the introductions, ending with, "Twyford's wards, you know."

That information, so casually dropped, clearly stunned both ladies. *"Twyford's?"* echoed Lady Sefton. Her mild eyes, up to now transfixed by the spectacle that was the Twinning sisters, shifted in bewilderment to Lady Benborough's face. "How on *earth...?*"

In a few well-chosen sentences, Augusta told her. Once their ladyships had recovered from their amusement, both at once promised vouchers for the girls to attend Almack's.

"My dear, if your girls attend, we'll have to lay on more refreshments. The gentlemen will be there in droves," said Lady Cowper, smiling in genuine amusement.

"Who knows? We might even prevail on Twyford himself to attend," mused Lady Sefton.

While Augusta thought that might be stretching

things a bit far, she was thankful for the immediate backing her two old friends had given her crusade to find four fashionable husbands for the Twinnings. The carriages remained together for some time as the two patronesses of Almack's learned more of His Grace of Twyford's wards. Augusta was relieved to find that all four girls could converse with ease. The two younger sisters prettily deferred to the elder two, allowing the more experienced Caroline, ably seconded by Sarah, to dominate the responses.

When they finally parted, Augusta gave the order to return to Mount Street. "Don't want to rush it," she explained to four enquiring glances. "Much better to let them come to us."

Two days later, the *ton* was still reeling from the discovery of the Duke of Twyford's wards. Amusement, from the wry to the ribald, had been the general reaction. Max had gritted his teeth and borne it, but the persistent demands of his friends to be introduced to his wards sorely tried his temper. He continued to refuse all such requests. He could not stop their eventual acquaintance but at least he did not need directly to foster it. Thus, it was in a far from benign mood that he prepared to depart Delmere House on that fine April morning, in the company of two of his particular cronies, Lord Darcy Hamilton and George, Viscount Pilborough.

As they left the parlour at the rear of the house and entered the front hallway, their conversation was interrupted by a knock on the street door. They paused in the rear of the hall as Hillshaw moved majestically past to answer it.

"I'm not at home, Hillshaw," said Max.

Hillshaw regally inclined his head. "Very good, Your Grace."

But Max had forgotten that Hillshaw had yet to experience the Misses Twinning *en masse*. Resistance was impossible and they came swarming over the threshold, in a frothing of lace and cambrics, bright smiles, laughing eyes and dancing curls.

The girls immediately spotted the three men, standing rooted by the stairs. Arabella reached Max first. "Dear guardian," she sighed languishingly, eyes dancing, "are you well?" She placed her small hand on his arm.

Sarah, immediately behind, came to his other side. "We hope you are because we want to ask your permission for something." She smiled matter-of-factly up at him.

Lizzie simply stood directly in front of him, her huge eyes trained on his face, a smile she clearly knew to be winning suffusing her countenance. "Please?"

Max raised his eyes to Hillshaw, still standing dumb by the door. The sight of his redoubtable henchman rolled up by a parcel of young misses caused his lips to twitch. He firmly denied the impulse to laugh. The Misses Twinning were outrageous already and needed no further encouragement. Then his eyes met Caroline's.

She had hung back, watching her sisters go through their paces, but as his eyes touched her, she moved forward, her hand outstretched. Max, quite forgetting the presence of all the others, took it in his.

"Don't pay any attention to them, Your Grace; I'm afraid they're sad romps."

"Not *romps*, Caro," protested Arabella, eyes fluttering over the other two men, standing mesmerized just behind Max.

"It's just that we heard it was possible to go riding in the Park but Lady Benborough said we had to have your permission," explained Sarah.

"So, here we are and can we?" asked Lizzie, big eyes beseeching.

"No," said Max, without further ado. As his aunt had observed, he knew every ploy. And the opportunities afforded by rides in the Park, where chaperons could be present but sufficiently remote, were endless. The first rule in a seduction was to find the opportunity to speak alone to the lady in question. And a ride in the Park provided the perfect setting.

Caroline's fine brows rose at his refusal. Max noticed that the other three girls turned to check their elder sister's response before returning to the attack.

"Oh, you can't mean that! How shabby!"

"Why on earth not?"

"We all ride well. I haven't been out since we were home."

Both Arabella and Sarah turned to the two gentlemen still standing behind Max, silent auditors to the extraordinary scene. Arabella fixed Viscount Pilborough with pleading eyes. "Surely there's nothing unreasonable in such a request?" Under the Viscount's besotted gaze, her lashes fluttered almost imperceptibly, before her lids decorously dropped, veiling those dancing eyes, the long lashes brushing her cheeks, delicately stained with a most becoming blush.

The Viscount swallowed. "Why on earth not, Max? Not an unreasonable request at all. Your wards would look very lovely on horseback."

Max, who was only too ready to agree on how lovely his wards would look in riding habits, bit back an oath. Ignoring Miss Twinning's laughing eyes, he glowered at the hapless Viscount.

Sarah meanwhile had turned to meet the blatantly admiring gaze of Lord Darcy. Not as accomplished a flirt as Arabella, she could nevertheless hold her own, and she returned his warm gaze with a serene smile. "Is there any real reason why we shouldn't ride?"

Her low voice, cool and strangely musical, made Darcy Hamilton wish there were far fewer people in Max's hall. In fact, his fantasies would be more complete if they were not in Max's hall at all. He moved towards Sarah and expertly captured her hand. Raising it to his lips, he smiled in a way that had thoroughly seduced more damsels than he cared to recall. He could well understand why Max did not wish his wards to ride. But, having met this Twinning sister, there was no way in the world he was going to further his friend's ambition.

His lazy drawl reached Max's ears. "I'm very much afraid, Max, dear boy, that you're going to have to concede. The opposition is quite overwhelming."

Max glared at him. Seeing the determination in his lordship's grey eyes and understanding his reasons only too well, he knew he was outnumbered on all fronts. His eyes returned to Caroline's face to find her regarding him quizzically. "Oh, very well!"

Her smile warmed him and at the prompting lift of her brows he introduced his friends, first to her, and then to her sisters in turn. The chattering voices washed over him, his friends' deeper tones running like a counterpoint in the cacophony. Caroline moved to his side.

"You're not seriously annoyed by us riding, are you?"

He glanced down at her. The stern set of his lips reluctantly relaxed. "I would very much rather you did not. However," he continued, his eyes roving to the group of her three sisters and his two friends, busy with noisy plans for their first ride that afternoon, "I can see that's impossible."

Caroline smiled. "We won't come to any harm, I assure you."

"Allow me to observe, Miss Twinning, that gallivanting about the London *ton* is fraught with rather more difficulty than you would have encountered in American society, nor yet within the circle to which you were accustomed in Hertfordshire."

A rich chuckle greeted his warning. "Fear not, dear guardian," she said, raising laughing eyes to his. Max noticed the dimple, peeking irrepressibly from beside her soft mouth. "We'll manage."

Naturally, Max felt obliged to join the riding party that afternoon. Between both his and Darcy Hamilton's extensive stables, they had managed to assemble suitable mounts for the four girls. Caroline had assured him that, like all country misses, they could ride very well. By the time they gained the Park, he had satisfied himself on that score. At least he need not worry over them losing control of the frisky horses and being thrown. But, as they were all as stunning as he had feared they would be, elegantly gowned in perfectly cut riding habits, his worries had not noticeably decreased.

As they ambled further into the Park, by dint of the simple expedient of reining in his dappled grey, he dropped to the rear of the group, the better to keep the three younger girls in view. Caroline, riding by his side, stayed with him. She threw him a laughing glance but made no comment.

As he had expected, they had not gone more than two hundred yards before their numbers were swelled by the appearance of Lord Tulloch and young Mr. Mitchell. But neither of these gentlemen seemed able to interrupt the rapport which, to Max's experienced eye, was developing with alarming rapidity between Sarah Twinning and Darcy Hamilton. Despite his fears, he grudgingly admitted the Twinning sisters knew a trick or two. Arabella flirted outrageously but did so with all gentlemen, none being able to claim any special consideration. Lizzie attracted the quieter men and was happy to converse on the matters currently holding the interest of the *ton*. Her natural shyness and understated youth, combined with her undeniable beauty, was a heady tonic for these more sober gentlemen. As they ventured deeper into the Park, Max was relieved to find Sarah giving Darcy

no opportunity to lead her apart. Gradually, his watch-
fulness relaxed. He turned to Caroline.

"Have you enjoyed your first taste of life in London?"

"Yes, thank you," she replied, grey eyes smiling.
"Your aunt has been wonderful. I can't thank you
enough for all you've done."

Max's brow clouded. As it happened, the last thing
he wanted was her gratitude. Here he was, thinking
along lines not grossly dissimilar from Darcy's present preoccupation, and the woman chose to thank
him. He glanced down at her as she rode beside him,
her face free of any worry, thoroughly enjoying the
moment. Her presence was oddly calming.

"What plans to you have for the rest of the week?"
he asked.

Caroline was slightly surprised by his interest but
replied readily. "We've been driving in the Park
every afternoon except today. I expect we'll continue
to appear, although I rather think, from now on, it
will be on horseback." She shot him a measuring
glance to see how he would take that. His face was
slightly grim but he nodded in acceptance. "Last evening, we went to a small party given by Lady Malling.
Your aunt said there are a few more such gatherings
in the next week which we should attend, to give
ourselves confidence in society."

Max nodded again. From the corner of his eye, he
saw Sarah avoid yet another of Darcy's invitations to
separate from the group. He saw the quick frown
which showed fleetingly in his friend's eyes. Serve
him right if the woman drove him mad. But, he knew,

Darcy was made of sterner stuff. The business of keeping his wards out of the arms of his friends was going to be deucedly tricky. Returning to contemplation of Miss Twinning's delightful countenance, he asked, "Has Aunt Augusta got you vouchers for Almack's yet?"

"Yes. We met Lady Sefton and Lady Cowper on our first drive in the Park."

Appreciating his aunt's strategy, Max grinned. "Trust Aunt Augusta."

Caroline returned his smile. "She's been very good to us."

Thinking that the unexpected company of four lively young women must have been a shock to his aunt's system, Max made a mental note to do anything in his power to please his aunt Benborough.

They had taken a circuitous route through the Park and only now approached the fashionable precincts. The small group almost immediately swelled to what, to Max, were alarming proportions, with every available gentleman clamouring for an introduction to his beautiful wards. But, to his surprise, at a nod from Caroline, the girls obediently brought their mounts closer and refused every attempt to draw them further from his protective presence. To his astonishment, they all behaved with the utmost decorum, lightened, of course, by their natural liveliness but nevertheless repressively cool to any who imagined them easy targets. Despite his qualms, he was impressed. They continued in this way until they reached the gates of the Park, by which time the group had dwindled to its original size and he could relax again.

He turned to Caroline, still by his side. "Can you guarantee they'll always behave so circumspectly, or was that performance purely for my benefit?" As her laughing eyes met his, he tried to decide whether they were greeny-grey or greyish-green. An intriguing question.

"Oh, we're experienced enough to know which way to jump, I assure you," she returned. After a pause, she continued, her voice lowered so only he could hear. "In the circumstances, we would not willingly do anything to bring disrepute on ourselves. We are very much aware of what we owe to you and Lady Benborough."

Max knew he should be pleased at this avowal of good intentions. Instead, he was aware of a curious irritation. He would certainly do everything in his power to reinforce her expressed sentiment with respect to the three younger girls, but to have Caroline Twinning espousing such ideals was not in keeping with his plans. Somehow, he was going to have to convince her that adherence to all the social strictures was not the repayment he, at least, would desire. The unwelcome thought that, whatever the case, she might now consider herself beholden to him, and would, therefore, grant him his wishes out of gratitude, very nearly made him swear aloud. His horse jibbed at the suddenly tightened rein and he pushed the disturbing thought aside while he dealt with the grey. Once the horse had settled again, he continued by Caroline's side as they headed back to Mount Street, a distracted frown at the back of his dark blue eyes.

* * *

Augusta Benborough flicked open her fan and plied it vigorously. Under cover of her voluminous skirts, she slipped her feet free of her evening slippers. She had forgotten how stifling the small parties, held in the run-up to the Season proper, could be. Every bit as bad as the crushers later in the Season. But there, at least, she would have plenty of her own friends to gossip with. The mothers and chaperons of the current batch of débutantes were a generation removed from her own and at these small parties they were generally the only older members present. Miriam Alford had elected to remain at Twyford House this evening, which left Augusta with little to do but watch her charges. And even that, she mused to herself, was not exactly riveting entertainment.

True, Max was naturally absent, which meant her primary interest in the entire business was in abeyance. Still, it was comforting to find Caroline treating all the gentlemen who came her way with the same unfailing courtesy and no hint of partiality. Arabella, too, seemed to be following that line, although, in her case, the courtesy was entirely cloaked in a lightly flirtatious manner. In any other young girl, Lady Benborough would have strongly argued for a more demure style. But she had watched Arabella carefully. The girl had quick wits and a ready tongue. She never stepped beyond what was acceptable, though she took delight in sailing close to the wind. Now, convinced that no harm would come of Arabella's artful play, Augusta nodded benignly as that young lady strolled by, accompanied by the inevitable gaggle of besotted gentlemen.

One of their number was declaiming,

     "'My dearest flower,
     More beautiful by the hour,
     To you I give my heart.'"

Arabella laughed delightedly and quickly said, "My dear sir, I beg you spare my blushes! Truly, your verses do me more credit than I deserve. But surely, to do them justice, should you not set them down on parchment?" Anything was preferable to having them said aloud.

The budding poet, young Mr. Rawlson, beamed. "*Nothing* would give me greater pleasure, Miss Arabella. I'll away and transcribe them immediately. And dedicate them to your inspiration!" With a flourishing bow, he departed precipitately, leaving behind a silence pregnant with suppressed laughter.

This was broken by a snigger from Lord Shannon. "Silly puppy!"

As Mr. Rawlson was a year or two older than Lord Shannon, who himself appeared very young despite his attempts to ape the Corinthians, this comment itself caused some good-natured laughter.

"Perhaps, Lord Shannon, you would be so good as to fetch me some refreshment?" Arabella smiled sweetly on the hapless youngster. With a mutter which all interpreted to mean he was delighted to be of service to one so fair, the young man escaped.

With a smile, Arabella turned to welcome Viscount Pilborough to her side.

Augusta's eyelids drooped. The temperature in the

room seemed to rise another degree. The murmuring voices washed over her. Her head nodded. With a start, she shook herself awake. Determined to keep her mind active for the half-hour remaining, she sought out her charges. Lizzie was chattering animatedly with a group of débutantes much her own age. The youngest Twinning was surprisingly innocent, strangely unaware of her attractiveness to the opposite sex, still little more than a schoolgirl at heart. Lady Benborough smiled. Lizzie would learn soon enough; let her enjoy her girlish gossiping while she might.

A quick survey of the room brought Caroline to light, strolling easily on the arm of the most eligible Mr. Willoughby.

"It's so good of you to escort your sister to these parties, sir. I'm sure Miss Charlotte must be very grateful." Caroline found conversation with the reticent Mr. Willoughby a particular strain.

A faint smile played at the corners of Mr. Willoughby's thin lips. "Indeed, I believe she is. But really, there is very little to it. As my mother is so delicate as to find these affairs quite beyond her, it would be churlish of me indeed to deny Charlotte the chance of becoming more easy in company before she is presented."

With grave doubts over how much longer she could endure such ponderous conversation without running amok, Caroline seized the opportunity presented by passing a small group of young ladies, which included the grateful Charlotte, to stop. The introductions were quickly performed.

As she stood conversing with a Miss Denbright, an occupation which required no more than half her brain, Caroline allowed her eyes to drift over the company. Other than Viscount Pilborough, who was dangling after Arabella in an entirely innocuous fashion, and Darcy Hamilton, who was pursuing Sarah in a far more dangerous way, there was no gentleman in whom she felt the least interest. Even less than her sisters did she need the opportunity of the early parties to gain confidence. Nearly eighteen months of social consorting in the ballrooms and banquet halls in New York had given them all a solid base on which to face the London *ton*. And even more than her sisters, Caroline longed to get on with it. Time, she felt, was slipping inexorably by. Still, there were only four more days to go. And then, surely their guardian would reappear? She had already discovered that no other gentleman's eyes could make her feel quite the same breathless excitement as the Duke of Twyford's did. He had not called on them since that first ride in the Park, a fact which had left her with a wholly resented feeling of disappointment. Despite the common sense on which she prided herself, she had formed an irritating habit of comparing all the men she met with His domineering Grace and inevitably found them wanting. Such foolishness would have to stop. With a small suppressed sigh, she turned a charming smile on Mr. Willoughby, wishing for the sixteenth time that his faded blue eyes were of a much darker hue.

Satisfied that Caroline, like Lizzie and Arabella, needed no help from her, Lady Benborough moved her gaze on, scanning the room for Sarah's dark head. When her first survey drew no result, she sat up straighter, a slight frown in her eyes. Darcy Hamilton was here, somewhere, drat him. He had attended every party they had been to this week, a fact which of itself had already drawn comment. His attentions to Sarah were becoming increasingly marked. Augusta knew all the Hamiltons. She had known Darcy's father and doubted not the truth of the 'like father, like son' adage. But surely Sarah was too sensible to... She wasted no time in completing that thought but started a careful, methodical and entirely well-disguised visual search. From her present position, on a slightly raised dais to one side, she commanded a view of the whole room. Her gaze passed over the alcove set in the wall almost directly opposite her but then returned, caught by a flicker of movement within the shadowed recess.

There they were, Sarah and, without doubt, Darcy Hamilton. Augusta could just make out the blur of colour that was Sarah's green dress. How typical of Darcy. They were still in the room, still within sight, but, in the dim light of the alcove, almost private. As her eyes adjusted to the poor light, Augusta saw to her relief that, despite her fears and Darcy's reputation, they were merely talking, seated beside one another on a small setee. Still, to her experienced eye, there was a degree of familiarity in their pose, which, given that it must be unconscious, was all too revealing. With a sigh, she determined to have a word, if not several words, with Sarah, regarding the fascinations of men like Darcy Hamilton. She would have to do it, for Darcy's proclivities were too well-known to doubt.

She watched as Darcy leaned closer to Sarah.

"My dear," drawled Darcy Hamilton, "do you have any idea of the temptation you pose? Or the effect beauty such as yours has on mere men?"

His tone was lazy and warm, with a quality of velvety smoothness which fell like a warm cloak over Sarah's already hypersensitized nerves. He had flung one arm over the back of the settee and long fingers were even now twining in the soft curls at her nape. She knew she should move but could not. The sensations rippling down her spine were both novel and exhilarating. She was conscious of a ludicrous desire to snuggle into that warmth, to invite more soft words. But the desire which burned in his lordship's grey eyes was already frighteningly intense. She determinedly ignored the small reckless voice which urged her to encourage him and instead replied, "Why, no. Of course not."

Darcy just managed to repress a snort of disgust. Damn the woman! Her voice had held not the thread of a quaver. Calm and steady as a rock when his own pulses were well and truly racing. He simply did not believe it. He glanced down into her wide brown eyes, guileless as ever, knowing that his exasperation was showing. For a fleeting instant, he saw a glimmer of amusement and, yes, of triumph in the brown depths. But when he looked again, the pale face was once again devoid of emotion. His grey eyes narrowed.

Sarah saw his intent look and immediately dropped her eyes.

Her action confirmed Darcy's suspicions. By God, the chit was playing with him! The fact that Sarah could only be dimly aware of the reality of the danger she was flirting with was buried somewhere in the recesses of his mind. But, like all the Hamiltons, for him, desire could easily sweep aside all reason. In that instant, he determined he would have her, no matter what the cost. Not here, not now—neither place nor time was right. But some time, somewhere, Sarah Twinning would be his.

Augusta's attention was drawn by the sight of a mother gathering her two daughters and preparing to depart. As if all had been waiting for this signal, it suddenly seemed as if half the room was on their way. With relief, she turned to see Darcy lead Sarah from the alcove and head in her direction. As Caroline approached, closely followed by Lizzie and Arabella, Augusta Benborough wriggled her aching toes back into her slippers and rose. It was over. And in four days' time the Season would begin. As she smiled benignly upon the small army of gentlemen who had escorted her charges to her side, she reminded herself that, with the exception of Darcy Hamilton, there was none present tonight who would make a chaperon uneasy. Once in wider society, she would have no time to be bored. The Twinning sisters would certainly see to that.

# Chapter Four

Emma, Lady Mortland, thought Max savagely, had no right to the title. He would grant she was attractive, in a blowsy sort of way, but her conduct left much to be desired. She had hailed him almost as soon as he had entered the Park. He rarely drove there except when expediency demanded. Consequently, her ladyship had been surprised to see his curricle, drawn by his famous match bays, advancing along the avenue. He had been forced to pull up or run the silly woman down. The considerable difficulty in conversing at any length with someone perched six feet and more above you, particularly when that someone displayed the most blatant uninterest, had not discouraged Lady Mortland. She had done her best to prolong the exchange in the dim hope, Max knew, of gaining an invitation to ride beside him. She had finally admitted defeat and archly let him go, but not before issuing a thickly veiled invitation which he had had no compunction in declining. As she had been unwise enough to speak in the hearing of two gentlemen of her acquaintance, her resulting embarrassment was entirely her own fault. He knew she entertained hopes, totally unfounded, of becoming his Duchess. Why she should imagine he would consider taking a woman with the morals of an alley cat to wife was beyond him.

As he drove beneath the trees, he scanned the carriages that passed, hoping to find his wards. He had not seen them since that first ride in the Park, a feat of self-discipline before which any other he had ever accomplished in his life paled into insignificance. Darcy Hamilton had put the idea into his head. His friend had returned with him to Delmere House after that first jaunt, vociferous in his complaints of the waywardness of Sarah Twinning. The fact that she was Max's ward had not subdued him in the least. Max had not been surprised; Darcy could be ruthlessly singleminded when hunting. It had been Darcy who had suggested that a short absence might make the lady more amenable and had departed with the firm resolve to give the Twinning girls the go-by for at least a week.

That had been six days ago. The Season was about to get under way and it was time to reacquaint himself with his wards. Having ascertained that their horses had not left his stable, he had had the bays put to and followed them to the Park. He finally spied the Twyford barouche drawn up to the side of the avenue. He pulled up alongside.

"Aunt Augusta," he said as he nodded to her. She beamed at him, clearly delighted he had taken the trouble to find them. His gaze swept over the other occupants of the carriage in an appraising and approving manner, then came to rest on Miss Twinning. She smiled sunnily back at him. Suddenly alert, Max's mind returned from where it had wandered and again counted heads. There was a total of five in the carriage but Miriam Alford was there, smiling vaguely at him. Which meant one of his wards was missing. He quelled the urge to immediately question his aunt, telling himself there would doubtless be some perfectly reasonable explanation. Perhaps one was merely unwell. His mind reverted to its main preoccupation.

Responding automatically to his aunt's social chatter, he took the first opportunity to remark, "But I can't keep my horses standing, ma'am. Perhaps Miss Twinning would like to come for a drive?"

He was immediately assured that Miss Twinning would and she descended from the carriage. He reached down to help her up beside him and they were off.

Caroline gloried in the brush of the breeze on her face as the curricle bowled along. Even reined in to the pace accepted in the Park, it was still infinitely more refreshing than the funereal plod favoured by Lady Benborough. That was undoubtedly the reason her spirits had suddenly soared. Even the sunshine seemed distinctly brighter.

"Not riding today?" asked Max.

"No. Lady Benborough felt we should not entirely desert the matrons."

Max smiled. "True enough. It don't do to put people's backs up unnecessarily."

Caroline turned to stare at him. "Your philosophy?'' Augusta had told her enough of their guardian's past to realise this was unlikely.

Max frowned. Miss Caroline Twinning was a great deal too knowing. Unprepared to answer her query, he changed the subject. ''Where's Sarah?''

''Lord Darcy took her up some time ago. Maybe we'll see them as we go around?''

Max suppressed the curse which rose to his lips. How many friends was he going to have left by the end of this Season? Another thought occurred. ''Has she been seeing much of him?''

A deep chuckle answered this and his uneasiness grew. ''If you mean has he taken to haunting us, no. On the other hand, he seems to have the entrée to all the salons we've attended this week.''

He should, he supposed, have anticipated his friend's duplicity. Darcy was, after all, every bit as experienced as he. Still, it rankled. He would have a few harsh words to say to his lordship when next they met. ''Has he been...particularly attentive towards her?''

''No,'' she replied in a careful tone, ''not in any unacceptable way.''

He looked his question and she continued, ''It's just that she's the only lady he pays any attention to at all. If he's not with Sarah, he either leaves or retires to the card tables or simply watches her from a distance.''

The description was so unlike the Darcy Hamilton he knew that it was on the tip of his tongue to verify they were talking about the same man. A sneaking suspicion that Darcy might, just might, be seriously smitten awoke in his mind. One black brow rose.

They paused briefly to exchange greetings with Lady Jersey, then headed back towards the barouche. Coming to a decision, Max asked, "What's your next major engagement?"

"Well, we go to the first of Almack's balls tomorrow, then it's the Billingtons' ball the next night."

The start of the Season proper. But there was no way he was going to cross the threshold of Almack's. He had not been near the place for years. Tender young virgins were definitely not on his menu these days. He did not equate that description with Miss Twinning. Nor, if it came to that, to her sisters. Uncertain what to do for the best, he made no response to the information, merely inclining his head to show he had heard.

Caroline was silent as the curricle retraced its journey. Max's questions had made her uneasy. Lord Darcy was a particular friend of his—surely Sarah was in no real danger with him? She stifled a small sigh. Clearly, their guardian's attention was wholly concentrated on their social performance. Which, of course, was precisely what a guardian should be concerned with. Why, then, did she feel such a keen sense of disappointment?

They reached the barouche to find Sarah already returned. One glance at her stormy countenance was sufficient to answer Max's questions. It seemed Darcy's plans had not prospered. Yet.

As he handed Caroline to the ground and acknowledged her smiling thanks, it occurred to him she had not expressed any opinion or interest in his week-long absence. So much for that tactic. As he watched her climb into the barouche, shapely ankles temporarily exposed, he realised he had made no headway during their interlude. Her sister's affair with his friend had dominated his thoughts. Giving his horses the office, he grimaced to himself. Seducing a young woman while acting as guardian to her three younger sisters was clearly going to be harder going than he had imagined.

Climbing the steps to Twyford House the next evening, Max was still in two minds over whether he was doing the right thing. He was far too wise to be overly attentive to Caroline, yet, if he did not make a push to engage her interest, she would shortly be the object of the attentions of a far larger circle of gentlemen, few of whom would hesitate to attend Almack's purely because they disliked being mooned over by very young women. He hoped, in his capacity as their guardian, to confine his attentions to the Twinning sisters and so escape the usual jostle of matchmaking mamas. They should have learned by now that he was not likely to succumb to their daughters' vapid charms. Still, he was not looking forward to the evening.

If truth were told, he had been hearing about his wards on all sides for the past week. They had caught the fancy of the *ton,* starved as it was of novelty. And their brand of beauty always had attraction. But what he had not heard was worrying him more. There had been more than one incident when, entering a room, he had been aware of at least one conversation abruptly halted, then smoothly resumed. Another reason to identify himself more closely with his wards. He reminded himself that three of them were truly his responsibility and, in the circumstances, the polite world would hold him responsible for Miss Twinning as well. His duty was clear.

Admitted to Twyford House, Max paused to exchange a few words with Millwade. Satisfied that all was running smoothly, he turned and stopped, all thought deserting him. Transfixed, he watched the Twinning sisters descend the grand staircase. Seen together, gorgeously garbed for the ball, they were quite the most heart-stopping sight he had beheld in many a year. His eyes rested with acclaim on each in turn, but stopped when they reached Caroline. The rest of the company seemed to dissolve in a haze as his eyes roamed appreciatively over the clean lines of her eau-de-Nil silk gown. It clung suggestively to her ripe figure, the neckline scooped low over her generous breasts. His hands burned with the desire to caress those tantalising curves. Then his eyes locked with hers as she crossed the room to his side, her hand extended to him. Automatically, he took it in his. Then she was speaking, smiling up at him in her usual confiding way.

"Thank you for coming. I do hope you'll not be too bored by such tame entertainment." Lady Benborough, on receiving Max's curt note informing them of his intention to accompany them to Almack's, had crowed with delight. When she had calmed, she had explained his aversion to the place.

So it was with an unexpected feeling of guilt that Caroline had come forward to welcome him. But, gazing into his intensely blue eyes, she could find no trace of annoyance or irritation. Instead, she recognised the same emotion she had detected the very first time they had met. To add to her confusion, he raised her hand to his lips, his eyes warm and entirely too knowing.

"Do you know, I very much doubt that I'll be bored at all?" her guardian murmured wickedly.

Caroline blushed vividly. Luckily, this was missed by all but Max in the relatively poor light of the hall and the bustle as they donned their cloaks. Both Lady Benborough and Miriam Alford were to go, cutting the odds between chaperons and charges. Before Max's intervention, the coach would have had to do two trips to King Street. Now, Caroline found that Augusta and Mrs. Alford, together with Sarah and Arabella, were to go in the Twyford coach while she and Lizzie were to travel with Max. Suddenly suspicious of her guardian's intentions, she was forced to accept the arrangement with suitable grace. As Max handed her into the carriage and saw her settled comfortably, she told herself she was a fool to read into his behaviour anything other than an attempt to trip her up. He was only amusing himself.

As if to confirm her supposition, the journey was unremarkable and soon they were entering the hallowed precincts of the Assembly Rooms. The sparsely furnished halls were already well filled with the usual mix of débutantes and unmarried young ladies, carefully chaperoned by their mamas in the hope of find-

ing a suitable connection among the unattached gentlemen strolling through the throng. It was a social
club to which it was necessary to belong. And it was
clear from their reception that, at least as far as the
gentlemen were concerned, the Twinning sisters definitely belonged. To Max's horror, they were almost
mobbed.

He stood back and watched the sisters artfully manage their admirers. Arabella had the largest court with
all the most rackety and dangerous blades. A more
discerning crowd of eminently eligible gentlemen had
formed around Sarah while the youthful Lizzie had
gathered all the more earnest of the younger men to
her. But the group around Caroline drew his deepest
consideration. There were more than a few highly
dangerous roués in the throng gathered about her but
all were experienced and none was likely to attempt
anything scandalous without encouragement. As he
watched, it became clear that all four girls had an
innate ability to choose the more acceptable among
their potential partners. They also had the happy
knack of dismissing the less favoured with real charm,
a not inconsiderable feat. The more he watched, the
more intrigued Max became. He was about to seek
clarification from his aunt, standing beside him, when
that lady very kindly answered his unspoken query.

"You needn't worry, y'know. Those girls have got
heads firmly on their shoulders. Ever since they
started going about, I've been bombarded with questions on who's eligible and who's not. Even Arabella,
minx that she is, takes good care to know who she's
flirting with.''

Max looked his puzzlement.

"Well," explained her ladyship, surprised by his obtuseness, "they're all set on finding husbands, of course!" She glanced up at him, eyes suddenly sharp, and added, "I should think you'd be thrilled—it means they'll be off your hands all the sooner."

"Yes. Of course," Max answered absently.

He stayed by his wards until they were claimed for the first dance. His sharp eyes had seen a number of less than desirable gentlemen approach the sisters, only to veer away as they saw him. If nothing else, his presence had achieved that much.

Searching through the crowd, he finally spotted Darcy Hamilton disappearing into one of the salons where refreshments were laid out.

"Going to give them the go-by for at least a week, huh?" he growled as he came up behind Lord Darcy.

Darcy choked on the lemonade he had just drunk.

Max gazed in horror at the glass in his friend's hand. "No! Bless me, Darcy! You turned temperate?"

Darcy grimaced. "Have to drink something and seemed like the best of a bad lot." His wave indicated the unexciting range of beverages available. "Thirsty work, getting a dance with one of your wards."

"Incidentally—" intoned Max in the manner of one about to pass judgement.

But Darcy held up his hand. "No. Don't start. I don't need any lectures from you on the subject. And you don't need to bother, anyway. Sarah Twinning has her mind firmly set on marriage and there's not a damned thing I can do about it."

Despite himself, Max could not resist a grin. "No luck?"

"None!" replied Darcy, goaded. "I'm almost at the stage of considering offering for her but I can't be sure she wouldn't reject me, and *that* I couldn't take."

Max, picking up a glass of lemonade himself, became thoughtful.

Suddenly, Darcy roused himself. "Do you know what she told me yesterday? Said I spent too much time on horses and not enough on matters of importance. *Can* you believe it?"

He gestured wildly and Max nearly hooted with laughter. Lord Darcy's stables were known the length and breadth of England as among the biggest and best producers of quality horseflesh.

"I very much doubt that she appreciates your interest in the field," Max said placatingly.

"Humph," was all his friend vouchsafed.

After a pause, Darcy laid aside his glass. "Going to find Maria Sefton and talk her into giving Sarah permission to waltz with me. One thing she won't be able to refuse." With a nod to Max, he returned to the main hall.

For some minutes, Max remained as he was, his abstracted gaze fixed on the far wall. Then, abruptly, he replaced his glass and followed his friend.

"You want me to give *your ward* permission to waltz with you?" Lady Jersey repeated Max's request, clearly unable to decide whether it was as innocuous as he represented or whether it had an ulterior motive concealed within and if so, what.

"It's really not such an odd request," returned Max, unperturbed. "She's somewhat older than the rest and, as I'm here, it seems appropriate."

"Hmm." Sally Jersey simply did not believe there was not more to it. She had been hard-pressed to swallow her astonishment when she had seen His Grace of Twyford enter the room. And she was even more amazed that he had not left as soon as he had seen his wards settled. But he was, after all, Twyford. And Delmere and Rotherbridge, what was more. So, if he wanted to dance with his ward… She shrugged. "Very well. Bring her to me. If you can separate her from her court, that is."

Max smiled in a way that reminded Lady Jersey of the causes of his reputation. "I think I'll manage," he drawled, bowing over her hand.

Caroline was surprised that Max had remained at the Assembly Rooms for so long. She lost sight of him for a while, and worked hard at forcing herself to pay attention to her suitors, for it was only to be expected their guardian would seek less tame entertainment elsewhere. But then his tall figure reappeared at the side of the room. He seemed to be scanning the multitude, then, over a sea of heads, his eyes met hers. Caroline fervently hoped the peculiar shock which went through her was not reflected in her countenance. After a moment, unobtrusively, he made his way to her side.

Under cover of the light flirtation she was engaged

in with an ageing baronet, Caroline was conscious of
the sudden acceleration of her heartbeat and the con-
striction that seemed to be affecting her breathing.
Horrendously aware of her guardian's blue eyes, she
felt her nervousness grow as he approached despite
her efforts to remain calm.

But, when he gained her side and bowed over her
hand in an almost bored way, uttering the most com-
monplace civilities and engaging her partner in a discussion of some sporting event, the anticlimax
quickly righted her mind for her.

Quite how it was accomplished she could not have
said, but Max succeeded in excusing them to her
court, on the grounds that he had something to discuss
with his ward. Finding herself on his arm, strolling
apparently randomly down the room, she turned to
him and asked, "What was it you wished to say to
me?"

He glanced down at her and she caught her breath.
That devilish look was back in his eyes as they rested
on her, warming her through and through. What on
earth was he playing at?

"Good heavens, my ward. And I thought you up
to all the rigs. Don't you know a ruse when you hear
it?"

The tones of his voice washed languorously over
Caroline, leaving a sense of relaxation in their wake.
She made a grab for her fast-disappearing faculties.
Interpreting his remark to mean that his previously
bored attitude had also been false, Caroline was left
wondering what the present reality meant. She made

a desperate bid to get their interaction back on an acceptable footing. "Where are we going?"

Max smiled. "We're on our way to see Lady Jersey."

"Why?"

"Patience, sweet Caroline," came the reply, all the more outrageous for its tone. "All will be revealed forthwith."

They reached Lady Jersey's side where she stood just inside the main room.

"There you are, Twyford!"

The Duke of Twyford smoothly presented his ward. Her ladyship's prominent eyes rested on the curtsying Caroline, then, as the younger woman rose, widened with a suddenly arrested expression. She opened her mouth to ask the question burning the tip of her tongue but caught His Grace's eye and, reluctantly swallowing her curiosity, said, "My dear Miss Twinning. Your guardian has requested you to be given permission to waltz and I have no hesitation in granting it. And, as he is here, I present the Duke as a suitable partner."

With considerable effort, Caroline managed to school her features to impassivity. Luckily, the musicians struck up at that moment, so that she barely had time to murmur her thanks to Lady Jersey before Max swept her on to the floor, leaving her ladyship, intrigued, staring after them.

Caroline struggled to master the unnerving sensation of being in her guardian's arms. He was holding her closer than strictly necessary, but, as they twirled down the room, she realised that to everyone else they presented a perfect picture of the Duke of Twyford doing the pretty by his eldest ward. Only she was close enough to see the disturbing glint in his blue eyes and hear the warmth in his tone as he said, "My dear ward, what a very accomplished dancer you are. Tell me, what other talents do you have that I've yet to sample?"

For the life of her, Caroline could not tear her eyes from his. She heard his words and understood their meaning but her brain refused to react. No shock, no scandalized response came to her lips. Instead, her mind was completely absorbed with registering the unbelievable fact that, despite their relationship of guardian and ward, Max Rotherbridge had every intention of seducing her. His desire was clear in the heat of his blue, blue gaze, in the way his hand at her back seemed to burn through the fine silk of her gown, in the gentle caress of his long fingers across her knuckles as he twirled her about the room under the long noses of the biggest gossips in London.

Mesmerized, she had sufficient presence of mind to keep a gentle smile fixed firmly on her face but her thoughts were whirling even faster than her feet. With a superhuman effort, she forced her lids to drop, screening her eyes from his. "Oh, we Twinnings have many accomplishments, dear guardian." To her relief, her voice was clear and untroubled. "But I'm desolated to have to admit that they're all hopelessly mundane."

A rich chuckle greeted this. "Permit me to tell you, my ward, that, for the skills I have in mind, your qualifications are more than adequate." Caroline's eyes flew to his. She could hardly believe her ears. But Max continued before she could speak, his blue eyes holding hers, his voice a seductive murmur. "And while you naturally lack experience, I assure you that can easily, and most enjoyably, be remedied."

It was too much. Caroline gave up the struggle to divine his motives and made a determined bid to reinstitute sanity. She smiled into the dark face above hers and said, quite clearly, "This isn't happening."

For a moment, Max was taken aback. Then, his sense of humour surfaced. "No?"

"Of course not," Caroline calmly replied. "You're my guardian and I'm your ward. Therefore, it is simply not possible for you to have said what you just did."

Studying her serene countenance, Max recognised the strategy and reluctantly admired her courage for adopting it. As things stood, it was not an easy defence for him to overcome. Reading in the grey-green eyes a determination not to be further discomposed, Max, too wise to push further, gracefully yielded.

"So what do you think of Almack's?" he asked.

Relieved, Caroline took the proffered olive branch and their banter continued on an impersonal level.

At the end of the dance, Max suavely surrendered her to her admirers, but not without a glance which, if she had allowed herself to think about it, would have made Caroline blush. She did not see him again until it was time for them to quit the Assembly Rooms. In order to survive the evening, she had sternly refused to let her mind dwell on his behaviour.

Consequently, it had not occurred to her to arrange to exchange her place in her guardian's carriage for one in the Twyford coach. When Lizzie came to tug at her sleeve with the information that the others had already left, she perceived her error. But the extent of her guardian's foresight did not become apparent until they were halfway home.

She and Max shared the forward facing seat with Lizzie curled up in a corner opposite them. On departing King Street, they preserved a comfortable silence—due to tiredness in Lizzie's case, from being too absorbed with her thoughts in her case and, as she suddenly realised, from sheer experience in the case of her guardian.

They were still some distance from Mount Street when, without warning, Max took her hand in his. Surprised, she turned to look up at him, conscious of his fingers moving gently over hers. Despite the darkness of the carriage, his eyes caught hers. Deliberately, he raised her hand and kissed her fingertips. A delicious tingle raced along Caroline's nerves, followed by a second of increased vigour as he turned her hand over and placed a lingering kiss on her wrist. But they were nothing compared to the galvanising shock that hit her when, without giving any intimation of his intent, he bent his head and his lips found hers.

From Max's point of view, he was behaving with admirable restraint. He knew Lizzie was sound asleep and that his manipulative and normally composed eldest ward was well out of her depth. Yet he reined in his desires and kept the kiss light, his lips moving gently over hers, gradually increasing the pressure until she parted her lips. He savoured the warm sweetness of her mouth, then, inwardly smiling at the response she had been unable to hide, he withdrew and watched as her eyes slowly refocused.

Caroline, eyes round, looked at him in consternation. Then her shocked gaze flew to Lizzie, still curled in her corner.

"Don't worry. She's sound asleep." His voice was deep and husky in the dark carriage.

Caroline, stunned, felt oddly reassured by the sound. Then she felt the carriage slow.

"And you're safe home," came the gently mocking voice.

In a daze, Caroline helped him wake Lizzie and then Max very correctly escorted them indoors, a smile of wicked contentment on his face.

Arabella stifled a wistful sigh and smiled brightly at the earnest young man who was guiding her around the floor in yet another interminable waltz. It had taken only a few days of the Season proper for her to sort through her prospective suitors. And come to the unhappy conclusion that none matched her requirements. The lads were too young, the men too old. There seemed to be no one in between. Presumably many were away with Wellington's forces, but surely there were those who could not leave the important business of keeping England running? And surely not all of them were old? She could not describe her ideal man, yet was sure she would instantly know when she met him. She was convinced she would feel it, like a thunderbolt from the blue. Yet no male of her acquaintance increased her heartbeat one iota.

Keeping up a steady and inconsequential conversation with her partner, something she could do half asleep, Arabella sighted her eldest sister, elegantly waltzing with their guardian. Now there was a coil. There was little doubt in Arabella's mind of the cause of Caroline's bright eyes and slightly flushed countenance. She looked radiant. But could a guardian marry his ward? Or, more to the point, was their guardian intent on marriage or had he some other arrangement in mind? Still, she had complete faith in Caroline. There had been many who had worshipped at her feet with something other than matrimony in view, yet her eldest sister had always had their measure. True, none had affected her as Max Rotherbridge clearly did. But Caroline knew the ropes, few better.

"I'll escort you back to Lady Benborough."

The light voice of her partner drew her thoughts back to the present. With a quick smile, Arabella declined. "I think I've torn my flounce. I'll just go and pin it up. Perhaps you could inform Lady Benborough that I'll return immediately?" She smiled dazzlingly upon the young man. Bemused, he bowed and moved away into the crowd. Her flounce was perfectly intact but she needed some fresh air and in no circumstances could she have borne another half-hour of that particular young gentleman's serious discourse.

She started towards the door, then glanced back to see Augusta receive her message without apparent perturbation. Arabella turned back to the door and immediately collided with a chest of quite amazing proportions.

"Oh!"

For a moment, she thought the impact had winded her. Then, looking up into the face of the mountain she had met, she realised it wasn't that at all. It was the thunderbolt she had been waiting for.

Unfortunately, the gentleman seemed unaware of this momentous happening. "My apologies, m'dear. Didn't see you there."

The lazy drawl washed over Arabella. He was tall, very tall, and seemed almost as broad, with curling blond hair and laughing hazel eyes. He had quite the most devastating smile she had ever seen. Her knees felt far too weak to support her if she moved, so she stood still and stared, mouthing she knew not what platitudes.

The gentleman seemed to find her reaction amusing. But, with a polite nod and another melting smile, he was gone.

Stunned, Arabella found herself standing in the doorway staring at his retreating back. Sanity returned with a thump. Biting back a far from ladylike curse, she swept out in search of the withdrawing-room. The use of a borrowed fan and the consumption of a glass of cool water helped to restore her outward calm. Inside, her resentment grew.

No gentleman simply excused himself and walked away from her. That was her role. Men usually tried to stay by her side as long as possible. Yet this man had seemed disinclined to linger. Arabella was not vain but wondered what was more fascinating than herself that he needs must move on so abruptly. Surely he had felt that strange jolt just as she had? Maybe he wasn't a ladies' man? But no. The memory of the decided appreciation which had glowed so warmly in his hazel eyes put paid to that idea. And, now she came to think of it, the comprehensive glance which had roamed suggestively over most of her had been decidedly impertinent.

Arabella returned to the ballroom determined to bring her large gentleman to heel, if for no better reason than to assure herself she had been mistaken in him. But frustration awaited her. He was not there. For the rest of the evening, she searched the throng but caught no glimpse of her quarry. Then, just before the last dance, another waltz, he appeared in the doorway from the card-room.

Surrounded by her usual court, Arabella was at her effervescent best. Her smile was dazzling as she openly debated, laughingly teasing, over who to bestow her hand on for this last dance. Out of the corner of her eye, she watched the unknown gentleman approach. And walk past her to solicit the hand of a plain girl in an outrageously overdecorated pink gown.

Arabella bit her lip in vexation but managed to conceal it as severe concentration on her decision. As the musicians struck up, she accepted handsome Lord Tulloch as her partner and studiously paid him the most flattering attention for the rest of the evening.

## Chapter Five

Max was worried. Seriously worried. Since that first night at Almack's, the situation between Sarah Twinning and Darcy Hamilton had rapidly deteriorated to a state which, from experience, he knew was fraught with danger. As he watched Sarah across Lady Overton's ballroom, chatting with determined avidity to an eminently respectable and thoroughly boring young gentleman, his brows drew together in a considering frown. If, at the beginning of his guardianship, anyone had asked him where his sympathies would lie, with the Misses Twinning or the gentlemen of London, he would unhesitatingly have allied himself with his wards, on the grounds that four exquisite but relatively inexperienced country misses would need all the help they could get to defend their virtue successfully against the highly knowledgeable rakes extant within the *ton*. Now, a month later, having gained first-hand experience of the tenacious perversity of the Twinning sisters, he was not so sure.

His behaviour with Caroline on the night of their first visit to Almack's had been a mistake. How much of a mistake had been slowly made clear to him over the succeeding weeks. He was aware of the effect he had on her, had been aware of it from the first time he had seen her in his library at Delmere House. But in order to make any use of that weapon, he had to have her to himself. A fact, unfortunately, that she had worked out for herself. Consequently, whenever he approached her, he found her surrounded either by admirers who had been given too much encouragement for him to dismiss easily or one or more of her far too perceptive sisters. Lizzie, it was true, was not attuned to the situation between her eldest sister and their guardian. But he had unwisely made use of her innocence, to no avail as it transpired, and was now unhappily certain he would get no further opportunity by that route. Neither Arabella nor Sarah was the least bit perturbed by his increasingly blatant attempts to be rid of them. He was sure that, if he was ever goaded into ordering them to leave their sister alone with him, they would laugh and refuse. And tease him unmercifully about it, what was more. He had already had to withstand one episode of Arabella's artful play, sufficiently subtle, thank God, so that the others in the group had not understood her meaning.

His gaze wandered to where the third Twinning sister held court, seated on a chaise surrounded by ardent swains, her huge eyes wickedly dancing with mischief. As he watched, she tossed a comment to one of the circle and turned, her head playfully tilted, to throw a glance of open invitation into the handsome face of a blond giant standing before her. Max stiffened. Hell and the devil! He would have to put a stop to that game, and quickly. He had no difficulty in recognising the large frame of Hugo, Lord Denbigh. Although a few years younger than himself, in character and accomplishments there was little to choose between them. Under his horrified gaze, Hugo took advantage of a momentary distraction which had succeeded in removing attention temporarily from Arabella to lean forward and whisper something, Max could guess what, into her ear. The look she gave him in response made Max set his jaw grimly. Then, Hugo extended one large hand and Arabella, adroitly excusing herself to her other admirers, allowed him to lead her on to the floor. A waltz was just starting up.

Knowing there was only so much Hugo could do on a crowded ballroom floor, Max made a resolution to call on his aunt and wards on the morrow, firmly determined to acquaint them with his views on encouraging rakes. Even as the idea occurred, he groaned. How on earth could he tell Arabella to cease her flirtation with Hugo on the grounds he was a rake when he was himself trying his damnedest to seduce her sister and his best friend was similarly occupied with Sarah? He had known from the outset that this crazy situation would not work.

Reminded of what had originally prompted him to stand just inside the door between Lady Overton's ballroom and the salon set aside for cards and quietly study the company, Max returned his eyes to Sarah Twinning. Despite her assured manner, she was on edge, her hands betraying her nervousness as they played with the lace on her gown. Occasionally, her eyes would lift fleetingly to the door behind him.

While to his experienced eye she was not looking her best, Darcy, ensconced in the card-room, was looking even worse. He had been drinking steadily throughout the evening and, although far from drunk, was fast attaining a dangerous state. Suffering from Twinning-induced frustration himself, Max could readily sympathise. He sincerely hoped his pursuit of the eldest Miss Twinning would not bring him so low. His friendship with Darcy Hamilton stretched back over fifteen years. In all that time he had never seen his friend so affected by the desire of a particular woman. Like himself, Darcy was an experienced lover who liked to keep his affairs easy and uncomplicated. If a woman proved difficult, he was much more likely to shrug and, with a smile, pass on to greener fields. But with Sarah Twinning, he seemed unable to admit defeat.

The thought that he himself had no intention of letting the elder Miss Twinning escape and was, even now, under the surface of his preoccupation with his other wards, plotting to get her into his arms, and, ultimately, into his bed, surfaced to shake his self-confidence. His black brows rose a little, in self-mockery. One could hardly blame the girls for keeping them at arm's length. The Twinning sisters had never encouraged them to believe they were of easy virtue, nor that they would accept anything less than marriage. Their interaction, thus far, had all been part of the game. By rights, it was they, the rakes of London, who should now acknowledge the evident truth that, despite their bountiful attractions, the Twinnings were virtuous females in search of husbands. And, having acknowledged that fact, to desist from their pursuit of the fair ladies. Without conscious thought on his part, his eyes strayed to where Caroline stood amid a group, mostly men, by the side of the dance floor. She laughed and responded to some comment, her copper curls gleaming like rosy gold in the bright light thrown down by the chandeliers. As if feeling his gaze, she turned and, across the intervening heads, their eyes met. Both were still. Then, she smoothly turned back to her companions and Max, straightening his shoulders, moved further into the crowd. The trouble was, he did not think that he, any more than Darcy, could stop.

Max slowly passed through the throng, stopping here and there to chat with acquaintances, his intended goal his aunt, sitting in a blaze of glorious purple on a chaise by the side of the room. But before he had reached her, a hand on his arm drew him around to face the sharp features of Emma Mortland.

"Your Grace! It's been such an age since we've...talked." Her ladyship's brown eyes quizzed him playfully.

Her arch tone irritated Max. It was on the tip of his tongue to recommend she took lessons in flirting from Arabella before she tried her tricks on him. Instead, he took her hand from his sleeve, bowed over it and pointedly returned to her, "As you're doubtless aware, Emma, I have other claims on my time."

His careless use of her first name was calculated to annoy but Lady Mortland, having seen his absorption with his wards, particularly his eldest ward, over the past weeks, was fast coming to the conclusion that she should do everything in her power to bring Twyford to his knees or that tiara would slip through her fingers. As she was a female of little intelligence, she sincerely believed the attraction that had brought Max Rotherbridge to her bed would prove sufficient to induce him to propose. Consequently, she coyly glanced up at him through her long fair lashes and sighed sympathetically. "Oh, my dear, *I know*. I do *feel* for you. This business of being guardian to four country girls must be such a bore to you. But surely, as a diversion, you could manage to spare us some few hours?"

Not for the first time, Max wondered where women such as Emma Mortland kept their intelligence. In their pockets? One truly had to wonder. As he looked down at her, his expression unreadable, he realized that she was a year or so younger than Caroline. Yet, from the single occasion on which he had shared her bed, he knew the frills and furbelows she favoured disguised a less than attractive figure, lacking the curves that characterized his eldest ward. And Emma Mortland's energies, it seemed, were reserved for scheming. He had not been impressed. As he knew that a number of gentlemen, including Darcy Hamilton, had likewise seen her sheets, he was at a loss to understand why she continued to single him out. A caustic dismissal was about to leave his lips when, amid a burst of hilarity from a group just behind them, he heard the rich tones of his eldest ward's laugh.

On the instant, a plan, fully formed, came into his head and, without further consideration, he acted. He allowed a slow, lazy smile to spread across his face.

"How well you read me, my sweet," he drawled to the relieved Lady Mortland. Encouraged, she put her hand tentatively on his arm. He took it in his hand, intending to raise it to his lips, but to his surprise he could not quite bring himself to do so. Instead, he smiled meaningfully into her eyes. With an ease born of countless hours of practice, he instituted a conversation of the risqué variety certain to appeal to Lady Mortland. Soon, he had her gaily laughing and flirting freely with her eyes and her fan. Deliberately, he turned to lead her on to the floor for the waltz just commencing, catching, as he did, a look of innocent surprise on Caroline's face.

Grinning devilishly, Max encouraged Emma to the limits of acceptable flirtation. Then, satisfied with the scene he had created, as they circled the room, he raised his head to see the effect the sight of Lady Mortland in his arms was having on Caroline. To his chagrin, he discovered his eldest ward was no longer standing where he had last seen her. After a frantic visual search, during which he ignored Emma entirely, he located Caroline, also dancing, with the highly suitable Mr. Willoughby. That same Mr. Willoughby who, he knew, was becoming very particular in his attentions. Smothering a curse, Max half-heartedly returned his attention to Lady Mortland.

He had intended to divest himself of the encumbrance of her ladyship as soon as the dance ended but, as the music ceased, he realized they were next to Caroline and her erstwhile partner. Again, Emma found herself the object of Max's undeniable, if strangely erratic charm. Under its influence, she blossomed and bloomed. Max, with one eye on Caroline's now unreadable countenance, leaned closer to Emma to whisper an invitation to view the beauties of the moonlit garden. As he had hoped, she crooned her delight and, with an air of anticipated pleasure, allowed him to escort her through the long windows leading on to the terrace.

"Count me out." Darcy Hamilton threw his cards on to the table and pushed back his chair. None of the other players was surprised to see him leave. Normally an excellent player, tonight his lordship had clearly had his mind elsewhere. And the brandy he had drunk was hardly calculated to improve matters, although his gait, as he headed for the ballroom, was perfectly steady.

In the ballroom, Darcy paused to glance about. He saw the musicians tuning up and then sighted his prey.

Almost as if she sensed his approach, Sarah turned as he came up to her. The look of sudden wariness that came into her large eyes pricked his conscience and, consequently, his temper. "My dance, I think."

It was not, as he well knew, but before she could do more than open her mouth to deny him Darcy had swept her on to the floor.

They were both excellent dancers and, despite their current difficulties, they moved naturally and easily together. Which was just as well, as their minds were each completely absorbed in trying to gauge the condition of the other. Luckily, they were both capable of putting on a display of calmness which succeeded in deflecting the interest of the curious.

Sarah, her heart, as usual, beating far too fast, glanced up under her lashes at the handsome face above her, now drawn and slightly haggard. Her heart sank. She had no idea what the outcome of this strange relationship of theirs would be, but it seemed to be causing both of them endless pain. Darcy Hamilton filled her thoughts, day in, day out. But he had steadfastly refused to speak of marriage, despite the clear encouragement she had given him to do so. He had side-stepped her invitations, offering, instead, to introduce her to a vista of illicit delights whose temptation was steadily increasing with time. But she could not, would not accept. She would give anything in the world to be his wife but had no ambition to be his mistress. Lady Benborough had, with all kindness, dropped her a hint that he was very likely a confirmed bachelor, too wedded to his equestrian interests to be bothered with a wife and family, satisfied instead with mistresses and the occasional *affaire*. Surreptitiously studying his rigid and unyielding face, she could find no reason to doubt Augusta's assessment. If that was so, then their association must end. And the sooner the better, for it was breaking her heart.

Seeing her unhappiness reflected in the brown pools of her eyes, Darcy inwardly cursed. There were times he longed to hurt her, in retribution for the agony she was putting him through, but any pain she felt seemed to rebound, ten times amplified, back on him. He was, as Lady Benborough had rightly surmised, well satisfied with his bachelor life. At least, he had been, until he had met Sarah Twinning. Since then, nothing seemed to be right any more. Regardless of the response he knew he awoke in her, she consistently denied any interest in the delightful pleasures he was only too willing to introduce her to. Or rather, held the prospect of said pleasures like a gun at his head, demanding matrimony. He would be damned if he would yield to such tactics. He had long ago considered matrimony, the state of, in a calm and reasoned way, and had come to the conclusion that it held few benefits for him. The idea of being driven, forced, pushed into taking such a step, essentially by the strength of his own raging desires, horrified him, leaving him annoyed beyond measure, principally with himself, but also, unreasonably he knew, with the object of said desires. As the music slowed and halted, he looked down at her lovely face and determined to give her one last chance to capitulate. If she remained adamant, he would have to leave London until the end of the Season. He was quite sure he could not bear the agony any longer.

As Sarah drew away from him and turned towards the room, Darcy drew her hand through his arm and deftly steered her towards the long windows leading on to the terrace. As she realized his intention, she hung back. With a few quick words, he reassured her. "I just want to talk to you. Come into the garden."

Thus far, Sarah had managed to avoid being totally private with him, too aware of her inexperience to chance such an interview. But now, looking into his pale grey eyes and seeing her own unhappiness mirrored there, she consented with a nod and they left the ballroom.

A stone terrace extended along the side of the house, the balustrade broken here and there by steps leading down to the gardens. Flambeaux placed in brackets along the walls threw flickering light down into the avenues and any number of couples could be seen, walking and talking quietly amid the greenery.

Unhurriedly, Darcy led her to the end of the terrace and then down the steps into a deserted walk. They both breathed in the heady freshness of the night air, calming their disordered senses and, without the need to exchange words, each drew some measure of comfort from the other's presence. At the end of the path, a secluded summer-house stood, white paintwork showing clearly against the black shadows of the shrubbery behind it.

As Darcy had hoped, the summer-house was deserted. The path leading to it was winding and heavily screened. Only those who knew of its existence would be likely to find it. He ushered Sarah through the narrow door and let it fall quietly shut behind them. The moonlight slanted through the windows, bathing the room in silvery tints. Sarah stopped in the middle of the circular floor and turned to face him. Darcy paused, trying to decide where to start, then crossed to stand before her, taking her hands in his. For some moments, they stood thus, the rake and the maid, gazing silently into each other's eyes. Then Darcy bent his head and his lips found hers.

Sarah, seduced by the setting, the moonlight and the man before her, allowed him to gather her, unresisting, into his arms. The magic of his lips on hers was a more potent persuasion than any she had previously encountered. Caught by a rising tide of passion, she was drawn, helpless and uncaring, beyond the bounds of thought. Her lips parted and gradually the kiss deepened until, with the moonlight washing in waves over then, he stole her soul.

It was an unintentionally intimate caress which abruptly shook the stars from her eyes and brought her back to earth with an unsteady bump. Holding her tightly within one arm, Darcy had let his other hand slide, gently caressing, over her hip, intending to draw her more firmly against him. But the feel of his hand, scorching through her thin evening dress, sent shock waves of such magnitude through Sarah's pliant body that she pulled back with a gasp. Then, as horrified realization fell like cold water over her heated flesh, she tore herself from his arms and ran.

For an instant, Darcy, stunned both by her response and by her subsequent reaction, stood frozen in the middle of the floor. A knot of jonquil ribbon from Sarah's dress had caught on the button of his cuff and impatiently he shook it free, then watched, fascinated, as it floated to the ground. The banging of the wooden door against its frame had stilled. Swiftly, he crossed the floor and, opening the door, stood in the aperture, listening to her footsteps dying in the spring night. Then, smothering a curse, he followed.

Sarah instinctively ran away from the main house, towards the shrubbery which lay behind the summerhouse. She did not stop to think or reason, but just ran. Finally, deep within the tall clipped hedges and the looming bushes, her breath coming in gasps, she came to a clearing, a small garden at the centre of the shrubbery. She saw a marble bench set in an arbour. Thankfully, she sank on to it and buried her face in her hands.

Darcy, following, made for the shrubbery, her hurrying footsteps echoing hollowly on the gravel walks giving him the lead. But once she reached the grassed avenues between the high hedges, her feet made no sound. Penetrating the dark alleys, he was forced to go slowly, checking this way and that to make sure he did not pass her by. So quite fifteen minutes had passed before he reached the central garden and saw the dejected figure huddled on the bench.

In that time, sanity of sorts had returned to Sarah's mind. Her initial horror at her weakness had been replaced by the inevitable reaction. She was angry. Angry at herself, for being so weak that one kiss could overcome all her defences; angry at Darcy, for having engineered that little scene. She was busy whipping up the necessary fury to face the prospect of not seeing him ever again, when he materialized at her side. With a gasp, she came to her feet.

Relieved to find she was not crying, as he had thought, Darcy immediately caught her hand to prevent her flying from him again.

Stung by the shock his touch always gave her, intensified now, she was annoyed to discover, Sarah tried to pull her hand away. When he refused to let her go, she said, her voice infused with an iciness designed to freeze, "Kindly release me, Lord Darcy."

On hearing her voice, Darcy placed the emotion

that was holding her so rigid. The knowledge that she was angry, nay, furious, did nothing to improve his own temper, stirred to life by her abrupt flight. Forcing his voice to a reasonableness he was far from feeling, he said, "If you'll give me your word you'll not run away from me, I'll release you."

Sarah opened her mouth to inform him she would not so demean herself as to run from him when the knowledge that she just had, and might have reason to do so again, hit her. She remained silent. Darcy, accurately reading her mind, held on to her hand.

After a moment's consideration, he spoke. "I had intended, my dear, to speak to you of our…curious relationship."

Sarah, breathing rapidly and anxious to end the interview, immediately countered, "I really don't think there's anything to discuss."

A difficult pause ensued, then, "So you would deny there's anything between us?"

The bleakness in his voice shook her, but she determinedly put up her chin, turning away from him as far as their locked hands would allow. "Whatever's between us is neither here nor there," she said, satisfied with the lightness she had managed to bring to her tone.

Her satisfaction was short-lived. Taking advantage of her movement, Darcy stepped quickly behind her, the hand still holding hers reaching across her, his arm wrapping around her waist and drawing her hard against him. His other hand came to rest on her shoulder, holding her still. He knew the shock it would give her, to feel his body against hers, and heard with grim satisfaction the hiss of her indrawn breath.

Sarah froze, too stunned to struggle, the sensation of his hard body against her back, his arm wound like steel about her waist, holding her fast, driving all rational thought from her brain. Then his breath wafted the curls around her ear. His words came in a deep and husky tone, sending tingling shivers up and down her spine.

"Well, sweetheart, there's very little between us now. So, perhaps we can turn our attention to our relationship?"

Sarah, all too well aware of how little there was between them, wondered in a moment of startling lucidity how he imagined that would improve her concentration. But Darcy's attention had already wandered. His lips were very gently trailing down her neck, creating all sorts of marvellous sensations which she tried very hard to ignore.

Then, he gave a deep chuckle. "As I've been saying these weeks past, my dear, you're wasted as a virgin. Now, if you were to become my mistress, just think of all the delightful avenues we could explore."

"I don't want to become your mistress!" Sarah almost wailed, testing the arm at her waist and finding it immovable.

"No?" came Darcy's voice in her ear. She had the impression he considered her answer for a full minute before he continued, "Perhaps we should extend your education a trifle, my dear. So you fully appreciate what you're turning down. We wouldn't want you to make the wrong decision for lack of a few minutes' instruction, would we?''

Sarah had only a hazy idea of what he could mean but his lips had returned to her throat, giving rise to those strangely heady swirls of pleasure that washed through her, sapping her will. ''Darcy, stop! You know you shouldn't be doing this!''

He stilled. ''Do I?''

Into the silence, a nightingale warbled. Sarah held her breath.

But, when Darcy spoke again, the steel threading his voice, so often sensed yet only now recognised, warned her of the futility of missish pleas.

''Yes. You're right. I know I shouldn't.'' His lips moved against her throat, a subtle caress. ''But what I want to do is make love to you. As you won't allow that, then this will have to do for now.''

Sarah, incapable of further words, simply shook her head, powerless to halt the spreading fires he was so skilfully igniting.

Afterwards, Darcy could not understand how it had happened. He was as experienced with women as Max and had never previously lost control as he did that night. He had intended to do no more than reveal to the perverse woman her own desires and give her some inkling of the pleasures they could enjoy together. Instead, her responses were more than he had bargained for and his own desires stronger than he had been prepared to admit. Fairly early in the engagement, he had turned her once more into his arms, so he could capture her lips and take the lesson further. And further it had certainly gone, until the moon sank behind the high hedges and left them in darkness.

How the hell was he to get rid of her? Max, Lady Mortland on his arm, had twice traversed the terrace. He had no intention of descending to the shadowy avenues. He had no intention of paying any further attention to Lady Mortland at all. Lady Mortland, on the other hand, was waiting for his attentions to begin and was rather surprised at his lack of ardour in keeping to the terrace.

They were turning at the end of the terrace, when Max, glancing along, saw Caroline come out of the ballroom, alone, and walk quickly to the balustrade and peer over. She was clearly seeking someone. Emma Mortland, prattling on at his side, had not seen her. With the reflexes necessary for being one of the more successful rakes in the *ton,* Max whisked her ladyship back into the ballroom via the door they were about to pass.

Finding herself in the ballroom once more, with the Duke of Twyford bowing over her hand in farewell, Lady Mortland put a hand to her spinning head. "Oh! But surely…"

"A guardian is never off duty for long, my dear," drawled Max, about to move off.

"Perhaps I'll see you in the Park, tomorrow?" asked Emma, convinced his departure had nothing to do with inclination.

Max smiled. "Anything's possible."

He took a circuitous route around the ballroom and exited through the same door he had seen his ward use. Gaining the terrace, he almost knocked her over as she returned to the ballroom, looking back over her shoulder towards the gardens.

"Oh!" Finding herself unexpectedly in her guardian's arms temporarily suspended Caroline's faculties.

From her face, Max knew she had not been looking for him. He drew her further into the shadows of the terrace, placing her hand on his arm and covering it comfortingly with his. "What is it?"

Caroline could not see any way of avoiding telling him. She fell into step beside him, unconsciously following his lead. "Sarah. Lizzie saw her leave the ballroom with Lord Darcy. More than twenty minutes ago. They haven't returned."

In the dim light, Max's face took on a grim look. He had suspected there would be trouble. He continued strolling towards the end of the terrace. "I know where they'll be. There's a summer-house deeper in the gardens. I think you had better come with me."

Caroline nodded and, unobtrusively, they made their way to the summer-house.

Max pushed open the door, then frowned at the empty room. He moved further in and Caroline followed. "Not here?"

Max shook his head, then bent to pick up a knot of ribbon from the floor.

Caroline came to see and took it from him. She crossed to the windows, turning the small cluster this way and that to gauge the colour.

"Is it hers?" asked Max as he strolled to her side.

"Yes. I can't see the colour well but I know the knot. It's a peculiar one. I made it myself."

"So they were here."

"But where are they now?"

"Almost certainly on their way back to the house," answered Max. "There's nowhere in this garden suitable for the purpose Darcy would have in mind. Presumably, your sister convinced him to return to more populated surroundings." He spoke lightly, but, in truth, was puzzled. He could not readily imagine Sarah turning Darcy from his purpose, not in his present mood, not in this setting. But he was sure there was nowhere else they could go.

"Well, then," said Caroline, dusting the ribbon, "we'd better go back, too."

"In a moment," said Max.

His tone gave Caroline an instant's warning. She put out a hand to fend him off. "No! This is *absurd*— you know it is."

Despite her hand, Max succeeded in drawing her into his arms, holding her lightly. "Absurd, is it? Well, you just keep on thinking how absurd it is, while I enjoy your very sweet lips." And he proceeded to do just that.

As his lips settled over hers, Caroline told herself she should struggle. But, for some mystical reason, her body remained still, her senses turned inward by his kiss. Under gentle persuasion, her lips parted and, with a thrill, she felt his gentle exploration teasing her senses, somehow drawing her deeper. Time seemed suspended and she felt her will weakening as she melted into his arms and they locked around her.

Max's mind was ticking in double time, evaluating the amenities of the summer-house and estimating

how long they could remain absent from the ballroom. He decided neither answer was appropriate. Seduction was an art and should not be hurried. Besides,
he doubted his eldest ward was quite ready to submit
yet. Reluctantly, he raised his head and grinned wolfishly at her. "Still absurd?"

Caroline's wits were definitely not connected. She
simply stared at him uncomprehendingly.

In face of this response, Max laughed and, drawing
her arm through his, steered her to the door. "I think
you're right. We'd better return."

Sanity returned to Sarah's mind like water in a
bucket, slowing filling from a dripping tap, bit by bit,
until it was full. For one long moment, she allowed
her mind to remain blank, savouring the pleasure of
being held so gently against him. Then, the world
returned and demanded her response. She struggled
to sit up and was promptly helped to her feet. She
checked her gown and found it perfectly tidy, bar one
knot of ribbon on her sleeve which seemed to have
gone missing.

Darcy, who had returned to earth long before, had
been engaged in some furious thinking. But, try as he
might, he could not imagine how she would react.
Like Max, it had been a long time since young virgins
had been his prey. As she stood, he tried to catch a
glimpse of her face in the dim light but she perversely
kept it averted. In the end, he caught her hands and
drew her to stand before him. "Sweetheart, are you
all right?"

Strangely enough, it was the note of sincerity in his

voice which snapped Sarah's control. Her head came up and, even in the darkness, her eyes flashed fire. "Of course I'm not all right! How *dare* you take advantage of me?"

She saw Darcy's face harden at her words and, in fury at his lack of comprehension, she slapped him.

For a minute, absolute silence reigned. Then a sob broke from Sarah as she turned away, her head bent to escape the look on Darcy's face.

Darcy, slamming a door on his emotions, so turbulent that even he had no idea what he felt, moved to rescue them both. In a voice totally devoid of all feeling, he said, "We had better get back to the house."

In truth, neither had any idea how long they had been absent. In silence, they walked side by side, careful not to touch each other, until, eventually, the terrace was reached. Sarah, crying but determined not to let the tears fall, blinked hard, then mounted the terrace steps by Darcy's side. At the top, he turned to her. "It would be better, I think, if you went in first."

Sarah, head bowed, nodded and went.

Caroline and Max regained the ballroom and both glanced around for their party. Almost immediately, Lizzie appeared by her sister's side on the arm of one of her youthful swains. She prettily thanked him and dismissed him before turning to her sister and their guardian. "Sarah came back just after you left to look for her. She and Lady Benborough and Mrs. Alford have gone home."

"Oh?" It was Max's voice which answered her. "Why?"

Lizzie cast a questioning look at Caroline and received a nod in reply. "Sarah was upset about something."

Max was already scanning the room when Lizzie's voice reached him. "Lord Darcy came in a little while after Sarah. He's left now, too."

With a sigh, Max realized there was nothing more to be done that night. They collected Arabella and departed Overton House, Caroline silently considering Sarah's problem and Max wondering if he was going to have to wait until his friend solved his dilemma before he would be free to settle his own affairs.

In truth, neither had any idea how long they had both waited in silence, they walked side by side, careful not to touch each other, until, eventually, the corner was reached. Sarah, content but determined not to let the tears fall, allowed hand, then regained the manner of Lord Darcy's side. At the top, he turned to her. "It would be better, I think, if you went in alone."

Sarah, head bowed, nodded and went in.

Caroline and Max re-entered the ballroom and both glanced around for short party. Almost immediately, Lizzie appeared by her side on the arm of one of her would-be suitors. She pulled herself free, and then sent him before turning to her aunt and their guardian. "Sarah came back just after you had been gone long. She and Lady Harborough and Mr. Willoughby have gone home."

## Chapter Six

Max took a long sip of his brandy and savoured the smooth warmth as it slid down his throat. He stretched his legs to the fire. The book he had been trying to reach rested open, on his thighs, one strong hand holding it still. He moved his shoulders slightly, settling them into the comfort of well padded leather and let his head fall back against the chair.

It was the first night since the beginning of the Season that he had had a quiet evening at home. And he needed it. Who would have thought his four wards would make such a drastic change in a hitherto well-ordered existence? Then he remembered. He had. But he had not really believed his own dire predictions. And the only reason he was at home tonight was because Sarah, still affected by her brush with Darcy the night before, had elected to remain at home and Caroline had stayed with her. He deemed his aunt Augusta and Miriam Alford capable of chaperoning the two younger girls between them. After the previous night, it was unlikely they would allow any liberties.

Even now, no one had had an accounting of what had actually taken place between Darcy and Sarah. But, knowing Darcy, his imagination had supplied a quantity of detail. He had left Delmere House at noon that day with the full intention of running his lordship to earth and demanding an explanation. He had finally found him at Manton's Shooting Gallery, culping wafer after wafer with grim precision. One look at his friend's face had been enough to cool his temper. He had patiently waited until Darcy, having dispatched all the wafers currently in place, had thrown the pistol down with an oath and turned to him.

"Don't ask!"

So he had preserved a discreet silence on the subject and together they had rolled about town, eventually ending in Cribb's back parlour, drinking Blue Ruin. Only then had Darcy reverted to the topic occupying both their minds. "I'm leaving town."

"Oh?"

His lordship had run a hand through his perfectly cut golden locks, disarranging them completely, in a gesture Max had never, in all their years together, seen him use. "Going to Leicestershire. I need a holiday."

Max had nodded enigmatically. Lord Darcy's principal estates lay in Leicestershire and always, due to the large number of horses he raised, demanded attention. But in general, his lordship managed to run his business affairs quite comfortably from town.

"No, by God! I've got a better idea. I'll go to Ireland. It's further away."

As Max knew, Lord Darcy's brother resided on the

family estates in Ireland. Still, he had said nothing, patiently waiting for what he had known would come.

Darcy had rolled his glass between his hands, studying the swirling liquid with apparent interest. "About Sarah."

"Mmm?" Max had kept his own eyes firmly fixed on his glass.

"I didn't."

"Oh?"

"No. But I'm not entirely sure she knows what happened." Darcy had drained his glass, using the opportunity to watch Max work this out.

Finally, comprehension had dawned. A glimmer of a smile had tugged at the corners of His Grace of Twyford's mouth. "Oh."

"Precisely. I thought I'd leave it in your capable hands."

"Thank you!" Max had replied. Then he had groaned and dropped his head into his hands. "How the hell do you imagine I'm going to find out what she believes and then explain it to her if she's wrong?" His mind had boggled at the awful idea.

"I thought you might work through Miss Twinning," Darcy had returned, grinning for the first time that day.

Relieved to see his friend smile, even at his expense, Max had grinned back. "I've not been pushing the pace quite as hard as you. Miss Twinning and I have some way to go before we reach the point where such intimate discussion would be permissible."

"Oh, well," Darcy had sighed. "I only hope you have better luck than I."

"Throwing in the towel?"

Darcy had shrugged. "I wish I knew." A silence had ensued which Darcy eventually broke. "I've got to get away."

"How long will you be gone?"

Another shrug. "Who knows? As long as it takes, I suppose."

He had left Darcy packing at Hamilton House and returned to the comfort of his own home to spend a quiet evening in contemplation of his wards. Their problems should really not cause surprise. At first sight, he had known what sort of men the Twinning girls would attract. And there was no denying they responded to such men. Even Arabella seemed hellbent on tangling with rakes. Thankfully, Lizzie seemed too quiet and gentle to take the same road—three rakes in any family should certainly be enough.

Family? The thought sobered him. He sat, eyes on the flames leaping in the grate, and pondered the odd notion.

His reverie was interrupted by sounds of an arrival. He glanced at the clock and frowned. Too late for callers. What now? He reached the hall in time to see Hillshaw and a footman fussing about the door.

"Yes, it's all right, Hillshaw, I'm not an invalid, you know!"

The voice brought Max forward. "Martin!"

The tousled brown head of Captain Martin Rotherbridge turned to greet his older brother. A winning grin spread across features essentially a more boyish version of Max's own. "Hello, Max. I'm back, as you see. Curst Frenchies put a hole in my shoulder."

Max's gaze fell to the bulk of bandaging distorting the set of his brother's coat. He clasped the hand held out to him warmly, his eyes raking the other's face. "Come into the library. Hillshaw?"

"Yes, Your Grace. I'll see to some food."

When they were comfortably ensconced by the fire, Martin with a tray of cold meat by his side and a large balloon of his brother's best brandy in his hand, Max asked his questions.

"No, you're right," Martin answered to one of these. "It wasn't just the wound, though that was bad enough. They tell me that with rest it'll come good in time." Max waited patiently. His brother fortified himself before continuing. "No. I sold out simply because, now the action's over, it's deuced boring over there. We sit about and play cards half the day. And the other half, we just sit and reminisce about all the females we've ever had." He grinned at his brother in a way Caroline, for one, would have recognised. "Seemed to me I was running out of anecdotes. So I decided to come home and lay in a fresh stock."

Max returned his brother's smile. Other than the shoulder wound, Martin was looking well. The difficult wound and slow convalescence had not succeeded in erasing the healthy glow from outdoor living which burnished his skin and, although there were lines present which had not been there before, these merely seemed to emphasize the fact that Martin Rotherbridge had seen more than twenty-five summers and was an old hand in many spheres. Max was delighted to hear he had returned to civilian life. Aside from his genuine concern for a much loved sibling, Martin was now the heir to the Dukedom of Twyford. While inheriting the Delmere holdings, with which he was well-acquainted, would have proved no difficulty to Martin, the Twyford estates were a different matter. Max eyed the long, lean frame stretched out in the chair before him and wondered where to begin. Before he had decided, Martin asked, "So how do you like being 'Your Grace'?"

In a few pithy sentences, Max told him. He then embarked on the saga of horrors examination of his uncle's estate had revealed, followed by a brief description of their present circumstances. Seeing the shadow of tiredness pass across Martin's face, he curtailed his report, saying instead, "Time for bed, stripling. You're tired."

Martin started, then grinned sleepily at Max's use of his childhood tag. "What? Oh, yes. I'm afraid I'm not up to full strength yet. And we've been travelling since first light."

Max's hand at his elbow assisted him to rise from the depth of the armchair. On his feet, Martin stretched and yawned. Seen side by side, the similarity between the brothers was marked. Max was still a few inches taller and his nine years' seniority showed in the heavier musculature of his chest and shoulders. Other than that, the differences were few— Martin's hair was a shade lighter than Max's dark mane and his features retained a softness Max's lacked, but the intensely blue eyes of the Rotherbridges shone in both dark faces.

Martin turned to smile at his brother. "It's good to be home."

* * *

"Good morning. Hillshaw, isn't it? I'm Lizzie Twinning. I've come to return a book to His Grace."

Although he had only set eyes on her once before, Hillshaw remembered his master's youngest ward perfectly. As she stepped daintily over the threshold of Delmere House, a picture in a confection of lilac muslin, he gathered his wits to murmur, "His Grace is not presently at home, miss. Perhaps his secretary, Mr. Cummings, could assist you." Hillshaw rolled one majestic eye toward a hovering footman who immediately, if reluctantly, disappeared in the direction of the back office frequented by the Duke's secretary.

Lizzie, allowing Hillshaw to remove her half-cape, looked doubtful. But all she said was, "Wait here for me, Hennessy. I shan't be long." Her maid, who had dutifully followed her in, sat primly on the edge of a chair by the wall and, under the unnerving stare of Hillshaw, lowered her round-eyed gaze to her hands.

Immediately, Mr. Joshua Cummings came hurrying forward from the dimness at the rear of the hall. "Miss Lizzie? I'm afraid His Grace has already left the house, but perhaps I may be of assistance?" Mr. Cummings was not what one might expect of a nobleman's secretary. He was of middle age and small and round and pale, and, as Lizzie later informed her sisters, looked as if he spent his days locked away perusing dusty papers. In a sense, he did. He was a single man and, until taking his present post, had lived with his mother on the Rotherbridge estate in Surrey. His family had long been associated with the Rotherbridges and he was sincerely devoted to that family's interests. Catching sight of the book in

Lizzie's small hand, he smiled. "Ah, I see you have brought back Lord Byron's verses. Perhaps you'd like to read his next book? Or maybe one of Mrs. Linfield's works would be more to your taste?"

Lizzie smiled back. On taking up residence at Twyford House, the sisters had been disappointed to find that, although extensive, the library there did not hold any of the more recent fictional works so much discussed among the *ton*. Hearing of their complaint, Max had revealed that his own library did not suffer from this deficiency and had promised to lend them any books they desired. But, rather than permit the sisters free rein in a library that also contained a number of works less suitable for their eyes, he had delegated the task of looking out the books they wanted to his secretary. Consequently, Mr. Cummings felt quite competent to deal with the matter at hand.

"If you'd care to wait in the drawing room, miss?" Hillshaw moved past her to open the door. With another dazzling smile, Lizzie handed the volume she carried to Mr. Cummings, informing him in a low voice that one of Mrs. Linfield's novels would be quite acceptable, then turned to follow Hillshaw. As she did so, her gaze travelled past the stately butler to rest on the figure emerging from the shadow of the library door. She remained where she was, her grey-brown eyes growing rounder and rounder, as Martin Rotherbridge strolled elegantly forward.

After the best night's sleep he had had in months, Martin had felt ready to resume normal activities but, on descending to the breakfast parlour, had discovered his brother had already left the house to call in at Tattersall's. Suppressing the desire to pull on his coat and follow, Martin had resigned himself to awaiting Max's return, deeming it wise to inform his brother in person that he was setting out to pick up the reins of his civilian existence before he actually did so. Knowing his friends, and their likely reaction to his reappearance among them, he was reasonably certain he would not be returning to Delmere House until the following morning. And he knew Max would worry unless he saw for himself that his younger brother was up to it. So, with a grin for his older brother's affection, he had settled in the library to read the morning's news sheets. But, after months of semi-invalidism, his returning health naturally gave rise to returning spirits. Waiting patiently was not easy. He had been irritably pacing the library when his sharp ears had caught the sound of a distinctly feminine voice in the hall. Intrigued, he had gone to investigate.

Setting eyes on the vision gracing his brother's hall, Martin's immediate thought was that Max had taken to allowing his ladybirds to call at his house. But the attitudes of Hillshaw and Cummings put paid to that idea. The sight of a maid sitting by the door confirmed his startled perception that the vision was indeed a young lady. His boredom vanishing like a cloud on a spring day, he advanced.

Martin allowed his eyes to travel, gently, so as not to startle her, over the delicious figure before him. Very nice. His smile grew. The silence around him penetrated his mind, entirely otherwise occupied. "Hillshaw, I think you'd better introduce us."

Hillshaw almost allowed a frown to mar his impassive countenance. But he knew better than to try to avoid the unavoidable. Exchanging a glance of fellow feeling with Mr. Cummings, he obliged in sternly disapproving tones. "Captain Martin Rotherbridge, Miss Lizzie Twinning. The young lady is His Grace's youngest ward, sir."

With a start, Martin's gaze, which had been locked with Lizzie's, flew to Hillshaw's face. "Ward?" He had not been listening too well last night when Max had been telling him of the estates, but he was sure his brother had not mentioned any wards.

With a thin smile, Hillshaw inclined his head in assent.

Lizzie, released from that mesmerising gaze, spoke up, her soft tones a dramatic contrast to the masculine voices. "Yes. My sisters and I are the Duke's wards, you know." She held out her hand. "How do you do? I didn't know the Duke had a brother. I've only dropped by to exchange some books His Grace lent us. Mr. Cummings was going to take care of it."

Martin took the small gloved hand held out to him and automatically bowed over it. Straightening, he moved to her side, placing her hand on his arm and holding it there. "In that case, Hillshaw's quite right. You should wait in the drawing-room." The relief on Hillshaw's and Mr. Cummings's faces evaporated at his next words. "And I'll keep you company."

As Martin ushered Lizzie into the drawing-room and pointedly shut the door in Hillshaw's face, the Duke's butler and secretary looked at each other helplessly. Then Mr. Cummings scurried away to find the required books, leaving Hillshaw to look with misgiving at the closed door of the drawing-room.

Inside, blissfully unaware of the concern she was engendering in her guardian's servants, Lizzie smiled trustingly up at the source of that concern.

"Have you been my brother's ward for long?" Martin asked.

"Oh, no!" said Lizzie. Then, "That is, I suppose, yes." She looked delightfully befuddled and Martin could not suppress a smile. He guided her to the chaise and, once she had settled, took the chair opposite her so that he could keep her bewitching face in full view.

"It depends, I suppose," said Lizzie, frowning in her effort to gather her wits, which had unaccountably scattered, "on what you'd call long. Our father died eighteen months ago, but then the other Duke—your uncle, was he not?—was our guardian. But when we came back from America, your brother had assumed the title. So then he was our guardian."

Out of this jumbled explanation, Martin gleaned enough to guess the truth. "Did you enjoy America? Were you there long?"

Little by little his questions succeeded in their aim and in short order, Lizzie had relaxed completely and was conversing in a normal fashion with her guardian's brother.

Listening to her description of her home, Martin shifted, trying to settle his shoulder more comfortably. Lizzie's sharp eyes caught the awkward movement and descried the wad of bandaging cunningly concealed beneath his coat.

"You're injured!" She leaned forward in concern. "Does it pain you dreadfully?"

"No, no. The enemy just got lucky, that's all. Soon be right as rain, I give you my word."

"You were in the army?" Lizzie's eyes had grown round. "Oh, please tell me all about it. It must have been so exciting!"

To Martin's considerable astonishment, he found himself recounting for Lizzie's benefit the horrors of the campaign and the occasional funny incident which had enlivened their days. She did not recoil but listened avidly. He had always thought he was a dab hand at interrogation but her persistent questioning left him reeling. She even succeeded in dragging from him the reason he had yet to leave the house. Her ready sympathy, which he had fully expected to send him running, enveloped him instead in a warm glow, a sort of prideful care which went rapidly to his head.

Then Mr. Cummings arrived with the desired books. Lizzie took them and laid them on a side-table beside her, patently ignoring the Duke's secretary who was clearly waiting to escort her to the front door. With an ill-concealed grin, Martin dismissed him. "It's all right, Cummings. Miss Twinning has taken pity on me and decided to keep me entertained until my brother returns."

Lizzie, entirely at home, turned a blissful smile on Mr. Cummings, leaving that gentleman with no option but to retire.

An hour later, Max crossed the threshold to be met by Hillshaw, displaying, quite remarkably, an emotion very near agitation. This was instantly explained. "Miss Lizzie's here. In the drawing-room with Mr. Martin."

Max froze. Then nodded to his butler. "Very good, Hill-shaw." His sharp eyes had already taken in the bored face of the maid sitting in the shadows. Presumably, Lizzie had been here for some time. His face was set in grim lines as his hand closed on the handle of the drawing-room door.

The sight which met his eyes was not at all what he had expected. As he shut the door behind him, Martin's eyes lifted to his, amused understanding in the blue depths. He was seated in an armchair and Lizzie occupied the nearest corner of the chaise. She was presently hunched forward, pondering what lay before her on a small table drawn up between them. As Max rounded the chaise, he saw to his stupefaction that they were playing checkers.

Lizzie looked up and saw him. "Oh! You're back. I was just entertaining your brother until you returned." Max blinked but Lizzie showed no consciousness of the implication of her words and he discarded the notion of enlightening her.

Then Lizzie's eyes fell on the clock on the mantelshelf. "Oh, dear! I didn't realize it was so late. I must go. Where are those books Mr. Cummings brought?"

Martin fetched them for her and, under the highly sceptical gaze of his brother, very correctly took leave of her. Max, seeing the expression in his brother's eyes as they rested on his youngest ward, almost groaned aloud. This was really too much.

Max saw Lizzie out, then returned to the library. But before he could launch into his inquisition, Martin got in first. "You didn't tell me you had inherited four wards."

"Well, I have," said Max, flinging himself into an armchair opposite the one his brother had resumed.

"Are they all like that?" asked Martin in awe.

Max needed no explanation of what "that" meant. He answered with a groan, "Worse!"

Eyes round, Martin did not make the mistake of imagining the other Twinning sisters were antidotes. His gaze rested on his brother for a moment, then his face creased into a wide smile. "Good lord!"

Max brought his blue gaze back from the ceiling and fixed it firmly on his brother. "Precisely. That being so, I suggest you revise the plans you've been making for Lizzie Twinning."

Martin's grin, if anything, became even broader. "Why so? It's you who's their guardian, not I. Besides, you don't seriously expect me to believe that, if our situations were reversed, you'd pay any attention to such restrictions?" When Max frowned, Martin continued. "Anyway, good heavens, you must have seen it for yourself. She's like a ripe plum, ready for the picking." He stopped at Max's raised hand.

"Permit me to fill you in," drawled his older brother. "For a start, I've nine years on you and there's nothing about the business you know that I don't. However, quite aside from that, I can assure you the Twinning sisters, ripe though they may be, are highly unlikely to fall into anyone's palms without a prior proposal of marriage."

A slight frown settled over Martin's eyes. Not for a moment did he doubt the accuracy of Max's assessment. But he had been strongly attracted to Lizzie Twinning and was disinclined to give up the idea of converting her to his way of thinking. He looked up and blue eyes met blue. "Really?"

Max gestured airily. "Consider the case of Lord Darcy Hamilton." Martin looked his question. Max obliged. "Being much taken with Sarah, the second of the four, Darcy's been engaged in storming her citadel for the past five weeks and more. No holds barred, I might add. And the outcome you ask? As of yesterday, he's retired to his estates, to lick his wounds and, unless I miss my guess, to consider whether he can stomach the idea of marriage."

"Good lord!" Although only peripherally acquainted with Darcy Hamilton, Martin knew he was one of Max's particular friends and that his reputation in matters involving the fairer sex was second only to Max's own.

"Exactly," nodded Max. "Brought low by a chit of a girl. So, brother dear, if it's your wish to tangle with any Twinnings, I suggest you first decide how much you're willing to stake on the throw."

As he pondered his brother's words, Martin noticed that Max's gaze had become abstracted. He only just caught the last words his brother said, musing, almost to himself. "For, brother mine, it's my belief the Twinnings eat rakes for breakfast."

The coach swayed, as it turned a corner and Arabella clutched the strap swinging by her head. As equilibrium returned, she settled her skirts once more and glanced at the other two occupants of the carriage. The glow from a street lamp momentarily lit the interior of the coach, then faded as the four horses hurried on. Arabella grinned into the darkness.

Caroline had insisted that she and not Lizzie share their guardian's coach. One had to wonder why. Too often these days, her eldest sister had the look of the cat caught just after it had tasted the cream. Tonight, that look of guilty pleasure, or, more specifically, the anticipation of guilty pleasure, was marked.

She had gone up to Caroline's room to hurry her sister along. Caroline had been sitting, staring at her reflection in the mirror, idly twisting one copper curl to sit more attractively about her left ear.

"Caro? Are you ready? Max is here."

"Oh!" Caroline had stood abruptly, then paused to cast one last critical glance over her pale sea-green dress, severely styled as most suited her ample charms, the neckline daringly *décolleté*. She had frowned, her fingers straying to the ivory swell of her breasts. "What do you think, Bella? Is it too revealing? Perhaps a piece of lace might make it a little less…?"

"Attractive?" Arabella had brazenly supplied. "To be perfectly frank, I doubt our guardian would approve a fichu."

The delicate blush that had appeared on Caroline's cheeks had been most informative. But, "Too true," was all her sister had replied.

Arabella looked across the carriage once more and caught the gleam of warm approval that shone in their guardian's eyes as they rested on Caroline. It was highly unlikely that the conservative Mr. Willoughby was the cause of her sister's blushes. That being so, what game was the Duke of Twyford playing? And, even more to the point, was Caro thinking of joining in?

Heaven knew, they had had a close enough call with Sarah and Lord Darcy. Nothing had been said of Sarah's strange affliction, yet they were all close enough for even the innocent Lizzie to have some inkling of the root cause. And while Max had been the soul of discretion in speaking privately to Caroline and Sarah in the hall before they had left, it was as plain as a pikestaff the information he had imparted had not included news of a proposal. Sarah's pale face had paled further. But the Twinnings were made of stern stuff and Sarah had shaken her head at Caro's look of concern.

The deep murmur of their guardian's voice came to her ears, followed by her sister's soft tones. Arabella's big eyes danced. She could not make out their words but those tones were oh, so revealing. But if Sarah was in deep waters and Caro was hovering on the brink, she, to her chagrin, had not even got her toes wet yet.

Arabella frowned at the moon, showing fleetingly between the branches of a tall tree. Hugo, Lord Denbigh. The most exasperating man she had ever met. She would give anything to be able to say she didn't care a button for him. Unfortunately, he was the only man who could make her tingle just by looking at her.

Unaware that she was falling far short of Caroline's expectations, Arabella continued to gaze out of the window, absorbed in contemplation of the means available for bringing one large gentleman to heel.

The heavy Twyford coach lumbered along in the wake of the sleek Delmere carriage. Lady Benborough put up a hand to right her wig, swaying perilously as they rounded a particularly sharp corner. For the first time since embarking on her nephew's crusade to find the Twinning girls suitable husbands, she felt a twinge of nervousness. She was playing with fire and she knew it. Still, she could not regret it. The sight of Max and Caroline together in the hall at Twyford House had sent a definite thrill through her old bones. As for Sarah, she doubted not that Darcy Hamilton was too far gone to desist, resist and retire. True, he might not know it yet, but time would certainly bring home to him the penalty he would have to pay to walk away from the snare. Her shrewd blue eyes studied the pale face opposite her. Even in the dim light, the strain of the past few days was evident. Thankfully, no one outside their party had been aware of that contretemps. So, regardless of what Sarah herself believed, Augusta had no qualms. Sarah was home safe; she could turn her attention elsewhere.

Arabella, the minx, had picked a particularly difficult nut to crack. Still, she could hardly fault the girl's taste. Hugo Denbigh was a positive Adonis, well-born, well-heeled and easy enough in his ways. Unfortunately, he was so easy to please that he seemed to find just as much pleasure in the presence of drab little girls as he derived from Arabella's rather more scintillating company. Gammon, of course, but how to alert Arabella to that fact? Or would it be more to the point to keep quiet and allow Hugo a small degree of success? As her mind drifted down that particular path, Augusta suddenly caught herself up and had the grace to look sheepish. What appalling thoughts for a chaperon!

Her gaze fell on Lizzie, sweet but far from demure in a gown of delicate silver gauze touched with colour in the form of embroidered lilacs. A soft, introspective smile hovered over her classically moulded lips. Almost a smile of anticipation. Augusta frowned. Had she missed something?

Mentally reviewing Lizzie's conquests, Lady Benborough was at a loss to account for the suppressed excitement evident, now she came to look more closely, in the way the younger girl's fingers beat an impatient if silent tattoo on the beads of her reticule. Clearly, whoever he was would be at the ball. She would have to watch her youngest charge like a hawk. Lizzie was too young, in all conscience, to be allowed the licence her more worldly sisters took for granted.

Relaxing back against the velvet squabs, Augusta smiled. Doubtless she was worrying over nothing. Lizzie might have the Twinning looks but surely she was too serious an innocent to attract the attentions of a rake? Three rakes she might land, the Twinnings being the perfect bait, but a fourth was bound to be wishful thinking.

# *Chapter Seven*

Martin puzzled over Max's last words on the Twinnings but it was not until he met the sisters that evening, at Lady Montacute's drum, that he divined what had prompted his brother to utter them. He had spent the afternoon dropping in on certain old friends, only to be, almost immediately, bombarded with requests for introductions to the Twinnings. He had come away with the definite impression that the best place to be that evening would be wherever the Misses Twinning were destined. His batman and valet, Jiggins, had turned up the staggering information that Max himself usually escorted his wards to their evening engagements. Martin had found this hard to credit, but when, keeping an unobtrusive eye on the stream of arrivals from a vantage-point beside a potted palm in Lady Montacute's ballroom, he had seen Max arrive surrounded by Twinning sisters, he had been forced to accept the crazy notion as truth. When the observation that the fabulous creature on his brother's arm was, in fact, his eldest ward finally penetrated his brain all became clear.

Moving rapidly to secure a dance with Lizzie, who smiled up at him with flattering welcome, Martin was close enough to see the expression in his brother's eyes as he bent to whisper something in Miss Twinning's ear, prior to relinquishing her to the attention of the circle forming about her. His brows flew and he pursed his lips in surprise. As his brother's words of that morning returned to him, he grinned. How much was Max prepared to stake?

For the rest of the evening, Martin watched and plotted and planned. He used his wound as an excuse not to dance, which enabled him to spend his entire time studying Lizzie Twinning. It was an agreeable pastime. Her silvery dress floated about her as she danced and the candlelight glowed on her sheening brown curls. With her natural grace, she reminded him of a fairy sprite, except that he rather thought such mythical creatures lacked the fulsome charms with which the Twinning sisters were so well-endowed. Due to his experienced foresight, Lizzie accommodatingly returned to his side after every dance, convinced by his chatter of the morning that he was in dire need of cheering up. Lady Benborough, to whom he had dutifully made his bow, had snorted in disbelief at his die-away airs but had apparently been unable to dissuade Lizzie's soft heart from bringing him continual succour. By subtle degrees, he sounded her out on each of her hopeful suitors and was surprised at his own relief in finding she had no special leaning towards any.

He started his campaign in earnest when the musicians struck up for the dance for which he *had* engaged her. By careful manoeuvring, they were seated in a sheltered alcove, free for the moment of her swains. Schooling his features to grave disappointment, he said, ''Dear Lizzie. I'm so sorry to disappoint you, but…'' He let his voice fade away weakly.

Lizzie's sweet face showed her concern. ''Oh! Do you not feel the thing? Perhaps I can get Mrs. Alford's smelling salts for you?''

Martin quelled the instinctive response to react to her suggestion in too forceful a manner. Instead, he waved aside her words with one limp hand. ''No! No! Don't worry about me. I'll come about shortly.'' He smiled forlornly at her, allowing his blue gaze to rest, with calculated effect, on her grey-brown eyes. ''But maybe you'd like to get one of your other beaux to dance with you? I'm sure Mr. Mallard would be only too thrilled.'' He made a move as if to summon this gentleman, the most assiduous of her suitors.

''Heavens, no!'' exclaimed Lizzie, catching his hand in hers to prevent the action. ''I'll do no such thing. If you're feeling poorly then of course I'll stay with you.'' She continued to hold his hand and, for his part, Martin made no effort to remove it from her warm clasp.

Martin closed his eyes momentarily, as if fighting off a sudden faintness. Opening them again, he said, ''Actually, I do believe it's all the heat and noise in here that's doing it. Perhaps if I went out on to the terrace for a while, it might clear my head.''

''The very thing!'' said Lizzie, jumping up.

Martin, rising more slowly, smiled down at her in

a brotherly fashion. "Actually, I'd better go alone. Someone might get the wrong idea if we both left."

"Nonsense!" said Lizzie, slightly annoyed by his implication that such a conclusion could, of course, have no basis in fact. "Why should anyone worry? We'll only be a few minutes and anyway, I'm your brother's ward, after all."

Martin made some small show of dissuading her, which, as he intended, only increased her resolution to accompany him. Finally, he allowed himself to be bullied on to the terrace, Lizzie's small hand on his arm, guiding him.

As supper time was not far distant, there were only two other couples on the shallow terrace, and within minutes both had returned to the ballroom. Martin, food very far from his mind, strolled down the terrace, apparently content to go where Lizzie led. But his sharp soldier's eyes had very quickly adjusted to the moonlight. After a cursory inspection of the surroundings, he allowed himself to pause dramatically as they neared the end of the terrace. "I really think..." He waited a moment, as if gathering strength, then continued, "I really think I should sit down."

Lizzie looked around in consternation. There were no benches on the terrace, not even a balustrade.

"There's a seat under that willow, I think," said Martin, gesturing across the lawn.

A quick glance from Lizzie confirmed this observation. "Here, lean on me," she said. Martin obligingly draped one arm lightly about her shoulders. As he felt her small hands gripping him about his waist, a pang of guilt shook him. She really was so trusting. A pity to destroy it.

They reached the willow and brushed through the long strands which conveniently fell back to form a curtain around the white wooden seat. Inside the chamber so formed, the moonbeams danced, sprinkling sufficient light to lift the gloom and allow them to see. Martin sank on to the seat with a convincing show of weakness. Lizzie subsided in a susurration of silks beside him, retaining her clasp on his hand and half turning the better to look into his face.

The moon was behind the willow and one bright beam shone through over Martin's shoulder to fall gently on Lizzie's face. Martin's face was in shadow, so Lizzie, smiling confidingly up at him, could only see that he was smiling in return. She could not see the expression which lit his blue eyes as they devoured her delicate face, then dropped boldly to caress the round swell of her breasts where they rose and fell invitingly below the demurely scooped neckline of her gown. Carefully, Martin turned his hand so that now he was holding her hand, not she his. Then he was still.

After some moments, Lizzie put her head on one side and softly asked, "Are you all right?"

It was on the tip of Martin's tongue to answer truthfully. No, he was not all right. He had brought her out here to commence her seduction and now some magical power was holding him back. What was the matter with him? He cleared his throat and answered huskily, "Give me a minute."

A light breeze wafted the willow leaves and the

light shifted. Lizzie saw the distracted frown which had settled over his eyes. Drawing her hand from his, she reached up and gently ran her fingers over his brow, as if to smooth the frown away. Then, to Martin's intense surprise, she leaned forward and, very gently, touched her lips to his.

As she drew away, Lizzie saw to her dismay that, if Martin had been frowning before, he was positively scowling now. "Why did you do that?" he asked, his tone sharp.

Even in the dim light he could see her confusion. "Oh, dear! I'm s...so sorry. Please excuse me! I shouldn't have done that."

"Damn right, you shouldn't have," Martin growled. His hand, which had fallen to the bench, was clenched hard with the effort to remain still and not pull the damn woman into his arms and devour her. He realized she had not answered his question. "But why did you?"

Lizzie hung her head in contrition. "It's just that you looked...well, so troubled. I just wanted to help." Her voice was a small whisper in the night.

Martin sighed in frustration. That sort of help he could do without.

"I suppose you'll think me very forward, but..." This time, her voice died away altogether.

What Martin did think was that she was adorable and he hurt with the effort to keep his hands off her. Now he came to think of it, while he had not had a headache when they came out to the garden, he certainly had one now. Repressing the desire to groan aloud, he straightened. "We'd better get back to the ballroom. We'll just forget the incident." As he drew her to her feet and placed her hand on his arm, an unwelcome thought struck him. "You don't go around kissing other men who look troubled, do you?"

The surprise in her face was quite genuine. "No! Of course not!"

"Well," said Martin, wondering why the information so thrilled him, "just subdue any of these sudden impulses of yours. Except around me, of course. I dare say it's perfectly all right with me, in the circumstances. You are my brother's ward, after all."

Lizzie, still stunned by her forward behaviour, and the sudden impulse that had driven her to it, smiled trustingly up at him.

Caroline smiled her practised smile and wished, for at least the hundredth time, that Max Rotherbridge were not their guardian. At least, she amended, not *her* guardian. He was proving a tower of strength in all other respects and she could only be grateful, both for his continuing support and protection, as well as his experienced counsel over the affair of Sarah and Lord Darcy. But there was no doubt in her mind that her own confusion would be immeasurably eased by dissolution of the guardianship clause which tied her so irrevocably to His Grace of Twyford.

While she circled the floor in the respectful arms of Mr. Willoughby who, she knew, was daily moving closer to a declaration despite her attempts to dampen his confidence, she was conscious of a wish that it was her guardian's far less gentle clasp she was in.

Mr. Willoughby, she had discovered, was worthy. Which was almost as bad as righteous. She sighed and covered the lapse with a brilliant smile into his mild eyes, slightly below her own. It was not that she despised short men, just that they lacked the ability to make her feel delicate and vulnerable, womanly, as Max Rotherbridge certainly could. In fact, the feeling of utter helplessness that seemed to overcome her every time she found herself in his powerful arms was an increasing concern.

As she and her partner turned with the music, she sighted Sarah, dancing with one of her numerous court, trying, not entirely successfully, to look as if she was enjoying it. Her heart went out to her sister. They had stayed at home the previous night and, in unusual privacy, thrashed out the happenings of the night before. While Sarah skated somewhat thinly over certain aspects, it had been clear that she, at least, knew her heart. But Max had taken the opportunity of a few minutes' wait in the hall at Twyford House to let both herself and Sarah know, in the most subtle way, that Lord Darcy had left town for his estates. She swallowed another sigh and smiled absently at Mr. Willoughby.

As the eldest, she had, in recent years, adopted the role of surrogate mother to her sisters. One unfortunate aspect of that situation was that she had no one to turn to herself. If the gentleman involved had been anyone other than her guardian, she would have sought advice from Lady Benborough. In the circumstances, that avenue, too, was closed to her. But, after that interlude in the Overtons's summer-house, she was abysmally aware that she needed advice. All he had to do was to take her into his arms and her well-ordered defences fell flat. And his kiss! The effect of that seemed totally to disorder her mind, let alone her senses. She had not yet fathomed what, exactly, he was about, yet it seemed inconceivable that he would seduce his own ward. Which fact, she ruefully admitted, but only to herself when at her most candid, was at the seat of her desire to no longer be his ward.

It was not that she had any wish to join the *demi-monde*. But face facts she must. She was nearly twenty-six and she knew what she wanted. She wanted Max Rotherbridge. She knew he was a rake and, if she had not instantly divined him standing as soon as she had laid eyes on him, Lady Benborough's forthright remarks on the subject left no room for doubt. But every tiny particle of her screamed that he was the one. Which was why she was calmly dancing with each of her most ardent suitors, careful not to give any one of them the slightest encouragement, while waiting for her guardian to claim her for the dance before supper. On their arrival in the over-heated ballroom, he had, in a sensual murmur that had wafted the curls over her ear and sent shivery tingles all the way down her spine, asked her to hold that waltz for him. She looked into Mr. Willoughby's pale eyes. And sighed.

"Sir Malcolm, I do declare you're flirting with me!" Desperation lent Arabella's bell-like voice a definite edge. Using her delicate feather fan to great purpose, she flashed her large eyes at the horrendously rich but essentially dim-witted Scottish baronet, managing meanwhile to keep Hugo, Lord Denbigh, in view. Her true prey was standing only feet away, conversing amiably with a plain matron with an even plainer daughter. What was the matter with him? She had tried every trick she knew to bring the great oaf to her tiny feet, yet he persistently drifted away. He would be politely attentive but seemed incapable of settling long enough even to be considered one of her court. She had kept the supper waltz free, declaring it to be taken to all her suitors, convinced he would ask her for that most favoured dance. But now, with supper time fast approaching, she suddenly found herself facing the prospect of having no partner at all. Her eyes flashing, she turned in welcome to Mr. Pritchard and Viscount Molesworth.

She readily captivated both gentlemen, skilfully steering clear of any lapse of her own rigidly imposed standards. She was an outrageous flirt, she knew, but a discerning flirt, and she had long made it her policy never to hurt anyone with her artless chatter. She enjoyed the occupation but it had never involved her heart. Normally, her suitors happily fell at her feet without the slightest assistance from her. But, now that she had at last found someone she wished to attract, she had, to her horror, found she had less idea of how to draw a man to her side than plainer girls who had had to learn the art.

To her chagrin, she saw the musicians take their places on the rostrum. There was only one thing to do. She smiled sweetly at the three gentlemen around her. "My dear sirs," she murmured, her voice mysteriously low, "I'm afraid I must leave you. No! Truly. Don't argue." Another playful smile went around. "Until later, Sir Malcolm, Mr. Pritchard, my lord." With a nod and a mysterious smile she moved away, leaving the three gentlemen wondering who the lucky man was.

Slipping through the crowd, Arabella headed for the exit to the ballroom. Doubtless there would be an antechamber somewhere where she could hide. She was not hungry anyway. She timed her exit to coincide with the movement of a group of people across the door, making it unlikely that anyone would see her retreat. Once in the passage, she glanced about. The main stairs lay directly in front of her. She glanced to her left in time to see two ladies enter one of the rooms. The last thing she needed was the endless chatter of a withdrawing-room. She turned purposefully to her right. At the end of the dimly lit corridor, a door stood open, light from the flames of a hidden fire flickering on its panels. She hurried down the corridor and, looking in, saw a small study. It was empty. A carafe and glasses set in readiness on a small table suggested it was yet another room set aside for the use of guests who found the heat of the ballroom too trying. With a sigh of relief, Arabella entered. After some consideration, she left the door open.

She went to the table and poured herself a glass of water. As she was replacing the glass, she heard voices approaching. Her eyes scanned the room and lit on the deep window alcove; the curtain across it, if fully drawn, would make it a small room. On the thought, she was through, drawing the heavy curtain tightly shut.

In silence, her heart beating in her ears, she listened as the voices came nearer and entered the room, going towards the fire. She waited a moment, breathless, but no one came to the curtain. Relaxing, she turned. And almost fell over the large pair of feet belonging to the gentleman stretched at his ease in the armchair behind the curtain.

"Oh!" Her hand flew to her lips in her effort to smother the sound. "What are you doing here?" she whispered furiously.

Slowly, the man turned his head towards her. He smiled. "Waiting for you, my dear."

Arabella closed her eyes tightly, then opened them again but he was still there. As she watched, Lord Denbigh unfurled his long length and stood, magnificent and, suddenly, to Arabella at least, oddly intimidating, before her. In the light of the full moon spilling through the large windows, his tawny eyes roved appreciatively over her. He caught her small hand in his and raised it to his lips. "I didn't think you'd be long."

His lazy tones, pitched very low, washed languidly over Arabella. With a conscious effort, she tried to break free of their hypnotic hold. "How could you know I was coming here? *I* didn't."

"Well," he answered reasonably, "I couldn't think where else you would go, if you didn't have a partner for the supper waltz."

He *knew!* In the moonlight, Arabella's fiery blush faded into more delicate tints but the effect on her temper was the same. "You oaf!" she said in a fierce whisper, aiming a stinging slap at the grin on his large face. But the grin grew into a smile as he easily caught her hand and drew it down and then behind her, drawing her towards him. He captured her other hand as well and imprisoned that in the same large hand behind her back.

"Lord Denbigh! Let me go!" Arabella pleaded, keeping her voice low for fear the others beyond the curtain would hear. How hideously embarrassing to be found in such a situation. And now she had another problem. What was Hugo up to? As her anger drained, all sorts of other emotions came to the fore. She looked up, her eyes huge and shining in the moonlight, her lips slightly parted in surprise.

Hugo lifted his free hand and one long finger traced the curve of her full lower lip.

Even with only the moon to light his face, Arabella saw the glimmer of desire in his eyes. "Hugo, let me go. Please?"

He smiled lazily down at her. "In a moment, sweetheart. After I've rendered you incapable of scratching my eyes out."

His fingers had taken hold of her chin and he waited to see the fury in her eyes before he chuckled and bent his head until his lips met hers.

Arabella had every intention of remaining aloof from his kisses. Damn him—he'd tricked her! She tried to whip up her anger, but all she could think of was how wonderfully warm his lips felt against hers. And what delicious sensations were running along her nerves. Everywhere. Her body, entirely of its own volition, melted into his arms.

She felt, rather than heard, his deep chuckle as his arms shifted and tightened about her. Finding her hands free and resting on his shoulders, she did not quite know what to do with them. Box his ears? In the end, she twined them about his neck, holding him close.

When Hugo finally lifted his head, it was to see the stars reflected in her eyes. He smiled lazily down at her. "Now you have to admit that's more fun than waltzing."

Arabella could think of nothing to say.

"No quips?" he prompted.

She blushed slightly. "We should be getting back." She tried to ease herself from his embrace but his arms moved not at all.

Still smiling in that sleepy way, he shook his head. "Not yet. That was just the waltz. We've supper to go yet." His lips lightly brushed hers. "And I'm ravenously hungry."

Despite the situation, Arabella nearly giggled at the boyish tone. But she became much more serious when his lips returned fully to hers, driving her into far deeper waters than she had ever sailed before.

But he was experienced enough correctly to gauge her limits, to stop just short and retreat, until they were sane again. Later, both more serious than was their wont, they returned separately to the ballroom.

Despite her strategies, Arabella was seen as she slipped from the ballroom. Max, returning from the

card-room where he had been idly passing his time
until he could, with reasonable excuse, gravitate to
the side of his eldest ward, saw the bright chestnut
curls dip through the doorway and for an instant had
thought that Caroline was deserting him. But his
sharp ears had almost immediately caught the husky
tone of her laughter from a knot of gentlemen near
by and he realised it must have been Arabella, most
like Caroline in colouring, whom he had seen.

But he had more serious problems on his mind than
whether Arabella had torn her flounce. His pursuit of
the luscious Miss Twinning, or, rather, the difficulties
which now lay in his path to her, were a matter for
concern. The odd fact that he actually bothered to
dance with his eldest ward had already been noted.
As there were more than a few ladies among the *ton*
who could give a fairly accurate description of his
preferences in women, the fact that Miss Twinning's
endowments brought her very close to his ideal had
doubtless not been missed. However, he cared very
little for the opinions of others and foresaw no real
problem in placating the *ton* after the deed was done.
What was troubling him was the unexpected behaviour of the two principals in the affair, Miss Twinning
and himself.

With respect to his prey, he had miscalculated on
two counts. Firstly, he had imagined it would take a
concerted effort to seduce a twenty-five-year-old
woman who had lived until recently a very retired
life. Instead, from the first, she had responded so
freely that he had almost lost his head. He was too
experienced not to know that it would take very little

of his persuasion to convince her to overthrow the tenets of her class and come to him. It irritated him beyond measure that the knowledge, far from spurring him on to take immediate advantage of her vulnerability, had made him pause and consider, in a most disturbing way, just what he was about. His other mistake had been in thinking that, with his intensive knowledge of the ways of the *ton,* he would have no difficulty in using his position as her guardian to create opportunities to be alone with Caroline. Despite— or was it because of?—her susceptibility towards him, she seemed able to avoid his planned tête-à-têtes with ease and, with the exception of a few occasions associated with some concern over one or other of her sisters, had singularly failed to give him the opportunities he sought. And seducing a woman whose mind was filled with worry over one of her sisters was a task he had discovered to be beyond him.

He had, of course, revised his original concept of what role Caroline was to play in his life. However, he was fast coming to the conclusion that he would have to in some way settle her sisters' affairs before either he or Caroline would have time to pursue their own destinies. But life, he was fast learning, was not all that simple. In the circumstances, the *ton* would expect Miss Twinning's betrothal to be announced before that of her sisters. And he was well aware he had no intention of giving his permission for any gentleman to pay his addresses to Miss Twinning. As he had made no move to clarify for her the impression of his intentions he had originally given her, he did not delude himself that she might not accept some man like Willoughby, simply to remove herself from the temptation of her guardian. Yet if he told her she was not his ward, she would undoubtedly be even more vigilant with respect to himself and, in all probability, even more successful in eluding him.

There was, of course, a simple solution. But he had a perverse dislike of behaving as society dictated. Consequently, he had formed no immediate intention of informing Caroline of his change of plans. There was a challenge, he felt, in attempting to handle their relationship his way. Darcy had pushed too hard and too fast and, consequently, had fallen at the last fence. He, on the other hand, had no intention of rushing things. Timing was everything in such a delicate matter as seduction.

The congestion of male forms about his eldest ward brought a slight frown to his face. But the musicians obligingly placed bow to string, allowing him to extricate her from their midst and sweep her on to the floor.

He glanced down into her grey-green eyes and saw his own pleasure in dancing with her reflected there. His arm tightened slightly and her attention focused. "I do hope your sisters are behaving themselves?"

Caroline returned his weary question with a smile. "Assuming your friends are doing likewise, I doubt there'll be a problem."

Max raised his brows. So she knew at least a little of what had happened. After negotiating a difficult turn to avoid old Major Brumidge and his similarly ancient partner, he jettisoned the idea of trying to learn more of Sarah's thoughts in favour of spiking a more specific gun. "Incidently, apropos of your sisters' and your own fell intent, what do you wish me to say to the numerous beaux who seem poised to troop up the steps of Delmere House?"

He watched her consternation grow as she grappled with the sticky question. He saw no reason to tell her that, on his wards' behalf, he had already turned down a number of offers, none of which could be considered remotely suitable. He doubted they were even aware of the interest of the gentlemen involved.

Caroline, meanwhile, was considering her options. If she was unwise enough to tell him to permit any acceptable gentlemen to address them, they could shortly be bored to distraction with the task of convincing said gentlemen that their feelings were not reciprocated. On the other hand, giving Max Rotherbridge a free hand to choose their husbands seemed equally unwise. She temporized. "Perhaps it would be best if we were to let you know if we anticipated receiving an offer from any particular gentleman that we would wish to seriously consider."

Max would have applauded if his hands had not been so agreeably occupied. "A most sensible suggestion, my ward. Tell me, how long does it take to pin up a flounce?"

Caroline blinked at this startling question.

"The reason I ask," said Max as they glided to a halt, "is that Arabella deserted the room some minutes before the music started and, as far as I can see, has yet to return."

A frown appeared in Caroline's fine eyes but, in deference to the eyes of others, she kept her face free of care and her voice light. "Can you see if Lord Denbigh is in the room?"

Max did not need to look. "Not since I entered it." After a pause, he asked, "Is she seriously pursuing that line? If so, I fear she'll all too soon reach point non plus."

Caroline followed his lead as he offered her his arm and calmly strolled towards the supper-room. A slight smile curled her lips as, in the increasing crowd, she leaned closer to him to answer. "With Arabella, it's hard to tell. She seems so obvious, with her flirting. But that's really all superficial. In reality, she's rather reticent about such things."

Max smiled in reply. Her words merely confirmed his own reading of Arabella. But his knowledge of the relationship between Caroline and her sisters prompted him to add, "Nevertheless, you'd be well-advised to sound her out on that score. Hugo Denbigh, when all is said and done, is every bit as dangerous as…" He paused to capture her eyes with his own before, smiling in a devilish way, he continued, "I am."

Conscious of the eyes upon them, Caroline strove to maintain her composure. "How very…reassuring, to be sure," she managed.

The smile on Max's face broadened. They had reached the entrance of the supper-room and he paused in the doorway to scan the emptying ballroom. "If she hasn't returned in ten minutes, we'll have to go looking. But come, sweet ward, the lobster patties await."

With a flourish, Max led her to a small table where

they were joined, much to his delight, by Mr. Willoughby and a plain young lady, a Miss Spence. Mr. Willoughby's transparent intention of engaging the delightful Miss Twinning in close converse, ignoring the undemanding Miss Spence and Miss Twinning's guardian, proved to be rather more complicated than Mr. Willoughby, for one, had imagined. Under the subtle hand of His Grace of Twyford, Mr. Willoughby found himself the centre of a general discussion on philosophy. Caroline listened in ill-concealed delight as Max blocked every move poor Mr. Willoughby made to polarise the conversation. It became apparent that her guardian understood only too well Mr. Willoughby's state and she found herself caught somewhere between embarrassment and relief. In the end, relief won the day.

Eventually, routed, Mr. Willoughby rose, ostensibly to return Miss Spence to her parent. Watching his retreat with laughing eyes, Caroline returned her gaze to her guardian, only to see him look pointedly at the door from the ballroom. She glanced across and saw Arabella enter, slightly flushed and with a too-bright smile on her lips. She made straight for the table where Sarah was sitting with a number of others and, with her usual facility, merged with the group, laughing up at the young man who leapt to his feet to offer her his chair.

Caroline turned to Max, a slight frown in her eyes, to find his attention had returned to the door. She followed his gaze and saw Lord Denbigh enter.

To any casual observer, Hugo was merely coming late to the supper-room, his languid gaze and sleepy smile giving no hint of any more pressing emotion than to discover whether there were any lobster patties left. Max Rotherbridge, however, was a far from casual observer. As he saw the expression in his lordship's heavy-lidded eyes as they flicked across the room to where Arabella sat, teasing her company unmercifully, His Grace of Twyford's black brows rose in genuine astonishment. Oh, God! Another one?

Resigned to yet another evening spent with no progress in the matter of his eldest ward, Max calmly escorted her back to the ballroom and, releasing her to the attentions of her admirers, not without a particularly penetrating stare at two gentlemen of dubious standing who had had the temerity to attempt to join her circle, he prepared to quit the ballroom. He had hoped to have persuaded Miss Twinning to view the moonlight from the terrace. There was a useful bench he knew of, under a concealing willow, which would have come in handy. However, he had no illusions concerning his ability to make love to a woman who was on tenterhooks over the happiness of not one but two sisters. So he headed for the cardroom.

On his way, he passed Arabella, holding court once again in something close to her usual style. His blue gaze searched her face. As if sensing his regard, she turned and saw him. For a moment, she looked lost. He smiled encouragingly. After a fractional pause, she flashed her brilliant smile back and, putting up her chin, turned back to her companions, laughing at some comment.

Max moved on. Clearly, Caroline did have another problem on her hands. He paused at the entrance to the card-room and, automatically, scanned the packed ballroom. Turning, he was about to cross the threshold when a disturbing thought struck him. He turned back to the ballroom.

"Make up your mind! Make up your mind! Oh, it's you, Twyford. What are you doing at such an occasion? Hardly your style these days, what?"

Excusing himself to Colonel Weatherspoon, Max moved out of the doorway and checked the room again. Where was Lizzie? He had not seen her at supper, but then again he had not looked. He had mentally dubbed her the baby of the family but his rational mind informed him that she was far from too young. He was about to cross the room to where his aunt Augusta sat, resplendent in bronze bombazine, when a movement by the windows drew his eyes.

Lizzie entered from the terrace, a shy and entirely guileless smile on her lips. Her small hand rested with easy assurance on his brother's arm. As he watched, she turned and smiled up at Martin, a look so full of trust that a newborn lamb could not have bettered it. And Martin, wolf that he was, returned the smile readily.

Abruptly, Max turned on his heel and strode into the card-room. He needed a drink.

# Chapter Eight

Arabella swatted at the bumble-bee blundering noisily by her head. She was lying on her stomach on the stone surround of the pond in the courtyard of Twyford House, idly trailing her fingers in the cool green water. Her delicate mull muslin, petal-pink in hue, clung revealingly to her curvaceous form while a straw hat protected her delicate complexion from the afternoon sun. Most other young ladies in a similar pose would have looked childish. Arabella, with her strangely wistful air, contrived to look mysteriously enchanting.

Her sisters were similarly at their ease. Sarah was propped by the base of the sundial, her *bergère* hat shading her face as she threaded daisies into a chain. The dark green cambric gown she wore emphasized her arrestingly pale face, dominated by huge brown eyes, darkened now by the hint of misery. Lizzie sat beside the rockery, poking at a piece of embroidery with a noticeable lack of enthusiasm. Her sprigged mauve muslin proclaimed her youth yet its effect was ameliorated by her far from youthful figure.

Caroline watched her sisters from her perch in a cushioned hammock strung between two cherry trees. If her guardian could have seen her, he would undoubtedly have approved of the simple round gown of particularly fine amber muslin she had donned for the warm day. The fabric clung tantalizingly to her mature figure while the neckline revealed an expanse of soft ivory breasts.

The sisters had gradually drifted here, one by one, drawn by the warm spring afternoon and the heady scents rising from the rioting flowers which crammed the beds and overflowed on to the stone flags. The period between luncheon and the obligatory appearance in the Park was a quiet time they were coming increasingly to appreciate as the Season wore on. Whenever possible, they tended to spend it together, a last vestige, Caroline thought, of the days when they had only had each other for company.

Sarah sighed. She laid aside her hat and looped the completed daisy chain around her neck. Cramming her headgear back over her dark curls, she said, "Well, what are we going to do?"

Three pairs of eyes turned her way. When no answer was forthcoming, she continued, explaining her case with all reasonableness, "Well, we can't go on as we are, can we? None of us is getting anywhere."

Arabella turned on her side better to view her sisters. "But what can we do? In your case, Lord Darcy's not even in London."

"True," returned the practical Sarah. "But it's just occurred to me that he must have friends still in London. Ones who would write to him, I mean. Other than our guardian.''

Caroline grinned. ''Whatever you do, my love, kindly explain all to me before you set the *ton* ablaze. I don't think I could stomach our guardian demanding an explanation and not having one to give him.''

Sarah chuckled. ''Has he been difficult?''

But Caroline would only smile, a secret smile of which both Sarah and Arabella took due note.

''He hasn't said anything about me, has he?'' came Lizzie's slightly breathless voice. Under her sisters' gaze, she blushed. ''About me and Martin,'' she mumbled, suddenly becoming engrossed in her *petit point*.

Arabella laughed. ''Artful puss. As things stand, you're the only one with all sails hoisted and a clear wind blowing. The rest of us are becalmed, for one reason or another.''

Caroline's brow had furrowed. ''Why do you ask? Has Max given you any reason to suppose he disapproves?''

''Well,'' temporized Lizzie, ''he doesn't seem entirely…happy, about us seeing so much of each other.''

Her attachment to Martin Rotherbridge had progressed in leaps and bounds. Despite Max's warning and his own innate sense of danger, Martin had not been able to resist the temptation posed by Lizzie Twinning. From that first undeniably innocent kiss he had, by subtle degrees, led her to the point where, finding herself in his arms in the gazebo in Lady Malling's garden, she had permitted him to kiss her again. Only this time, it had been Martin leading the way. Lizzie, all innocence, had been thoroughly enthralled by the experience and stunned by her own response to the delightful sensations it had engendered. Unbeknownst to her, Martin Rotherbridge had been stunned, too.

Belatedly, he had tried to dampen his own increasing desires, only to find, as his brother could have told him, that that was easier imagined than accomplished. Abstinence had only led to intemperance. In the end, he had capitulated and returned to spend every moment possible at Lizzie's side, if not her feet.

Lizzie was right in her assessment that Max disapproved of their association but wrong in her idea of the cause. Only too well-acquainted with his brother's character, their guardian entertained a grave concern that the frustrations involved in behaving with decorum in the face of Lizzie Twinning's bounteous temptations would prove overwhelming long before Martin was brought to admit he was in love with the chit. His worst fears had seemed well on the way to being realized when he had, entirely unintentionally, surprised them on their way back to the ballroom. His sharp blue eyes had not missed the glow in Lizzie's face. Consequently, the look he had directed at his brother, which Lizzie had intercepted, had not been particularly encouraging. She had missed Martin's carefree response.

Caroline, reasonably certain of Max's thoughts on the matter, realized these might not be entirely clear to Lizzie. But how to explain Max's doubts of his own brother to the still innocent Lizzie? Despite the fact that only a year separated her from Arabella, the disparity in their understandings, particularly with respect to the male of the species, was enormous. All three elder Twinnings had inherited both looks and dispositions from their father's family, which in part explained his aversion to women. Thomas Twinning had witnessed firsthand the dance his sisters had led all the men of their acquaintance before finally settling in happily wedded bliss. The strain on his father and himself had been considerable. Consequently, the discovery that his daughters were entirely from the same mould had prompted him to immure them in rural seclusion. Lizzie, however, had only inherited the Twinning looks, her gentle and often quite stubborn innocence deriving from the placid Eleanor. Viewing the troubled face of her youngest half-sister, Caroline decided the time had come to at least try to suggest to Lizzie's mind that there was often more to life than the strictly obvious. Aside from anything else, this time, she had both Sarah and Arabella beside her to help explain.

"I rather think, my love," commenced Caroline, "that it's not that Max would disapprove of the connection. His concern is more for your good name."

Lizzie's puzzled frown gave no indication of lightening. "But why should my being with his brother endanger my good name?"

Sarah gave an unladylike snort of laughter. "Oh, Lizzie, love! You're going to have to grow up, my dear. Our guardian's concerned because he knows what his brother's like and that, generally speaking, young ladies are not safe with him."

The effect of this forthright speech on Lizzie was galvanizing. Her eyes blazed in defence of her absent love. "Martin's not like that at all!"

"Oh, sweetheart, you're going to have to open your eyes!" Arabella bought into the discussion, sitting up the better to do so. "He's not only 'like that,' Martin Rotherbridge has made a career specializing in being 'like that.' He's a rake. The same as Hugo and Darcy Hamilton, too. And, of course, the greatest rake of them all is our dear guardian, who has his eye firmly set on Caro here. Rakes and Twinnings go together, I'm afraid. We attract them and they—" she put her head on one side, considering her words "—well, they attract us. It's no earthly good disputing the evidence."

Seeing the perturbation in Lizzie's face, Caroline sought to reassure her. "That doesn't mean that the end result is not just the same as if they were more conservative. It's just that, well, it very likely takes longer for such men to accept the…the desirability of marriage." Her eyes flicked to Sarah who, head bent and eyes intent on her fingers, was plaiting more daisies. "Time will, I suspect, eventually bring them around. The danger is in the waiting."

Lizzie was following her sister's discourse with difficulty. "But Martin's never…well, you know, tried to make love to me."

"Do you mean to say he's never kissed you?" asked Arabella in clear disbelief.

Lizzie blushed. "Yes. But I kissed him first."

"Lizzie!" The startled exclamation was drawn from all three sisters who promptly thereafter fell about laughing. Arabella was the last to recover. "Oh, my dear, you're more a Twinning than we'd thought!"

"Well, it was nice, I thought," said Lizzie, fast losing her reticence in the face of her sisters' teasing. "Anyway, what am I supposed to do? Avoid him? That wouldn't be much fun. And I don't think I could stop him kissing me, somehow. I rather like being kissed."

"It's not the kissing itself that's the problem," stated Sarah. "It's what comes next. And that's even more difficult to stop."

"Very true," confirmed Arabella, studying her slippered toes. "But if you want lessons in how to hold a rake at arm's length you shouldn't look to me. Nor to Sarah either. It's only Caro who's managed to hold her own so far." Arabella's eyes started to dance as they rested on her eldest sister's calm face. "But, I suspect, that's only because our dear guardian is playing a deep game."

Caroline blushed slightly, then reluctantly smiled. "Unfortunately, I'm forced to agree with you."

A silence fell as all four sisters pondered their rakes. Eventually, Caroline spoke. "Sarah, what are you planning?"

Sarah wriggled her shoulders against the sundial's pedestal. "Well, it occurred to me that perhaps I should make some effort to bring things to a head. But if I did the obvious, and started wildly flirting with a whole bevy of gentlemen, then most likely I'd only land myself in the suds. For a start, Darcy would very likely not believe it and I'd probably end with a very odd reputation. I'm not good at it, like Bella.''

Arabella put her head on one side, the better to observe her sister. ''I could give you lessons,'' she offered.

''No,'' said Caroline. ''Sarah's right. It wouldn't wash.'' She turned to Lizzie to say, ''Another problem, my love, is that rakes know all the tricks, so bamming them is very much harder.''

''Too true,'' echoed Arabella. She turned again to Sarah. ''But if not that, what, then?''

A wry smile touched Sarah's lips. ''I rather thought the pose of the maiden forlorn might better suit me. Nothing too obvious, just a subtle withdrawing. I'd still go to all the parties and balls, but I'd just become quieter and ever so gradually, let my...what's the word, Caro? My despair? My broken heart? Well, whatever it is, show through.''

Her sisters considered her plan and found nothing to criticise. Caroline summed up their verdict. ''In truth, my dear, there's precious little else you could do.''

Sarah's eyes turned to Arabella. ''But what are you going to do about Lord Denbigh?''

Arabella's attention had returned to her toes. She wrinkled her pert nose. ''I really don't know. I can't make him jealous; as Caro said, he knows all those tricks. And the forlorn act would not do for me.''

Arabella had tried every means possible to tie down the elusive Hugo but that large gentleman seemed to view her attempts with sleepy humour, only bestirring himself to take advantage of any tactical error she made. At such times, as Arabella had found to her confusion and consternation, he could move with ruthless efficiency. She was now very careful not to leave any opening he could exploit to be private with her.

"Why not try...?" Caroline broke off, suddenly assailed by a twinge of guilt at encouraging her sisters in their scheming. But, under the enquiring gaze of Sarah and Arabella, not to mention Lizzie, drinking it all in, she mentally shrugged and continued. "As you cannot convince him of your real interest in any other gentleman, you'd be best not to try, I agree. But you could let him understand that, as he refused to offer marriage, and you, as a virtuous young lady, are prevented from accepting any other sort of offer, then, with the utmost reluctance and the deepest regret, you have been forced to turn aside and consider accepting the attentions of some other gentleman."

Arabella stared at her sister. Then, her eyes started to dance. "Oh, Caro!" she breathed. "What a perfectly marvellous plan!"

"Shouldn't be too hard for you to manage," said Sarah. "Who are the best of your court for the purpose? You don't want to raise any overly high expectations on their parts but you've loads of experience in playing that game."

Arabella was already deep in thought. "Sir Humphrey Bullard, I think. And Mr. Stone. They're both sober enough and in no danger of falling in love with me. They're quite coldly calculating in their approach to matrimony; I doubt they have hearts to lose. They both want an attractive wife, preferably with money, who would not expect too much attention from them. To their minds, I'm close to perfect but to scramble for my favours would be beneath them. They should be perfect for my charade.''

Caroline nodded. ''They sound just the thing.''

''Good! I'll start tonight,'' said Arabella, decision burning in her huge eyes.

''But what about you, Caro?'' asked Sarah with a grin. ''We've discussed how the rest of us should go on, but you've yet to tell us how you plan to bring our dear guardian to his knees.''

Caroline smiled, the same gently wistful smile that frequently played upon her lips these days. ''If I knew that, my dears, I'd certainly tell you.'' The last weeks had seen a continuation of the unsatisfactory relationship between His Grace of Twyford and his eldest ward. Wary of his ability to take possession of her senses should she give him the opportunity, Caroline had consistently avoided his invitations to dally alone with him. Indeed, too often in recent times her mind had been engaged in keeping a watchful eye over her sisters, something their perceptive guardian seemed to understand. She could not fault him for his support and was truly grateful for the understated manner in which he frequently set aside his own inclinations to assist her in her concern for her siblings. In fact, it had occurred to her that, far from being a lazy guardian, His Grace of Twyford was very much *au fait* with the activities of each of his wards. Lately, it had seemed to her that her sisters' problems were deflecting a considerable amount of his energies from his pursuit of herself. So, with a twinkle in her eyes, she said, "If truth be told, the best plan I can think of to further my own ends is to assist you all in achieving your goals as soon as may be. Once free of you three, perhaps our dear guardian will be able to concentrate on me."

It was Lizzie who initiated the Twinning sisters' friendship with the two Crowbridge girls, also being presented that year. The Misses Crowbridge, Alice and Amanda, were very pretty young ladies in the manner which had been all the rage until the Twinnings came to town. They were pale and fair, as ethereal as the Twinnings were earthy, as fragile as the Twinnings were robust, and, unfortunately for them, as penniless as the Twinnings were rich. Consequently, the push to find well-heeled husbands for the Misses Crowbridge had not prospered.

Strolling down yet another ballroom, Lady Mott's as it happened, on the arm of Martin, of course, Lizzie had caught the sharp words uttered by a large woman of horsey mien to a young lady, presumably her daughter, sitting passively at her side. "Why can't you two be like that? Those girls simply walk off with any man they fancy. All it needs is a bit of push. But you and Alice..." The rest of the tirade had been swallowed up by the hubbub around them. But the words returned to Lizzie later, when, retiring to the withdrawing-room to mend her hem which Martin very carelessly had stood upon, she found the room empty except for the same young lady, huddled in a pathetic bundle, trying to stifle her sobs.

As a kind heart went hand in hand with Lizzie's

innocence, it was not long before she had befriended Amanda Crowbridge and learned of the difficulty facing both Amanda and Alice. Lacking the Twinning sisters' confidence and abilities, the two girls, thrown without any preparation into the heady world of the *ton*, found it impossible to converse with the elegant gentlemen, becoming tongue-tied and shy, quite unable to attach the desired suitors. To Lizzie, the solution was obvious.

Both Arabella and Sarah, despite having other fish to fry, were perfectly willing to act as tutors to the Crowbridge girls. Initially, they agreed to this more as a favour to Lizzie than from any more magnanimous motive, but as the week progressed they became quite absorbed with their protégées. For the Crowbridge girls, being taken under the collective wing of the three younger Twinnings brought a cataclysmic change to their social standing. Instead of being left to decorate the wall, they now spent their time firmly embedded amid groups of chattering young people. Drawn ruthlessly into conversations by the artful Arabella or Sarah at her most prosaic, they discovered that talking to the swells of the *ton* was not, after all, so very different from conversing with the far less daunting lads at home. Under the steady encouragement provided by the Twinnings, the Crowbridge sisters slowly unfurled their petals.

Caroline and His Grace of Twyford watched the growing friendship from a distance and were pleased to approve, though for very different reasons. Having ascertained that the Crowbridges were perfectly acceptable acquaintances, although their mother, for all her breeding, was, as Lady Benborough succinctly put it, rather too pushy, Caroline was merely pleased that her sisters had found some less than scandalous distraction from their romantic difficulties. Max, on the other hand, was quick to realize that with the three younger girls busily engaged in this latest exploit, which kept them safely in the ballrooms and salons, he stood a much better chance of successfully spending some time, in less populated surroundings, with his eldest ward.

In fact, as the days flew past, his success in his chosen endeavour became so marked that Caroline was forced openly to refuse any attempt to detach her from her circle. She had learned that their relationship had become the subject of rampant speculation and was now seriously concerned at the possible repercussions, for herself, for her sisters and for him. Max, reading her mind with consummate ease, paid her protestations not the slightest heed. Finding herself once more in His Grace's arms and, as usual, utterly helpless, Caroline was moved to remonstrate. "What on earth do you expect to accomplish by all this? I'm your *ward*, for heaven's sake!"

A deep chuckle answered her. Engaged in tracing her left brow, first with one long finger, then with his lips, Max had replied, "Consider your time spent with me as an educational experience, sweet Caro. As Aunt Augusta was so eager to point out," he continued, transferring his attention to her other brow, "who better than your guardian to demonstrate the manifold dangers to be met with among the *ton?*"

She was prevented from telling him what she

thought of his reasoning, in fact, was prevented from thinking at all, when his lips moved to claim hers and she was swept away on a tide of sensation she was coming to appreciate all too well. Emerging, much later, pleasantly witless, she found herself the object of His Grace's heavy-lidded blue gaze. "Tell me, my dear, if you were not my ward, would you consent to be private with me?"

Mentally adrift, Caroline blinked in an effort to focus her mind. For the life of her she could not understand his question, although the answer seemed clear enough. "Of course not!" she lied, trying unsuccessfully to ease herself from his shockingly close embrace.

A slow smile spread across Max's face. As the steel bands around her tightened, Caroline was sure he was laughing at her.

Another deep chuckle, sending shivers up and down her spine, confirmed her suspicion. Max bent his head until his lips brushed hers. Then, he drew back slightly and blue eyes locked with grey. "In that case, sweet ward, you have some lessons yet to learn."

Bewildered, Caroline would have asked for enlightenment but, reading her intent in her eyes, Max avoided her question by the simple expedient of kissing her again. Irritated by his cat-and-mouse tactics, Caroline tried to withdraw from participation in this strange game whose rules were incomprehensible to her. But she quickly learned that His Grace of Twyford had no intention of letting her backslide. Driven, in the end, to surrender to the greater force, Caroline

relaxed, melting into his arms, yielding body, mind
and soul to his experienced conquest.

It was at Lady Richardson's ball that Sir Ralph
Keighly first appeared as a cloud on the Twinnings's
horizon. Or, more correctly, on the Misses Crowbridge's horizon, although by that stage, it was much
the same thing. Sir Ralph, with a tidy estate in Gloucestershire, was in London to look for a wife. His
taste, it appeared, ran to sweet young things of the
type personified by the Crowbridge sisters, Amanda
Crowbridge in particular. Unfortunately for him, Sir
Ralph was possessed of an overwhelming self-conceit
combined with an unprepossessing appearance. He
was thus vetoed on sight as beneath consideration by
the Misses Crowbridge and their mentors.

However, Sir Ralph was rather more wily than he
appeared. Finding his attentions to Amanda Crowbridge compromised by the competing attractions of
the large number of more personable young men who
formed the combined Twinning-Crowbridge court, he
retired from the lists and devoted his energies to cul-
tivating Mr. and Mrs. Crowbridge. In this, he
achieved such notable success that he was invited to
attend Lady Richardson's ball with the Crowbridges.
Despite the tearful protestations of both Amanda and
Alice at his inclusion in their party, when they crossed
the threshold of Lady Richardson's ballroom,
Amanda, looking distinctly seedy, had her hand on
Sir Ralph's arm.

At her parents' stern instruction, she was forced to
endure two waltzes with Sir Ralph. As Arabella acidly

observed, if it had been at all permissible, doubtless Amanda would have been forced to remain at his side for the entire ball. As it was, she dared not join her friends for supper but, drooping with dejection, joined Sir Ralph and her parents.

To the three Twinnings, the success of Sir Ralph was like waving a red rag to a bull. Without exception, they took it as interference in their, up until then, successful development of their protégées. Even Lizzie was, metaphorically speaking, hopping mad. But the amenities offered by a ball were hardly conducive to a council of war, so, with admirable restraint, the three younger Twinnings devoted themselves assiduously to their own pursuits and left the problem of Sir Ralph until they had leisure to deal with it appropriately.

Sarah was now well down the road to being acknowledged as having suffered an unrequited love. She bore up nobly under the strain but it was somehow common knowledge that she held little hope of recovery. Her brave face, it was understood, was on account of her sisters, as she did not wish to ruin their Season by retiring into seclusion, despite this being her most ardent wish. Her large brown eyes, always fathomless, and her naturally pale and serious face were welcome aids in the projection of her new persona. She danced and chatted, yet the vitality that had burned with her earlier in the Season had been dampened. That, at least, was no more than the truth.

Arabella, all were agreed, was settling down to the sensible prospect of choosing a suitable connection. As Hugo Denbigh had contrived to be considerably

more careful in his attentions to Arabella than Darcy
Hamilton had been with Sarah, the gossips had never
connected the two. Consequently, the fact that Lord
Denbigh's name was clearly absent from Arabella's
list did not in itself cause comment. But, as the Twinning sisters had been such a hit, the question of who
precisely Arabella would choose was a popular topic
for discussion. Speculation was rife and, as was often
the case in such matters, a number of wagers had
already been entered into the betting books held by
the gentlemen's clubs. According to rumour, both Mr.
Stone and Sir Humphrey Bullard featured as possible
candidates. Yet not the most avid watcher could dis-
cern which of these gentlemen Miss Arabella favoured.

Amid all this drama, Lizzie Twinning continued as
she always had, accepting the respectful attentions of
the sober young men who sought her out while reserving her most brilliant smiles for Martin Rotherbridge. As she was so young and as Martin wisely
refrained from any overtly amorous or possessive act
in public, most observers assumed he was merely
helping his brother with what must, all were agreed,
constitute a definite handful. Martin, finding her increasingly difficult to lead astray, was forced to live
with his growing frustrations and their steadily di-
minishing prospects for release.

The change in Amanda Crowbridge's fortunes
brought a frown to Caroline's face. She would not
have liked the connection for any of her sisters. Still,
Amanda Crowbridge was not her concern. As her sisters appeared to have taken the event philosophically

enough, she felt justified in giving it no further thought, reserving her energies, mental and otherwise, for her increasingly frequent interludes with her guardian.

Despite her efforts to minimize his opportunities, she found herself sharing his carriage on their return journey to Mount Street. Miriam Alford sat beside her and Max, suavely elegant and exuding a subtle aura of powerful sensuality, had taken the seat opposite her. Lady Benborough and her three sisters were following in the Twyford coach. As Caroline had suspected, their chaperon fell into a sound sleep before the carriage had cleared the Richardson House drive.

Gazing calmly at the moonlit fields, she calculated they had at least a forty-minute drive ahead of them. She waited patiently for the move she was sure would come and tried to marshal her resolve to deflect it. As the minutes ticked by, the damning knowledge slowly seeped into her consciousness that, if her guardian was to suddenly become afflicted with propriety and the journey was accomplished without incident, far from being relieved, she would feel let down, cheated of an eagerly anticipated treat. She frowned, recognizing her already racing pulse and the tense knot in her stomach that restricted her breathing for the symptoms they were. On the thought, she raised her eyes to the dark face before her.

He was watching the countryside slip by, the silvery light etching the planes of his face. As if feeling her gaze, he turned and his eyes met hers. For a moment, he read her thoughts and Caroline was visited by the dreadful certainty that he knew the truth she was struggling to hide. Then, a slow, infinitely wicked smile spread across his face. Caroline stopped breathing. He leaned forward. She expected him to take her hand and draw her to sit beside him. Instead, his strong hands slipped about her waist and, to her utter astonishment, he lifted her across and deposited her in a swirl of silks on his lap.

"Max!" she gasped.

"Sssh. You don't want to wake Mrs. Alford. She'd have palpitations."

Horrified, Caroline tried to get her feet to the ground, wriggling against the firm clasp about her waist. Almost immediately, Max's voice sounded in her ear, in a tone quite different from any she had previously heard. "Sweetheart, unless you cease wriggling your delightful *derriére* in such an enticing fashion, this lesson is likely to go rather further than I had intended."

Caroline froze. She held her breath, not daring to so much as twitch. Then Max's voice, the raw tones of an instant before no longer in evidence, washed over her in warm approval. "Much better."

She turned to face him, carefully keeping her hips still. She placed her hands on his chest in an effort, futile, she knew, to fend him off. "Max, this is madness. You must stop doing this!"

"Why? Don't you like it?" His hands were moving gently on her back, his touch scorching through the thin silk of her gown.

Caroline ignored the sardonic lift of his black brows and the clear evidence in his eyes that he was laughing at her. She found it much harder to ignore the sensations his hands were drawing forth. Forcing her face into strongly disapproving lines, she answered his first question, deeming it prudent to conveniently forget the second. "I'm your *ward*, remember? You know I am. You told me so yourself."

"A fact you should strive to bear in mind, my dear."

Caroline wondered what he meant by that. But Max's mind, and hands, had shifted their focus of attention. As his hands closed over her breasts, Caroline nearly leapt to her feet. *"Max!"*

But, "Sssh," was all her guardian said as his lips settled on hers.

# Chapter Nine

The Twyford Coach was also the scene of considerable activity, though of a different sort. Augusta, in sympathy with Mrs. Alford, quickly settled into a comfortable doze which the whisperings of the other occupants of the carriage did nothing to disturb. Lizzie, Sarah and Arabella, incensed by Amanda's misfortune, spent some minutes giving vent to their feelings.

"It's not as if Sir Ralph's such a good catch, even," Sarah commented.

"Certainly not," agreed Lizzie with uncharacteristic sharpness. "It's really too bad! Why, Mr. Minchbury is almost at the point of offering for her and he has a much bigger estate, besides being much more attractive. And Amanda *likes* him, what's more."

"Ah," said Arabella, wagging her head sagely, "but he's not been making up to Mrs. Crowbridge, has he? That woman must be all about in her head, to think of giving little Amanda to Keighly."

"Well," said Sarah decisively, "what are we going to do about it?"

Silence reigned for more than a mile as the sisters considered the possibilities. Arabella eventually spoke into the darkness. "I doubt we'd get far discussing matters with the Crowbridges."

"Very true," nodded Sarah. "And working on Amanda's equally pointless. She's too timid."

"Which leaves Sir Ralph," concluded Lizzie. After a pause, she went on: "I know we're not precisely to his taste, but do you think you could do it, Bella?"

Arabella's eyes narrowed as she considered Sir Ralph. Thanks to Hugo, she now had a fairly extensive understanding of the basic attraction between men and women. Sir Ralph was, after all, still a man. She shrugged. "Well, it's worth a try. I really can't see what else we can do."

For the remainder of the journey, the sisters' heads were together, hatching a plan.

Arabella started her campaign to steal Sir Ralph from Amanda the next evening, much to the delight of Amanda. When she was informed in a whispered aside of the Twinnings' plan for her relief, Amanda's eyes had grown round. Swearing to abide most faithfully by any instructions they might give her, she had managed to survive her obligatory two waltzes with Sir Ralph in high spirits, which Sarah later informed her was not at all helpful. Chastised, she begged pardon and remained by Sarah's side as Arabella took to the floor with her intended.

As Sir Ralph had no real affection for Amanda, it took very little of Arabella's practised flattery to make him increasingly turn his eyes her way. But, to the

Twinnings' consternation, their plan almost immediately developed a hitch.

Their guardian was not at all pleased to see Sir
Ralph squiring Arabella. A message from him, re-
layed by both Caroline and Lady Benborough, to the
effect that Arabella should watch her step, pulled Arabella up short. A hasty conference, convened in the
withdrawing-room, agreed there was no possibility of
gaining His Grace's approval for their plan. Likewise,
none of the three sisters had breathed a word of their
scheme to Caroline, knowing that, despite her affection for them, there were limits to her forbearance.

"But we can't just give up!" declared Lizzie in
trenchant tones.

Arabella was nibbling the end of one finger. "No.
We won't give up. But we'll have to reorganize. You
two," she said, looking at Sarah and Lizzie, quite
ignoring Amanda and Alice who were also present,
"are going to have to cover for me. That way, I won't
be obviously spending so much time with Sir Ralph,
but he'll still be thinking about me. You must tell Sir
Ralph that our guardian disapproves but that, as I'm
head over heels in love with him, I'm willing to go
against the Duke's wishes and continue to see him."
She frowned, pondering her scenario. "We'll have to
be careful not to paint our dear guardian in too strict
colours. The story is that we're sure he'll eventually
come around, when he sees how attached I am to Sir
Ralph. Max knows I'm a flighty, flirtatious creature
and so doubts of the strength of my affections. That
should be believable enough."

"All right," Sarah nodded. "We'll do the ground-work and you administer the *coup de grâce*."

And so the plan progressed.

For Arabella, the distraction of Sir Ralph came at an opportune time in her juggling of Sir Humphrey and Mr. Stone. It formed no part of her plans for either of these gentlemen to become too particular. And while her sober and earnest consideration of their suits had, she knew, stunned and puzzled Lord Denbigh, who watched with a still sceptical eye, her flirtation with Sir Ralph had brought a strange glint to his hazel orbs.

In truth, Hugo had been expecting Arabella to flirt outrageously with her court in an attempt to make him jealous and force a declaration. He had been fully prepared to sit idly by, watching her antics from the sidelines with his usual sleepily amused air, waiting for the right moment to further her seduction. But her apparent intention to settle for a loveless marriage had thrown him. It was not a reaction he had expected. Knowing what he did of Arabella, he could not stop himself from thinking what a waste it would be. True, as the wife of a much older man, she was likely to be even more receptive to his own suggestions of a discreet if illicit relationship. But the idea of her well-endowed charms being brutishly enjoyed by either of her ageing suitors set his teeth on edge. Her sudden pursuit of Sir Ralph Keighly, in what he was perceptive enough to know was not her normal style, seriously troubled him, suggesting as it did some deeper intent. He wondered whether she knew what she was about. The fact that she continued to encourage

Keighly despite Twyford's clear disapproval further increased his unease.

Arabella, sensing his perturbation, continued to tread the difficult path she had charted, one eye on him, the other on her guardian, encouraging Sir Ralph with one hand while using the other to hold back Sir Humphrey and Mr. Stone. As she confessed to her sisters one morning, it was exhausting work.

Little by little, she gained ground with Sir Ralph, their association camouflaged by her sisters' ploys. On the way back to the knot of their friends, having satisfactorily twirled around Lady Summerhill's ballroom, Arabella and Sir Ralph were approached by a little lady, all in brown.

Sir Ralph stiffened.

The unknown lady blushed. "How do you do?" she said, taking in both Arabella and Sir Ralph in her glance. "I'm Harriet Jenkins," she explained helpfully to Arabella, then, turning to Sir Ralph, said, "Hello, Ralph," in quite the most wistful tone Arabella had ever heard.

Under Arabella's interested gaze, Sir Ralph became tongue-tied. He perforce bowed over the small hand held out to him and managed to say, "Mr. Jenkins's estates border mine."

Arabella's eyes switched to Harriet Jenkins. "My father," she supplied.

Sir Ralph suddenly discovered someone he had to exchange a few words with and precipitately left them. Arabella looked down into Miss Jenkins's large eyes, brown, of course, and wondered. "Have you lately come to town, Miss Jenkins?"

Harriet Jenkins drew her eyes from Sir Ralph's departing figure and dispassionately viewed the beauty before her. What she saw in the frank hazel eyes prompted her to reply, "Yes. I was...bored at home. So my father suggested I come to London for a few weeks. I'm staying with my aunt, Lady Cottesloe."

Arabella was only partly satisfied with this explanation. Candid to a fault, she put the question in her mind. "Pardon me, Miss Jenkins, but are you and Sir Ralph...?"

Miss Jenkins's wistfulness returned. "No. Oh, you're right in thinking I want him. But Ralph has other ideas. I've known him from the cradle, you see. And I suppose familiarity breeds contempt." Suddenly realizing to whom she was speaking, she blushed and continued, "Not that I could hope to hold a candle to the London beauties, of course."

Her suspicions confirmed, Arabella merely laughed and slipped an arm through Miss Jenkins's. "Oh, I shouldn't let that bother you, my dear." As she said the words, it occurred to her that, if anything, Sir Ralph was uncomfortable and awkward when faced with beautiful women, as evidenced by his behaviour with either herself or Amanda. It was perfectly possible that some of his apparent conceit would drop away when he felt less threatened; for instance, in the presence of Miss Jenkins.

Miss Jenkins had stiffened at Arabella's touch and her words. Then, realizing the kindly intent behind them, she relaxed. "Well, there's no sense in deceiving myself. I suppose I shouldn't say so, but Ralph and I were in a fair way to being settled before he took this latest notion of looking about before he made up his mind irrevocably. I sometimes think it was simply fear of tying the knot that did it.''

"Very likely," Arabella laughingly agreed as she steered Miss Jenkins in the direction of her sisters.

"My papa was furious and said I should give him up. But I convinced him to let me come to London, to see how things stood. Now, I suppose, I may as well go home."

"Oh, on no account should you go home yet awhile, Miss Jenkins!" said Arabella, a decided twinkle in her eye. "May I call you Harriet? Harriet, I'd like you to meet my sisters."

The advent of Harriet Jenkins caused a certain amount of reworking of the Twinnings' plan for Sir Ralph. After due consideration, she was taken into their confidence and willingly joined the small circle of conspirators. In truth, her appearance relieved Arabella's mind of a nagging worry over how she was to let Sir Ralph down after Amanda accepted Mr. Minchbury, who, under the specific guidance of Lizzie, was close to popping the question. Now, all she had to do was to play the hardened flirt and turn Sir Ralph's bruised ego into Harriet's tender care. All in all, things were shaping up nicely.

However, to their dismay, the Twinnings found that Mrs. Crowbridge was not yet vanquished. The news of her latest ploy was communicated to them two days later, at Beckenham, where they had gone to watch a balloon ascent. The intrepid aviators had yet to arrive at the field, so the three Twinnings had de-

scended from their carriage and, together with the
Misses Crowbridge and Miss Jenkins, were strolling
elegantly about the field, enjoying the afternoon sunshine and a not inconsiderable amount of male attention. It transpired that Mrs. Crowbridge had invited
Sir Ralph to pay a morning call and then, on the
slightest of pretexts, had left him alone with Amanda
for quite twenty minutes. Such brazen tactics left
them speechless. Sir Ralph, to do him justice, had not
taken undue advantage.

"He probably didn't have time to work out the
odds against getting Arabella versus the benefits of
Amanda," said Sarah with a grin. "Poor man! I can
almost pity him, what with Mrs. Crowbridge after him
as well."

All the girls grinned but their thoughts quickly returned to their primary preoccupation. "Yes, but,"
said Lizzie, voicing a fear already in both Sarah's and
Arabella's minds, "if Mrs. Crowbridge keeps behaving like this, she might force Sir Ralph to offer for
Amanda by tricking him into compromising her."

"I'm afraid that's only too possible," agreed Harriet. "Ralph's very gullible." She shook her head in
such a deploring way that Arabella and Sarah were
hard put to it to smother their giggles.

"Yes, but it won't do," said Amanda, suddenly.
"I know my mother. She'll keep on and on until she
succeeds. You've got to think of some way of...of
removing Sir Ralph quickly."

"For his sake as well as your own," agreed Harriet. "The only question is, how?"

Silence descended while this conundrum revolved

in their minds. Further conversation on the topic was necessarily suspended when they were joined by a number of gentlemen disinclined to let the opportunity of paying court to such a gaggle of very lovely young ladies pass by. As His Grace of Twyford's curricle was conspicuously placed among the carriages drawn up to the edge of the field, the behaviour of said gentlemen remained every bit as deferential as within the confines of Almack's, despite the sylvan setting.

Mr. Mallard was the first to reach Lizzie's side, closely followed by Mr. Swanston and Lord Brookfell. Three other fashionable exquisites joined the band around Lizzie, Amanda, Alice and Harriet, and within minutes an unexceptionable though thoroughly merry party had formed. Hearing one young gentleman allude to the delicate and complementary tints of the dresses of the four younger girls as "pretty as a posy," Sarah could not resist a grimace, purely for Arabella's benefit. Arabella bit hard on her lip to stifle her answering giggle. Both fell back a step or two from the younger crowd, only to fall victim to their own admirers.

Sir Humphrey Bullard, a large man of distinctly florid countenance, attempted to capture Arabella's undivided attention but was frustrated by the simultaneous arrival of Mr. Stone, sleekly saturnine, on her other side. Both offered their arms, leaving Arabella, with a sunshade to juggle, in a quandary. She laughed and shook her head at them both. "Indeed, gentlemen, you put me to the blush. What can a lady do under such circumstances?"

"Why, make your choice, m'dear," drawled Mr. Stone, a strangely determined glint in his eye.

Arabella's eyes widened at this hint that Mr. Stone, at least, was not entirely happy with being played on a string. She was rescued by Mr. Humphrey, irritatingly aware that he did not cut such a fine figure as Mr. Stone. "I see the balloonists have arrived. Perhaps you'd care to stroll to the enclosure and watch the inflation, Miss Arabella?"

"We'll need to get closer if we're to see anything at all," said Sarah, coming up on the arm of Lord Tulloch.

By the time they reached the area cordoned off in the centre of the large field, a crowd had gathered. The balloon was already filling slowly. As they watched, it lifted from the ground and slowly rose to hover above the cradle slung beneath, anchored to the ground by thick ropes.

"It looks like such a flimsy contraption," said Arabella, eyeing the gaily striped silk balloon. "I wonder that anyone could trust themselves to it."

"They don't always come off unscathed, I'm sorry to say," answered Mr. Stone, his schoolmasterish tones evincing strong disapproval of such reckless behaviour.

"Humph!" said Sir Humphrey Bullard.

Arabella's eyes met Sarah's in mute supplication. Sarah grinned.

It was not until the balloon had taken off, successfully, to Arabella's relief, and the crowd had started to disperse that the Twinnings once more had leisure to contemplate the problem of Sir Ralph Keighly. Predictably, it was Sarah and Arabella who conceived the plot. In a few whispered sentences, they developed its outline sufficiently to see that it would require great attention to detail to make it work. As they would have no further chance that day to talk with the others in private, they made plans to meet the next morning at Twyford House. Caroline had mentioned her intention of visiting her old nurse, who had left the Twinnings' employ after her mother had died and hence was unknown to the younger Twinnings. Thus, ensconced in the back parlour of Twyford House, they would be able to give free rein to their thoughts. Clearly, the removal of Sir Ralph was becoming a matter of urgency.

Returning to their carriage, drawn up beside the elegant equipage bearing the Delmere crest, the three youngest Twinnings smiled serenely at their guardian, who watched them from the box seat of his curricle, a far from complaisant look in his eyes.

Max was, in fact, convinced that something was in the wind but had no idea what. His highly developed social antennae had picked up the undercurrents of his wards' plotting and their innocent smiles merely confirmed his suspicions. He was well aware that Caroline, seated beside him in a fetching gown of figured muslin, was not privy to their schemes. As he headed his team from the field, he smiled. His eldest ward had had far too much on her mind recently to have had any time free for scheming.

Beside him, Caroline remained in blissful ignorance of her sisters' aims. She had spent a thoroughly enjoyable day in the company of her guardian and was in charity with the world. They had had an excellent view of the ascent itself from the height of the box seat of the curricle. And when she had evinced the desire to stroll among the crowds, Max had readily escorted her, staying attentively by her side, his acerbic comments forever entertaining and, for once, totally unexceptionable. She looked forward to the drive back to Mount Street with unimpaired calm, knowing that in the curricle, she ran no risk of being subjected to another of His Grace's "lessons." In fact, she was beginning to wonder how many more lessons there could possibly be before the graduation ceremony. The thought brought a sleepy smile to her face. She turned to study her guardian.

His attention was wholly on his horses, the bays, as sweet a pair as she had ever seen. Her eyes fell to his hands as they tooled the reins, strong and sure. Remembering the sensations those hands had drawn forth as they had knowledgeably explored her body, she caught her breath and rapidly looked away. Keeping her eyes fixed on the passing landscape, she forced her thoughts into safer fields.

The trouble with Max Rotherbridge was that he invaded her thoughts, too, and, as in other respects, was wellnigh impossible to deny. She was fast coming to the conclusion that she should simply forget all else and give herself up to the exquisite excitements she found in his arms. All the social and moral strictures ever intoned, all her inhibitions seemed to be consumed to ashes in the fire of her desire. She was beginning to feel it was purely a matter of time before she succumbed. The fact that the idea did not fill her with trepidation but rather with a pleasant sense of anticipation was in itself, she felt, telling.

As the wheels hit the cobbles and the noise that was London closed in around them, her thoughts flew ahead to Lady Benborough, who had stayed at home recruiting her energies for the ball that night. It was only this morning, when, with Max, she had bid her ladyship goodbye, that the oddity in Augusta's behaviour had struck her. While the old lady had been assiduous in steering the girls through the shoals of the acceptable gentlemen of the *ton*, she had said nothing about her eldest charge's association with her nephew. No matter how Caroline viewed it, invoke what reason she might, there was something definitely odd about that. As she herself had heard the rumours about His Grace of Twyford's very strange relationship with his eldest ward, it was inconceivable that Lady Benborough had not been edified with their tales. However, far from urging her to behave with greater discretion towards Max, impossible task though that might be, Augusta continued to behave as if there was nothing at all surprising in Max Rotherbridge escorting his wards to a balloon ascent. Caroline wondered what it was that Augusta knew that she did not.

The twinning sisters attended the opera later that week. It was the first time they had been inside the ornate structure that was the Opera House; their progress to the box organized for them by their guardian was perforce slow as they gazed about them with interest. Once inside the box itself, in a perfect position in the first tier, their attention was quickly claimed by their fellow opera-goers. The pit below was a teeming sea of heads; the stylish crops of the fashionable young men who took perverse delight in rubbing shoulders with the masses bobbed amid the unkempt locks of the hoi polloi. But it was upon the occupants of the other boxes that the Twinnings' principal interest focused. These quickly filled as the time for the curtain to rise approached. All four were absorbed in nodding and waving to friends and acquaintances as the lights went out.

The first act consisted of a short piece by a little-known Italian composer, as the prelude to the opera itself, which would fill the second and third acts, before another short piece ended the performance. Caroline sat, happily absorbed in the spectacle, beside and slightly in front of her guardian. She was blissfully content. She had merely made a comment to Max a week before that she would like to visit the opera. Two days later, he had arranged it all. Now she sat, superbly elegant in a silver satin slip overlaid with bronzed lace, and revelled in the music, conscious, despite her preoccupation, of the warmth of the Duke of Twyford's blue gaze on her bare shoulders.

Max watched her delight with satisfaction. He had long ago ceased to try to analyze his reactions to Caroline Twinning; he was besotted and knew it. Her happiness had somehow become his happiness; in his view, nothing else mattered. As he watched, she turned and smiled, a smile of genuine joy. It was, he felt, all the thanks he required for the effort organizing such a large box at short notice had entailed. He returned her smile, his own lazily sensual. For a moment, their eyes locked. Then, blushing, Caroline turned back to the stage.

Max had little real interest in the performance, his past experiences having had more to do with the singer than the song. He allowed his gaze to move past Caroline to dwell on her eldest half-sister. He had not yet fathomed exactly what Sarah's ambition was, yet felt sure it was not as simple as it appeared. The notion that any Twinning would meekly accept unwedded solitude as her lot was hard to swallow. As Sarah sat by Caroline's side, dramatic as ever in a gown of deepest green, the light from the stage lit her face. Her troubles had left no mark on the classical lines of brow and cheek but the peculiar light revealed more clearly than daylight the underlying determination in the set of the delicate mouth and chin. Max's lips curved in a wry grin. He doubted that Darcy had heard the last of Sarah Twinning, whatever the outcome of his self-imposed exile.

Behind Sarah sat Lord Tulloch and Mr. Swanston, invited by Max to act as squires for Sarah and Arabella respectively. Neither was particularly interested in the opera, yet both had accepted the invitations with alacrity. Now, they sat, yawning politely behind their hands, waiting for the moment when the curtain would fall and they could be seen by the other attending members of the *ton*, escorting their exquisite charges through the corridors.

Arabella, too, was fidgety, settling and resetting her pink silk skirts and dropping her fan. She appeared to be trying to scan the boxes on the tier above. Max smiled. He could have told her that Hugo Denbigh hated opera and had yet to be seen within the portals of Covent Garden.

Lady Benborough, dragon-like in puce velvet, sat determinedly following the aria. Distracted by Arabella's antics, she turned to speak in a sharp whisper, whereat Arabella grudgingly subsided, a dissatisfied frown marring her delightful visage.

At the opposite end of the box sat Martin, with Lizzie by the parapet beside him. She was enthralled by the performance, hanging on every note that escaped the throat of the soprano performing the lead. Martin, most improperly holding her hand, evinced not the slightest interest in the buxom singer but gazed solely at Lizzie, a peculiar smile hovering about his lips. Inwardly, Max sighed. He just hoped his brother knew what he was about.

The aria ended and the curtain came down. As the applause died, the large flambeaux which lit the pit were brought forth and re-installed in their brackets. Noise erupted around them as everyone talked at once.

Max leaned forward to speak by Caroline's ear. "Come. Let's stroll."

She turned to him in surprise and he smiled. "That's what going to the opera is about, my dear. To see and be seen. Despite appearances, the most important performances take place in the corridors of Covent Garden, not on the stage."

"Of course," she returned, standing and shaking out her skirts. "How very provincial of me not to realize." Her eyes twinkled. "How kind of you, dear guardian, to attend so assiduously to our education."

Max took her hand and tucked it into his arm. As they paused to allow the others to precede them, he bent to whisper in her ear, "On the contrary, sweet Caro. While I'm determined to see your education completed, my interest is entirely selfish."

The wicked look which danced in his dark blue eyes made Caroline blush. But she was becoming used to the highly improper conversations she seemed to have with her guardian. "Oh?" she replied, attempting to look innocent and not entirely succeeding. "Won't I derive any benefit from my new-found knowledge?"

They were alone in the box, hidden from view of the other boxes by shadows. For a long moment, they were both still, blue eyes locked with grey-green, the rest of the world far distant. Caroline could not breathe; the intensity of that blue gaze and the depth of the passion which smouldered within it held her mesmerized. Then, his eyes still on hers, Max lifted her hand and dropped a kiss on her fingers. "My dear, once you find the key, beyond that particular door lies paradise. Soon, sweet Caro, very soon, you'll see."

Once in the corridor, Caroline's cheeks cooled. They were quickly surrounded by her usual court and Max, behaving more circumspectly than he ever had before, relinquished her to the throng. Idly, he strolled along the corridors, taking the opportunity to stretch his long legs. He paused here and there to exchange a word with friends but did not stop for long. His preoccupation was not with extending his acquaintance of the *ton.* His ramblings brought him to the corridor serving the opposite arm of the horseshoe of boxes. The bell summoning the audience to their seats for the next act rang shrilly. Max was turning to make his way back to his box when a voice hailed him through the crush.

"Your Grace!"

Max closed his eyes in exasperation, then opened them and turned to face Lady Mortland. He nodded curtly. "Emma."

She was on the arm of a young man whom she introduced and immediately dismissed, before turning to Max. "I think perhaps we should have a serious talk, Your Grace."

The hard note in her voice and the equally rock-like glitter in her eyes were not lost on the Duke of Twyford. Max had played the part of the fashionable rake for fifteen years and knew well the occupational hazards. He lifted his eyes from an uncannily thorough contemplation of Lady Mortland and sighted a small alcove, temporarily deserted. "I think perhaps you're right, my dear. But I suggest we improve our surroundings."

His hand under her elbow steered Emma towards the alcove. The grip of his fingers through her silk sleeve and the steely quality in his voice were a surprise to her ladyship, but she was determined that Max Rotherbridge should pay, one way or another, for her lost dreams.

They reached the relative privacy of the alcove. "Well, Emma, what's this all about?"

Suddenly, Lady Mortland was rather less certain of

her strategy. Faced with a pair of very cold blue eyes and an iron will she had never previously glimpsed, she vacillated. "Actually, Your Grace," she cooed, "I had rather hoped you would call on me and we could discuss the matter in…greater privacy."

"Cut line, Emma," drawled His Grace. "You knew perfectly well I have no wish whatever to be private with you."

The bald statement ignited Lady Mortland's temper. "Yes!" she hissed, fingers curling into claws. "Ever since you set eyes on that little harpy you call your ward, you've had no time for me!"

"I wouldn't, if I were you, make scandalous statements about a young lady to her guardian," said Max, unmoved by her spleen.

"Guardian, ha! Love, more like!"

One black brow rose haughtily.

"Do you deny it? No, of course not! Oh, there are whispers aplenty, let me tell you. But they're as nothing to the storm there'll be when I get through with you. I'll tell—Ow!"

Emma broke off and looked down at her wrist, imprisoned in Max's right hand. "L…let me go. Max, you're hurting me."

"Emma, you'll say nothing."

Lady Mortland looked up and was suddenly frightened. Max nodded, a gentle smile, which was quite terrifyingly cold, on his lips. "Listen carefully, Emma, for I'll say this once only. You'll not, verbally or otherwise, malign my ward—any of my wards— in any way whatever. Because, if you do, rest assured I'll hear about it. Should that happen, I'll ensure your stepson learns of the honours you do his father's memory by your retired lifestyle. Your income derives from the family estates, does it not?''

Emma had paled. "You...you wouldn't."

Max released her. "No. You're quite right. I wouldn't," he said. "Not unless you do first. Then, you may be certain that I would." He viewed the woman before him, with understanding if not compassion. "Leave be, Emma. What Caroline has was never yours and you know it. I suggest you look to other fields."

With a nod, Max left Lady Mortland and returned through the empty corridors to his box.

Caroline turned as he resumed his seat. She studied his face for a moment, then leaned back to whisper, "Is anything wrong?"

Max's gaze rested on her sweet face, concern for his peace of mind the only emotion visible. He smiled reassuringly and shook his head. "A minor matter of no moment." In the darkness he reached for her hand and raised it to his lips. With a smile, Caroline returned her attention to the stage. When she made no move to withdraw her hand, Max continued to hold it, mimicking Martin, placating his conscience with the observation that, in the dark, no one could see the Duke of Twyford holding hands with his eldest ward.

# Chapter Ten

Execution of the first phase of the Twinnings' master plot to rescue Amanda and Sir Ralph from the machinations of Mrs. Crowbridge fell to Sarah. An evening concert was selected as the venue most conducive to success. As Sir Ralph was tone deaf, enticing him from the real pleasure of listening to the dramatic voice of *Señorita Muscariña*, the Spanish soprano engaged for the evening, proved easier than Sarah had feared.

Sir Ralph was quite content to escort Miss Sarah for a stroll on the balcony, ostensibly to relieve the stuffiness in Miss Twinning's head. In the company of the rest of the *ton*, he knew Sarah was pining away and thus, he reasoned, he was safe in her company. That she was one of the more outstandingly opulent beauties he had ever set eyes on simply made life more complete. It was rare that he felt at ease with such women and his time in London had made him, more than once, wish he was back in the less demanding backwoods of Gloucestershire. Even now, despite his successful courtship of the beautiful, the effervescent, the gorgeous Arabella Twinning, there were times Harriet Jenkins's face reminded him of how much more comfortable their almost finalized relationship had been. In fact, although he tried his best to ignore them, doubts kept appearing in his mind, of whether he would be able to live up to Arabella's expectations once they were wed. He was beginning to understand that girls like Arabella—well, she was a woman, really—were used to receiving the most specific advances from the more hardened of the male population. Sir Ralph swallowed nervously, woefully aware that he lacked the abilities to compete with such gentlemen. He glanced at the pale face of the beauty beside him. A frown marred her smooth brow. He relaxed. Clearly, Miss Sarah's mind was not bent on illicit dalliance.

In thinking this, Sir Ralph could not have been further from the truth. Sarah's frown was engendered by her futile attempts to repress the surge of longing that had swept through her—a relic of that fateful evening in Lady Overton's shrubbery, she felt sure—when she had seen Darcy Hamilton's tall figure negligently propped by the door. She had felt the weight of his gaze upon her and, turning to seek its source, had met his eyes across the room. Fool that she was! She had had to fight to keep herself in her seat and not run across the room and throw herself into his arms. Then, an arch look from Arabella, unaware of Lord Darcy's return, had reminded her of her duty. She had put her hand to her head and Lizzie had promptly asked if she was feeling the thing. It had been easy enough to claim Sir Ralph's escort and leave the music-room.

But the thunderous look in Darcy's eyes as she did so had tied her stomach in knots.

Pushing her own concerns abruptly aside, she transferred her attention to the man beside her. "Sir Ralph, I hope you won't mind if I speak to you on a matter of some delicacy?"

Taken aback, Sir Ralph goggled.

Sarah ignored his startled expression. Harriet had warned her how he would react. It was her job to lead him by the nose. "I'm afraid things have reached a head with Arabella. I know it's not obvious; she's so reticent about such things. But I feel it's my duty to try to explain it to you. She's in such low spirits. Something must be done or she may even go into a decline."

It was on the tip of Sir Ralph's tongue to say that he had thought it was Sarah who was going into the decline. And the suggestion that Arabella, last seen with an enchanting sparkle in her big eyes, was in low spirits confused him utterly. But Sarah's next comment succeeded in riveting his mind. "You're the only one who can save her."

The practical tone in which Sarah brought out her statement lent it far greater weight than a more dramatic declaration. In the event, Sir Ralph's attention was all hers. "You see, although she would flay me alive for telling you, you should know that she was very seriously taken with a gentleman earlier in the Season, before you arrived. He played on her sensibilities and she was so vulnerable. Unfortunately, he was not interested in marriage. I'm sure I can rely on your discretion. Luckily, she learned of his true intentions before he had time to achieve them. But her heart was sorely bruised, of course. Now that she's found such solace in your company, we had hoped, my sisters and I, that you would not let her down.''

Sir Ralph was heard to mumble that he had no intention of letting Miss Arabella down.

"Ah, but you see," said Sarah, warming to her task, "what she needs is to be taken out of herself. Some excitement that would divert her from the present round of balls and parties and let her forget her past hurts in her enjoyment of a new love.''

Sir Ralph, quite carried away by her eloquence, muttered that yes, he could quite see the point in that.

"So you see, Sir Ralph, it's imperative that she be swept off her feet. She's very romantically inclined, you know.''

Sir Ralph, obediently responding to his cue, declared he was only too ready to do whatever was necessary to ensure Arabella's happiness.

Sarah smiled warmly, "In that case, I can tell you exactly what you must do.''

It took Sarah nearly half an hour to conclude her instructions to Sir Ralph. Initially, he had been more than a little reluctant even to discuss such an enterprise. But, by dwelling on the depth of Arabella's need, appealing quite brazenly to poor Sir Ralph's chivalrous instincts, she had finally wrung from him his sworn agreement to the entire plan.

In a mood of definite self-congratulation, she led the way back to the music-room and, stepping over the door sill, all but walked into Darcy Hamilton. His

hand at her elbow steadied her, but, stung by his
touch, she abruptly pulled away. Sir Ralph, who had
not previously met Lord Darcy, stopped in bewilderment, his eyes going from Sarah's burning face to his
lordship's pale one. Then, Darcy Hamilton became
aware of his presence. "I'll return Miss Twinning to
her seat."

Responding to the commanding tone, Sir Ralph
bowed and departed.

Sarah drew a deep breath. "How *dare* you?" she
uttered furiously as she made to follow Sir Ralph.

But Darcy's hand on her arm detained her.
"What's that...country bumpkin to you?" The in-
sulting drawl in his voice drew a blaze of fire from
Sarah's eyes.

But before she could wither him where she stood,
several heads turned their way. "Sssh!"

Without a word, Darcy turned her and propelled
her back out of the door.

"Disgraceful!" said Lady Malling to Mrs. Benn,
nodding by her side.

On the balcony, Sarah stood very still, quivering
with rage and a number of other more interesting
emotions, directly attributable to the fact that Darcy
was standing immediately behind her.

"Perhaps you'd like to explain what you were doing with that gentleman on the balcony for half an
hour and more?"

Sarah almost turned, then remembered how close
he was. She lifted her chin and kept her temper with
an effort. "That's hardly any affair of yours, my
lord."

Darcy frowned. "As a friend of your guardian—"

At that Sarah did turn, uncaring of the consequences, her eyes flashing, her voice taut. "As a friend of my guardian, you've been trying to seduce me ever since you first set eyes on me!"

"True," countered Darcy, his face like granite. "But not even Max has blamed me for that. Besides, it's what you Twinning girls expect, isn't it? Tell me, my dear, how many other lovesick puppies have you had at your feet since I left?"

It was on the tip of Sarah's tongue to retort that she had had no lack of suitors since his lordship had quit the scene. But, just in time, she saw the crevasse yawning at her feet. In desperation, she willed herself to calm, and coolly met his blue eyes, her own perfectly candid. "Actually, I find the entertainments of the *ton* have palled. Since you ask, I've formed the intention of entering a convent. There's a particularly suitable one, the Ursulines, not far from our old home."

For undoubtedly the first time in his adult life, Darcy Hamilton was completely nonplussed. A whole range of totally unutterable responses sprang to his lips. He swallowed them all and said, "You wouldn't be such a fool."

Sarah's brows rose coldly. For a moment she held his gaze, then turned haughtily to move past him.

"Sarah!" The word was wrung from him and then she was in his arms, her lips crushed under his, her head spinning as he gathered her more fully to him.

For Sarah, it was a repeat of their interlude in the shrubbery. As the kiss deepened, then deepened

again, she allowed herself a few minutes' grace, to
savour the paradise of being once more in his arms.

Then, she gathered her strength and tore herself
from his hold. For an instant, they remained frozen,
silently staring at each other, their breathing tumul-
tuous, their eyes liquid fire. Abruptly, Sarah turned
and walked quickly back into the music-room.

With a long-drawn-out sigh, Darcy Hamilton
leaned upon the balustrade, gazing unseeingly at the
well-manicured lawns.

His Grace of Twyford carefully scrutinized Sarah
Twinning's face as she returned to the music-room
and joined her younger sisters in time to applaud the
singer's operatic feats. Caroline, seated beside him,
had not noticed her sister's departure from the room,
nor her short-lived return. As his gaze slid gently over
Caroline's face and noted the real pleasure the music
had brought her, he decided that he had no intention
of informing her of her sister's strange behaviour.
That there was something behind the younger Twinnings's interest in Sir Ralph Keighly he did not doubt.
But whatever it was, he would much prefer that Caroline was not caught up in it. He was becoming accustomed to having her complete attention and found
himself reluctant to share it with anyone.

He kept a watchful eye on the door to the balcony
and, some minutes later, when the singer was once
more in full flight, saw Darcy Hamilton enter and,
unobtrusively, leave the room. His eyes turning once
more to the bowed dark head of Sarah Twinning, Max
sighed. Darcy Hamilton had been one of the coolest

hands in the business. But in the case of Sarah Twinning his touch seemed to have deserted him entirely. His friend's disintegration was painful to watch. He had not yet had time to do more than nod a greeting to Darcy when he had seen him enter the room. Max wondered what conclusions he had derived from his sojourn in Ireland. Whatever they were, he wryly suspected that Darcy would be seeking him out soon enough.

Which, of course, was likely to put a time limit on his own affair. His gaze returned to Caroline and, as if in response, she turned to smile up at him, her eyes unconsciously warm, her lips curving invitingly. Regretfully dismissing the appealing notion of creating a riot by kissing her in the midst of the cream of the *ton*, Max merely returned the smile and watched as she once more directed her attention to the singer. No, he did not need to worry. She would be his long before her sisters' affairs became pressing.

The masked ball given by Lady Penbright was set to be one of the highlights of an already glittering Season. Her ladyship had spared no expense. Her ballroom was draped in white satin and the terraces and trellised walks with which Penbright House was lavishly endowed were lit by thousands of Greek lanterns. The music of a small orchestra drifted down from the minstrels' gallery, the notes falling like petals on the gloriously covered heads of the *ton*. By decree, all the guests wore long dominos, concealing their evening dress, hoods secured over the ladies' curls to remove even that hint of identity. Fixed masks concealing the upper face were the order, far harder to penetrate than the smaller and often more bizarre hand-held masks, still popular in certain circles for flirtation. By eleven, the Penbright ball had been accorded the ultimate accolade of being declared a sad crush and her ladyship retired from her position by the door to join in the revels with her guests.

Max, wary of the occasion and having yet to divine the younger Twinnings' secret aim, had taken special note of his wards' dresses when he arrived at Twyford House to escort them to the ball. Caroline he would have no difficulty in detecting; even if her domino in a subtle shade of aqua had not been virtually unique, the effect her presence had on him, he had long ago noticed, would be sufficient to enable him to unerringly find her in a crowded room blindfold. Sarah, looking slightly peaked but carrying herself with the grace he expected of a Twinning, had flicked a moss-green domino over her satin dress which was in a paler shade of the same colour. Arabella had been struggling to settle the hood of a delicate rose-pink domino over her bright curls while Lizzie's huge grey eyes had watched from the depths of her lavender hood. Satisfied he had fixed the particular tints in his mind, Max had ushered them forth.

On entering the Penbright ballroom, the three younger Twinnings melted into the crowd but Caroline remained beside Max, anchored by his hand under her elbow. To her confusion, she found that one of the major purposes of a masked ball seemed to be to allow those couples who wished to spend an entire evening together without creating a scandal to do so.

Certainly, her guardian appeared to have no intention of quitting her side.

While the musicians were tuning up, she was approached in a purposeful manner by a grey domino, under which she had no difficulty in recognizing the slight frame of Mr. Willoughby. The poor man was not entirely sure of her identity and Caroline gave him no hint. He glared at the tall figure by her side, which resulted in a slow, infuriating grin spreading across that gentleman's face. Then, as Mr. Willoughby cleared his throat preparatory to asking the lady in the aqua domino for the pleasure of the first waltz, Max got in before him.

After her second waltz with her guardian, who was otherwise behaving impeccably, Caroline consented to a stroll about the rooms. The main ballroom was full and salons on either side took up the overflow. A series of interconnecting rooms made Caroline's head spin. Then, Max embarked on a long and involved anecdote which focused her attention on his masked face and his wickedly dancing eyes.

She should, of course, have been on her guard, but Caroline's defences against her dangerous guardian had long since fallen. Only when she had passed through the door he held open for her, and discovered it led into a bedroom, clearly set aside for the use of any guests overcome by the revels downstairs, did the penny drop. As she turned to him, she heard the click of the lock falling into its setting. And then Max stood before her, his eyes alight with an emotion she dared not define. That slow grin of his, which by itself turned her bones to jelly, showed in the shifting light from the open windows.

She put her hands on his shoulders, intending to hold him off, yet there was no strength behind the gesture and instead, as he drew her against him, her arms of their own accord slipped around his neck. She yielded in that first instant, as his lips touched hers, and Max knew it. But he saw no reason for undue haste. Savouring the feel of her, the taste of her, he spun out their time, giving her the opportunity to learn of each pleasure as it came, gently guiding her to the chaise by the windows, never letting her leave his arms or that state of helpless surrender she was in.

Caroline Twinning was heady stuff, but Max remembered he had a question for her. He drew back to gaze at her as she lay, reclining against the colourful cushions, her eyes unfocused as his long fingers caressed the satin smoothness of her breasts as they had once before in the carriage on the way back from the Richardsons' ball, with Miriam Alford snoring quietly in the corner. "Caro?"

Caroline struggled to make sense of his voice through the haze of sensation clouding her mind. "Mmm?"

"Sweet Caro," he murmured wickedly, watching her efforts. "If you recall, I once asked you if, were I not your guardian, you would permit me to be alone with you. Do you still think, if that was the case, you'd resist?"

To Caroline, the question was so ridiculous that it broke through to her consciousness, submerged beneath layers of pleasurable sensation. A slight frown came to her eyes as she wondered why on earth he kept asking such a hypothetical question. But his hands had stilled so it clearly behoved her to answer it. "I've always resisted you," she declared. "It's just that I've never succeeded in impressing that fact upon you. Even if you weren't my guardian, I'd still try to resist you." Her eyes closed and she gave up the attempt at conversation as his hands resumed where they had left off. But all too soon they stilled again.

"What do you mean, *even* if I weren't your guardian?"

Caroline groaned. "Max!" But his face clearly showed that he wanted her answer, so she explained with what patience she could muster. "This, you and me, together, would be scandalous enough if you weren't my guardian, but you are, so it's ten times worse." She closed her eyes again. "You must know that."

Max did, but it had never occurred to him that she would have readily accepted his advances even had he not had her guardianship to tie her to him. His slow smile appeared. He should have known. Twinnings and rakes, after all. Caroline, her eyes still closed, all senses focused on the movement of his hands upon her breasts, did not see the smile, nor the glint in her guardian's very blue eyes that went with it. But her eyes flew wide open when Max bent his head and took one rosy nipple into his mouth.

"Oh!" She tensed and Max lifted his head to grin wolfishly at her. He cocked one eyebrow at her but she was incapable of speech. Then, deliberately, his eyes holding hers, he lowered his head to her other breast, feeling her tense in his arms against the anticipated shock. Gradually, she relaxed, accepting that sensation too. Slowly, he pushed her further, knowing he would meet no resistance. She responded freely, so much so that he was constantly drawing back, trying to keep a firm hold on his much tried control. Experienced as he was, Caroline Twinning was something quite outside his previous knowledge.

Soon, they had reached that subtle point beyond which there would be no turning back. He knew it, though he doubted she did. And, to his amazement, he paused, then gently disengaged, drawing her around to lean against his chest so that he could place kisses in the warm hollow of her neck and fondle her breasts, ensuring she would stay blissfully unaware while he did some rapid thinking.

The pros were clear enough, but she would obviously come to him whenever he wished, now or at any time in the future. Such as tomorrow. The cons were rather more substantial. Chief among these was that tonight they would have to return to the ball afterwards, usually a blessing if one merely wanted to bed a woman, not spend the entire night with her. But, if given the choice, he would prefer to spend at least twenty-four hours in bed with Caroline, a reasonable compensation for his forbearance to date. Then, too, there was the very real problem of her sisters. Despite the preoccupation of his hands, he knew that a part of his mind was taken up with the question of what they were doing while he and his love were otherwise engaged. He would infinitely prefer to be able to devote his entire attention to the luscious person in his arms. He sighed. His body did not like what his mind was telling it. Before he could change his decision, he pulled Caroline closer and bent to whisper in her ear. "Caro?"

She murmured his name and put her hand up to his face. Max smiled. "Sweetheart, much as I'd like to complete your education here and now, I have a dreadful premonition of what hideous scandals your sisters might be concocting with both of us absent from the ballroom."

He knew it was the right excuse to offer, for her mind immediately reasserted itself. "Oh, dear," she sighed, disappointment ringing clearly in her tone, deepening Max's smile. "I suspect you're right."

"I know I'm right," he said, straightening and sitting her upright. "Come, let's get you respectable again."

As soon as she felt sufficiently camouflaged from her guardian's eye by the gorgeously coloured throng, Lizzie Twinning made her way to the ballroom window further from the door. It was the meeting place Sarah had stipulated where Sir Ralph was to await further instructions. He was there, in a dark green domino and a black mask.

Lizzie gave him her hand. "Good!" The hand holding hers trembled. She peered into the black mask. "You're not going to let Arabella down, are you?"

To her relief, Sir Ralph swallowed and shook his head. "No. Of course not. I've got my carriage waiting, as Miss Sarah suggested. I wouldn't dream of deserting Miss Arabella.''

Despite the weakness in his voice, Lizzie was satisfied. "It's all right," she assured him. "Arabella is wearing a rose-pink domino. It's her favourite colour so you should recognise it. We'll bring her to you, as we said we would. Don't worry," she said, giving his hand a squeeze, "it'll all work out for the best, you'll see." She patted his hand and, returning it to him, left him. As she moved down the ballroom, she scanned the crowd and picked out Caroline in her aqua domino waltzing with a black domino who could only be their guardian. She grinned to herself and the next instant, walked smack into a dark blue domino directly in her path.

"Oh!" She fell back and put up a hand to her mask, which had slipped.

"Lizzie," said the blue domino in perfectly recognizable accents, "what were you doing talking to Keighly?"

"Martin! What a start you gave me. My mask nearly fell. Wh…what do you mean?"

"I mean, Miss Innocence," said Martin sternly, taking her arm and compelling her to walk beside him on to the terrace, "that I saw you come into the ballroom and then, as soon as you were out of Max's sight, make a bee-line for Keighly. Now, out with it! What's going on?"

Lizzie was in shock. What was she to do? Not for a moment did she imagine that Martin would agree to turn a blind eye to their scheme. But she was not a very good liar. Still, she would have to try. Luckily, the mask hid most of her face and her shock had kept her immobile, gazing silently up at him in what could be taken for her usual innocent manner. "But I don't know what you mean, Martin. I know I talked to Sir Ralph, but that was because he was the only one I recognized."

The explanation was so reasonable that Martin felt his sudden suspicion was as ridiculous as it had seemed. He felt decidedly foolish. "Oh."

"But now you're here," said Lizzie, putting her hand on his arm. "So I can talk to you."

Martin's usual grin returned. "So you can." He raised his eyes to the secluded walks, still empty as the dancing had only just begun. "Why don't we explore while we chat?"

Lately, Lizzie had been in the habit of refusing such invitations but tonight she was thankful for any suggestion that would distract Martin from their enterprise. So she nodded and they stepped off the terrace on to the gravel. They followed a path into the shrubbery. It wended this way and that until the house was a glimmer of light and noise beyond the screening bushes. They found an ornamental stream and followed it to a lake. There was a small island in the middle with a tiny summer-house, reached by a rustic bridge. They crossed over and found the door of the summer-house open.

"Isn't this lovely?" said Lizzie, quite enchanted by the scene. Moonbeams danced in a tracery of light created by the carved wooden shutters. The soft swish of the water running past the reed-covered banks was the only sound to reach their ears.

"Mmm, yes, quite lovely," murmured Martin, enchanted by something quite different. Even Lizzie in her innocence heard the warning in his tone but she turned only in time to find herself in his arms. Martin tilted her face up and smiled gently down at her. "Lizzie, sweet Lizzie. Do you have any idea how beautiful you are?"

Lizzie's eyes grew round. Martin's arms closed around her, gentle yet quite firm. It seemed unbelievable that their tightness could be restricting her breathing, yet she found herself quite unable to draw breath. And the strange light in Martin's eyes was making her dizzy. She had meant to ask her sisters for guidance on how best to handle such situations but, due to her absorption with their schemes, it had slipped her mind. She suspected this was one of those points where using one's wits came into it. But, as her tongue seemed incapable of forming any words, she could only shake her head and hope that was acceptable.

"Ah," said Martin, his grin broadening. "Well, you're so very beautiful, sweetheart, that I'm afraid I can't resist. I'm going to kiss you again, Lizzie. And it's going to be thoroughly enjoyable for both of us." Without further words, he dipped his head and, very gently, kissed her. When she did not draw back, he continued the caress, prolonging the sensation until he felt her response. Gradually, with the moonlight washing over them, he deepened the kiss, then, as she continued to respond easily, gently drew her further into his arms. She came willingly and Martin was suddenly unsure of the ground rules. He had no wish to frighten her, innocent as she was, yet he longed to take their dalliance further, much further. He gently increased the pressure of his lips on hers until they parted for him. Slowly, continually reminding himself of her youth, he taught her how pleasurable a kiss could be. Her responses drove him to seek more.

Kisses were something Lizzie felt she could handle. Being held securely in Martin's arms was a delight. But when his hand closed gently over her breast she gasped and pulled away. The reality of her feelings hit her. She burst into tears.

"Lizzie?" Martin, cursing himself for a fool, for pushing her too hard, gathered her into his arms, ignoring her half-hearted resistance. "I'm sorry, Lizzie. It was too soon, I know. Lizzie? Sweetheart?"

Lizzie gulped and stifled her sobs. "It's true!" she said, her voice a tear-choked whisper. "They said you were a rake and you'd want to take me to bed and I didn't believe them but it's *true*." She ended this astonishing speech on a hiccup.

Martin, finding much of her accusation difficult to deny, fastened on the one aspect that was not clear. "They—who?"

"Sarah and Bella and Caro. They said you're *all* rakes. You and Max and Lord Darcy and Lord Denbigh. They said there's something about us that means we attract rakes."

Finding nothing in all this that he wished to dispute, Martin kept silent. He continued to hold Lizzie, his face half buried in her hair. "What did they suggest you should do about it?" he eventually asked, unsure if he would get an answer.

The answer he got was unsettling. "Wait."

*Wait.* Martin did not need to ask what for. He knew.

Very much later in the evening, when Martin had escorted Lizzie back to the ballroom, Max caught sight of them from the other side of the room. He had been forced to reassess his original opinion of the youngest Twinning's sobriety. Quite how such a youthful innocent had managed to get Martin into her toils he could not comprehend, but one look at his brother's face, even with his mask in place, was enough to tell him she had succeeded to admiration. Well, he had warned him.

Arabella's role in the great plan was to flirt so outrageously that everyone in the entire room would be certain that it was indeed the vivacious Miss Twinning under the rose-pink domino. None of the conspirators had imagined this would prove at all difficult and, true to form, within half an hour Arabella had convinced the better part of the company of her identity. She left one group of revellers, laughing gaily, and was moving around the room, when she found she had walked into the arms of a large, black-domino-clad figure. The shock she received from the contact immediately informed her of the identity of the gentleman.

"Oh, sir! You quite overwhelm me!"

"In such a crowd as this, my dear? Surely you jest?"

"Would you contradict a lady, sir? Then you're no gentlemen, in truth."

"In truth, you're quite right, sweet lady. Gentlemen lead such boring lives."

The distinctly seductive tone brought Arabella up short. He could not know who she was, could he? As if in answer to her unspoken question, he asked, "And who might you be, my lovely?"

Arabella's chin went up and she playfully retorted, "Why, that's not for you to know, sir. My reputation might be at stake, simply for talking to so unconventional a gentleman as you."

To her unease, Hugo responded with a deep and attractive chuckle. Their light banter continued, Arabella making all the customary responses, her quick ear for repartee saving her from floundering when his returns made her cheeks burn. She flirted with Hugo to the top of her bent. And hated every minute of it. He did not know who she was, yet was prepared to push an unknown lady to make an assignation with him for later in the evening. She was tempted to do so and then confront him with her identity. But her heart failed her. Instead, when she could bear it no longer, she made a weak excuse and escaped.

They had timed their plan carefully, to avoid any possible mishap. The unmasking was scheduled for one o'clock. At precisely half-past twelve, Sarah and Sir Ralph left the ballroom and strolled in a convincingly relaxed manner down a secluded walk which led to a little gazebo. The gazebo was placed across the path and, beyond it, the path continued to a gate giving access to the carriage drive.

Within sight of the gazebo, Sarah halted. "Arabella's inside. I'll wait here and ensure no one interrupts.''

Sir Ralph swallowed, nodded once and left her. He climbed the few steps and entered the gazebo. In the dimness, he beheld the rose-pink domino, her mask still in place, waiting nervously for him to approach. Reverently, he went forward and then went down on one knee.

Sarah, watching from the shadows outside, grinned in delight. The dim figures exchanged a few words, then Sir Ralph rose and kissed the lady. Sarah held her breath, but all went well. Hand in hand, the pink domino and her escort descended by the opposite door of the gazebo and headed for the gate. To make absolutely sure of their success, Sarah entered the gazebo and stood watching the couple disappear through the gate. She waited, silently, then the click of horses' hooves came distantly on the breeze. With a quick smile, she turned to leave. And froze.

Just inside the door to the gazebo stood a tall, black-domino-clad figure, his shoulders propped negligently against the frame in an attitude so characteristic Sarah would have known him anywhere. ''Are you perchance waiting for an assignation, my dear?''

Sarah made a grab for her fast-disappearing wits. She drew herself up but, before she could speak, his voice came again. ''Don't run away. A chase through the bushes would be undignified at best and I would catch you all the same.''

Sarah's brows rose haughtily. She had removed her mask which had been irritating her and it hung by its strings from her fingers. She swung it back and forth nervously. "Run? Why should I run?" Her voice, she was pleased to find, was calm.

Darcy did not answer. Instead, he pushed away from the door and crossed the floor to stand in front of her. He reached up and undid his mask. Then his eyes caught hers. "Are you still set on fleeing to a convent?"

Sarah held his gaze steadily. "I am."

A wry smile, self-mocking, she thought, twisted his mobile mouth. "That won't do, you know. You're not cut out to be a bride of Christ."

"Better a bride of Christ than the mistress of any man." She watched the muscles in his jaw tighten.

"You think so?"

Despite the fact that she had known it would happen, had steeled herself to withstand it, her defences crumbled at his touch and she was swept headlong into abandonment, freed from restraint, knowing where the road led and no longer caring.

But when Darcy stooped and lifted her, to carry her to the wide cushioned seats at the side of the room, she shook her head violently. "Darcy, no!" Her voice caught on a sob. "Please, Darcy, let me go."

Her tears sobered him as nothing else could have. Slowly, he let her down until her feet touched the floor. She was openly crying, as if her heart would break. "Sarah?" Darcy put out a hand to smooth her brown hair.

Sarah had found her handkerchief and was mopping her streaming eyes, her face averted. "Please go, Darcy."

Darcy stiffened. For the first time in his adult life,

he wanted to take a woman into his arms purely to comfort her. All inclinations to make love to her had vanished at the first hint of her distress. But, sensing behind her whispered words a confusion she had yet to resolve, he sighed and, with a curt bow, did as she asked.

Sarah listened to his footsteps die away. She remained in the gazebo until she had cried herself out. Then, thankful for the at least temporary protection of her mask, she returned to the ballroom to tell her sisters and their protégées of their success.

Hugo scanned the room again, searching through the sea of people for Arabella. But the pink domino was nowhere in sight. He was as thoroughly disgruntled as only someone of a generally placid nature could become. Arabella had flirted outrageously with an unknown man. Admittedly him, but she had not known that. Here he had been worrying himself into a state over her getting herself stuck in a loveless marriage for no reason and underneath she was just a heartless flirt. A jade. Where the hell was she?

A small hand on his arm made him jump. But, contrary to the conviction of his senses, it was not Arabella but a lady in a brown domino with a brown mask fixed firmly in place. "'Ello, kind sir. You seem strangely lonely."

Hugo blinked. The lady's accent was heavily middle European, her tone seductively low.

"I'm all alone," sighed the lady in brown. "And as you seemed also alone, I thought that maybe we could cheer one another up, no?"

In spite of himself, Hugo's glance flickered over the lady. Her voice suggested a wealth of experience yet her skin, what he could see of it, was as delicate as a young girl's. The heavy mask she wore covered most of her face, even shading her lips, though he could see these were full and ripe. The domino, as dominos did, concealed her figure. Exasperated, Hugo sent another searching glance about the room in vain. Then, he looked down and smiled into the lady's hazel eyes. "What a very interesting idea, my dear. Shall we find somewhere to further develop our mutual acquaintance?"

He slipped an arm around the lady's waist and found that it was indeed very neat. She seemed for one instant to stiffen under his arm but immediately relaxed. Damn Arabella! She had driven him mad. He would forget her existence and let this lovely lady restore his sanity. "What did you say your name was, my dear?"

The lady smiled up at him, a wickedly inviting smile. "Maria Pavlovska," she said as she allowed him to lead her out of the ballroom.

They found a deserted ante-room without difficulty and, without waiting time in further, clearly unnecessary talk, Hugo drew Maria Pavlovska into his arms. She allowed him to kiss her and, to his surprise, raised no demur when he deepened the kiss. His senses were racing and her responses drove him wild. He let his hand wander and she merely chuckled softly, the sound suggesting that he had yet to reach her limit. He found a convenient armchair and pulled her on to his lap and let her drive him demented. She was the most satisfyingly responsive woman he had ever found. Bewildered by his good fortune, he smiled understandingly when she whispered she would leave him for a moment.

He sighed in anticipation and stretched his long legs in front of him as the door clicked shut.

As the minutes ticked by and Maria Pavlovska did not return, sanity slowly settled back into Hugo's fevered brain. Where the hell was she? She'd deserted him. Just like Arabella. The thought hit him with the force of a sledgehammer. *Just like Arabella?* No, he was imagining things. True, Maria Pavlovska had aroused him in a way he had begun to think only Arabella could. *Hell!* She had even *tasted* like Arabella. But Arabella's domino was pink. Maria Pavlovska's domino was brown. And, now he came to think of it, it had been a few inches too short; he had been able to see her pink slippers and the pink hem of her dress. Arabella's favourite colour was pink but pink was, after all, a very popular colour. Damn, where was she? Where were they? With a long-suffering sigh, Hugo rose and, forswearing all women, left to seek the comparative safety of White's for the rest of the night.

## Chapter Eleven

After returning to the ballroom with Caroline, Max found his temper unconducive to remaining at the ball. In short, he had a headache. His wards seemed to be behaving themselves, despite his premonitions, so there was little reason to remain at Penbright House. But the night was young and his interlude with Caroline had made it unlikely that sleep would come easily, so he excused himself to his eldest ward and his aunt, and left to seek entertainment of a different sort.

He had never got around to replacing Carmelita. There hardly seemed much point now. He doubted he would have much use for such women in future. He grinned to himself, then winced. Just at that moment, he regretted not having a replacement available. He would try his clubs—perhaps a little hazard might distract him.

The carriage had almost reached Delmere House when, on the spur of the moment, he redirected his coachman to a discreet house on Bolsover Street. Sending the carriage back to Penbright House, he entered the newest gaming hell in London. Naturally, the door was opened to His Grace of Twyford with an alacrity that brought a sardonic grin to His Grace's face. But the play was entertaining enough and the beverages varied and of a quality he could not fault. The hell claimed to be at the forefront of fashion and consequently there were a number of women present, playing the green baize tables or, in some instances, merely accompanying their lovers. To his amusement, Max found a number of pairs of feminine eyes turned his way, but was too wise to evince an interest he did not, in truth, feel. Among the patrons he found more than a few refugees from the Penbright ball, among them Darcy Hamilton.

Darcy was leaning against the wall, watching the play at the hazard table. He glowered as Max approached. "I noticed both you and your eldest ward were absent from the festivities for an inordinately long time this evening. Examining etchings upstairs, I suppose?"

Max grinned. "We were upstairs, as it happens. But it wasn't etchings I was examining."

Darcy nearly choked on his laughter. "Damn you, Max," he said when he could speak. "So you've won through, have you?"

A shrug answered him. "Virtually. But I decided the ball was not the right venue." The comment stunned Darcy but before he could phrase his next question Max continued. "Her sisters seem to be hatching some plot, though I'm dashed if I can see what it is. But when I left all seemed peaceful enough.'' Max's blue eyes went to his friend's face. ''What are you doing here?''

''Trying to avoid thinking,'' said Darcy succinctly.

Max grinned. ''Oh. In that case, come and play a hand of piquet.''

The two were old adversaries who only occasionally found the time to play against each other. Their skills were well-matched and before long their game had resolved into an exciting tussle which drew an increasing crowd of spectators. The owners of the hell, finding their patrons leaving the tables to view the contest, from their point an unprofitable exercise, held an urgent conference. They concluded that the cachet associated with having hosted a contest between two such well-known players was worth the expense. Consequently, the two combatants found their glasses continually refilled with the finest brandy and new decks of cards made readily available.

Both Max and Darcy enjoyed the battle, and as both were able to stand the nonsense, whatever the outcome, they were perfectly willing to continue the play for however long their interest lasted. In truth, both found the exercise a welcome outlet for their frustrations of the past weeks.

The brandy they both consumed made absolutely no impression on their play or their demeanour. Egged on by a throng of spectators, all considerably more drunk than the principals, the game was still underway at the small table in the first parlour when Lord McCubbin, an ageing but rich Scottish peer, entered with Emma Mortland on his arm.

Drawn to investigate the cause of the excitement,

Emma's bright eyes fell on the elegant figure of the Duke of Twyford. An unpleasant smile crossed her sharp features. She hung on Lord McCubbin's arm, pressing close to whisper to him.

"Eh? What? Oh, yes," said his lordship, somewhat incoherently. He turned to address the occupants of the table in the middle of the crowd. "Twyford! There you are! Think you've lost rather more than money tonight, what?"

Max, his hand poised to select his discard, let his eyes rise to Lord McCubbin's face. He frowned, an unwelcome premonition filling him as his lordship's words sank in. "What, exactly, do you mean by that, my lord?" The words were even and precise and distinctly deadly.

But Lord McCubbin seemed not to notice. "Why, dear boy, you've lost one of your wards. Saw her, clear as daylight. The flighty one in the damned pink domino. Getting into a carriage with that chap Keighly outside the Penbright place. Well, if you don't know, it's probably too late anyway, don't you know?"

Max's eyes had gone to Emma Mortland's face and seen the malicious triumph there. But he had no time to waste on her. He turned back to Lord McCubbin. "Which way did they go?"

The silence in the room had finally penetrated his lordship's foggy brain. "Er—didn't see. I went back to the ballroom."

Martin Rotherbridge paused, his hand on the handle of his bedroom door. It was past seven in the morning. He had sat up all night since returning from the ball, with his brother's brandy decanter to keep him company, going over his relationship with Lizzie Twinning. And still he could find only one solution. He shook his head and opened the door. The sounds of a commotion in the hall drifted up the stairwell. He heard his brother's voice, uplifted in a series of orders to Hillshaw, and then to Wilson. The tone of voice was one he had rarely heard from Max. It brought him instantly alert. Sleep forgotten, he strode back to the stairs.

In the library, Max was pacing back and forth before the hearth, a savage look on his face. Darcy Hamilton stood silently by the window, his face showing the effects of the past weeks, overlaid by the stress of the moment. Max paused to glance at the clock on the mantelshelf. "Seven-thirty," he muttered. "If my people haven't traced Keighly's carriage by eight-thirty, I'll have to send around to Twyford House." He stopped as a thought struck him. Why hadn't they sent for him anyway? It could only mean that, somehow or other, Arabella had managed to conceal her disappearance. He resumed his pacing. The idea of his aunt in hysterics, not to mention Miriam Alford, was a sobering thought. His own scandalous career would be nothing when compared to the repercussions from this little episode. He would wring Arabella's neck when he caught her.

The door opened. Max looked up to see Martin enter. "What's up?" asked Martin.

"Arabella!" said his brother, venom in his voice. "The stupid chit's done a bunk with Keighly."

*"Eloped?"* said Martin, his disbelief patent.

Max stopped pacing. "Well, I presume he means to marry her. Considering how they all insist on the proposal first, I can't believe she'd change her spots quite so dramatically. But if I have anything to say about it, she won't be marrying Keighly. I've a good mind to shove her into a convent until she comes to her senses!"

Darcy started, then smiled wryly. "I'm told there's a particularly good one near their old home."

Max turned to stare at him as if he had gone mad.

"But think of the waste," said Martin, grinning.

"Precisely my thoughts," nodded Darcy, sinking into an armchair. "Max, unless you plan to ruin your carpet, for God's sake sit down."

With something very like a growl, Max threw himself into the other armchair. Martin drew up a straight-backed chair from the side of the room and sat astride it, his arms folded over its back. "So what now?" he asked. "I've never been party to an elopement before."

His brother's intense blue gaze, filled with silent warning, only made him grin more broadly. "Well, how the hell should I know?" Max eventually exploded.

Both brothers turned to Darcy. He shook his head, his voice unsteady as he replied. "Don't look at me. Not in my line. Come to think of it, none of us has had much experience in trying to get women to marry us."

"Too true," murmured Martin. A short silence fell,

filled with uncomfortable thoughts. Martin broke it. "So, what's your next move?"

"Wilson's sent runners out to all the posting houses. I can't do a thing until I know which road they've taken."

At that moment, the door silently opened and shut again, revealing the efficient Wilson, a small and self-effacing man, Max's most trusted servitor. "I thought you'd wish to know, Your Grace. There's been no sightings of such a vehicle on any of the roads leading north, north-east or south. The man covering the Dover road has yet to report back, as has the man investigating the road to the south-west."

Max nodded. "Thank you, Wilson. Keep me informed as the reports come in."

Wilson bowed and left as silently as he had entered.

The frown on Max's face deepened. "Where would they go? Gretna Green? Dover? I know Keighly's got estates somewhere, but I never asked where." After a moment, he glanced at Martin. "Did Lizzie ever mention it?"

Martin shook his head. Then, he frowned. "Not but what I found her talking to Keighly as soon as ever they got to the ball this evening. I asked her what it was about but she denied there was anything in it." His face had become grim. "She must have known."

"I think Sarah knew too," said Darcy, his voice unemotional. "I saw her go out with Keighly, then found her alone in a gazebo not far from the carriage gate."

"Hell and the devil!" said Max. "They can't all

simultaneously have got a screw loose. What I can't understand is what's so attractive about *Keighly*?''

A knock on the door answered this imponderable question. At Max's command, Hillshaw entered. "Lord Denbigh desires a word with you, Your Grace."

For a moment, Max's face was blank. Then, he sighed. "Show him in, Hillshaw. He's going to have to know sooner or later."

As it transpired, Hugo already knew. As he strode into the library, he was scowling furiously. He barely waited to shake Max's hand and exchange nods with the other two men before asking, "Have you discovered which road they've taken?"

Max blinked and waved him to the armchair he had vacated, moving to take the chair behind the desk. "How did you know?"

"It's all over town," said Hugo, easing his large frame into the chair. "I was at White's when I heard it. And if it's reached that far, by later this morning your ward is going to be featuring in the very latest *on-dit* all over London. I'm going to wring her neck!"

This last statement brought a tired smile to Max's face. But, "You'll have to wait in line for that privilege," was all he said.

The brandy decanter, replenished after Martin's inroads, had twice made the rounds before Wilson again slipped noiselessly into the room. He cleared his throat to attract Max's attention. "A coach carrying a gentleman and a young lady wearing a rose-pink domino put in at the Crown at Acton at two this morning, Your Grace."

The air of despondency which had settled over the room abruptly lifted. "Two," said Max, his eyes going to the clock. "And it's well after eight now. So they must be past Uxbridge. Unless they made a long stop?"

Wilson shook his head. "No, Your Grace. They only stopped long enough to change horses." If anything, the little man's impassive face became even more devoid of emotion. "It seems the young lady was most anxious to put as much distance as possible behind them."

"As well she might," said Max, his eyes glittering. "Have my curricle put to. And good work, Wilson."

"Thank you, Your Grace." Wilson bowed and left. Max tossed off the brandy in his glass and rose.

"I'll come with you," said Hugo, putting his own glass down. For a moment, his eyes met Max's, then Max nodded.

"Very well." His gaze turned to his brother and Darcy Hamilton. "Perhaps you two could break the news to the ladies at Twyford House?"

Martin nodded.

Darcy grimaced at Max over the rim of his glass. "I thought you'd say that." After a moment, he continued, "As I said before, I'm not much of a hand at elopements and I don't know Keighly at all. But it occurs to me, Max, dear boy, that it's perfectly possible he might not see reason all that easily. He might even do something rash. So, aside from Hugo here, don't you think you'd better take those along with you?"

Darcy pointed at a slim wooden case that rested on

top of the dresser standing against the wall at the side of the room. Inside, as he knew, reposed a pair of Mr. Joseph Manton's duelling pistols, with which Max was considered a master.

Max hesitated, then shrugged. "I suppose you're right." He lifted the case to his desk-top and, opening it, quickly checked the pistols. They looked quite lethal, the long black barrels gleaming, the silver mountings glinting wickedly. He had just picked up the second, when the knocker on the front door was plied with a ruthlessness which brought a definite wince to all four faces in the library. The night had been a long one. A moment later, they heard Hillshaw's sonorous tones, remonstrating with the caller. Then, an unmistakably feminine voice reached their ears. With an oath, Max strode to the door.

Caroline fixed Hillshaw with a look which brooked no argument. "I wish to see His Grace *immediately*, Hillshaw."

Accepting defeat, Hillshaw turned to usher her to the drawing-room, only to be halted by his master's voice.

"Caro! What are you doing here?"

From the library door, Max strolled forward to take the hand Caroline held out to him. Her eyes widened as she took in the pistol he still held in his other hand. "Thank God I'm in time!" she said, in such heartfelt accents that Max frowned.

"It's all right. We've found out which road they took. Denbigh and I were about to set out after them. Don't worry, we'll bring her back."

Far from reassuring her as he had intended, his

matter-of-fact tone seemed to set her more on edge. Caroline clasped both her small hands on his arm. "No! You don't understand."

Max's frown deepened. He decided she was right. He could not fathom why she wished him to let Arabella ruin herself. "Come into the library."

Caroline allowed him to usher her into the apartment where they had first met. As her eyes took in the other occupants, she coloured slightly. "Oh, I didn't realize," she said.

Max waved her hesitation aside. "It's all right. They already know." He settled her in the armchair Hugo had vacated. "Caro, do you know where Keighly's estates are?"

Caroline was struggling with his last revelation. They already knew? How? "Gloucestershire, I think," she replied automatically. Then, her mind registered the fact that Max had laid the wicked-looking pistol he had been carrying on his desk, with its mate, no less, and was putting the box which she thought ought to contain them back, empty, on the dresser. A cold fear clutched at her stomach. Her voice seemed thin and reedy. "Max, what are you going to do with those?"

Max, still standing behind the desk, glanced down at the pistols. But it was Hugo's deep voice which answered her. "Have to make sure Keighly sees reason, ma'am," he explained gently. "Need to impress on him the wisdom of keeping his mouth shut over this."

Her mind spinning, Caroline looked at him blankly.

"But why? I mean, what can he say? Well, it's all so ridiculous."

"Ridiculous?" echoed Max, a grim set to his mouth.

"I'm afraid you don't quite understand, Miss Twinning," broke in Darcy. "The story's already all over town. But if Max can get her back and Keighly keeps his mouth shut, then it's just possible it'll all blow over, you see."

"But...but why should Max interfere?" Caroline put a hand to her head, as if to still her whirling thoughts.

This question was greeted by stunned silence. It was Martin who broke it. "But, dash it all! He's her *guardian!*"

For an instant, Caroline looked perfectly blank. "Is he?" she whispered weakly.

This was too much for Max. "You know perfectly well I am." It appeared to him that his Caro had all but lost her wits with shock. He reined in his temper, sorely tried by the events of the entire night, and said, "Hugo and I are about to leave to get Arabella back—"

"No!" The syllable was uttered with considerable force by Caroline as she leapt to her feet. It had the desired effect of stopping her guardian in his tracks. One black brow rose threateningly, but before he could voice his anger she was speaking again. "You *don't* understand! I didn't *think* you did, but you kept telling me you *knew.*"

Caroline's eyes grew round as she watched Max move around the desk and advance upon her. She waved one hand as if to keep him back and enunciated clearly, "Arabella did not go with Sir Ralph."

Max stopped. Then his eyes narrowed. "She was seen getting into a carriage with him in the Penbrights' drive."

Caroline shook her head as she tried to work this out. Then she saw the light. "A rose-pink domino was seen getting into Sir Ralph's carriage?"

At her questioning look, Max thought back to Lord McCubbin's words. Slowly, he nodded his head. "And you're sure it wasn't Arabella?"

"When I left Twyford House, Arabella was at the breakfast table."

"So who...?"

"Sarah?" came the strangled voice of Darcy Hamilton.

Caroline looked puzzled. "No. She's at home, too."

*"Lizzie?"*

Martin's horrified exclamation startled Caroline. She regarded him in increasing bewilderment. "Of course not. She's at Twyford House."

By now, Max could see the glimmer of reason for what seemed like the first time in hours. "So who went with Sir Ralph?"

"Miss Harriet Jenkins," said Caroline.

*"Who?"* The sound of four male voices in puzzled unison was very nearly too much for Caroline. She sank back into her chair and waved them back to their seats. "Sit down and I'll explain."

With wary frowns, they did as she bid them.

After a pause to marshal her thoughts, Caroline began. "It's really all Mrs. Crowbridge's fault. She decided she wanted Sir Ralph for a son-in-law. Sir Ralph had come to town because he took fright at the thought of the marriage he had almost contracted with Miss Jenkins in Gloucestershire." She glanced up, but none of her audience seemed to have difficulty understanding events thus far. "Mrs. Crowbridge kept throwing Amanda in Sir Ralph's way. Amanda did not like Sir Ralph and so, to help out, and especially because Mr. Minchbury had almost come to the point with Amanda and she favoured his suit, Arabella started flirting with Sir Ralph, to draw him away from Amanda." She paused, but no questions came. "Well, you, Max, made that a bit difficult when you told Arabella to behave herself with respect to Sir Ralph. But they got around that by sharing the work, as it were. It was still Arabella drawing Sir Ralph off, but the other two helped to cover her absences. Then, Miss Jenkins came to town, following Sir Ralph. She joined in the…the plot. I gather Arabella was to hold Sir Ralph off until Mr. Minchbury proposed and then turn him over to Miss Jenkins."

Max groaned and Caroline watched as he put his head in his hand. "Sir Ralph has my heart-felt sympathy," he said. He gestured to her. "Go on."

"Well, then Mrs. Crowbridge tried to trap Sir Ralph by trying to put him in a compromising situation with Amanda. After that, they all decided something drastic needed to be done, to save both Sir Ralph and Amanda. At the afternoon concert, Sarah wheedled a declaration of sorts from Sir Ralph over Arabella and got him to promise to go along with their plan. He thought Arabella was about to go into a decline and had to be swept off her feet by an elopement.''

''My sympathy for Sir Ralph has just died,'' said Max. ''What a slow-top if he believed that twaddle!''

''So that's what she was doing on the balcony with him,'' said Darcy. ''She was there for at least half an hour.''

Caroline nodded. ''She said she had had to work on him. But Harriet Jenkins has known Sir Ralph from the cradle and had told her how best to go about it.''

When no further comment came, Caroline resumed her story. ''At the Penbrights's ball last night, Lizzie had the job of making sure Sir Ralph had brought his carriage and would be waiting for Sarah when she came to take him to the rendezvous later.''

''And that's why she went to talk to Keighly as soon as you got in the ballroom,'' said Martin, putting his piece of the puzzle into place.

''All Arabella had to do was flirt outrageously as usual, so that everyone, but particularly Sir Ralph, would be convinced it was her in the rose-pink domino. At twelve-twenty, Arabella swapped dominos with Harriet Jenkins and Harriet went down to a gazebo by the carriage gate.''

''Oh, God!'' groaned Hugo Denbigh. The horror in his voice brought all eyes to him. He had paled. ''What was the colour? Of the second domino?''

Caroline stared at him. ''Brown.''

''Oh, no! I should have guessed. But her *accent*.'' Hugo dropped his head into his large hands.

For a moment, his companions looked on in total bewilderment. Then Caroline chuckled, her eyes dancing. "Oh. Did you meet Maria Pavlovska?"

"Yes, I did!" said Hugo, emerging from his depression. "Allow me to inform you, Miss Twinning, that your sister is a minx!"

"I know that," said Caroline. "Though I must say, it's rather trying of her." In answer to Max's look of patent enquiry, she explained. "Maria Pavlovska was a character Arabella acted in a play on board ship. A Polish countess of—er—" Caroline broke off, blushing.

"Dubious virtue," supplied Hugo, hard pressed.

"Well, she was really very good at it," said Caroline.

Looking at Hugo's flushed countenance, none of the others doubted it.

"Where was I?" asked Caroline, trying to appear unconscious. "Oh, yes. Well, all that was left to do was to get Sir Ralph to the gazebo. Sarah apparently did that."

Darcy nodded. "Yes. I saw her."

Max waited for more. His friend's silence brought a considering look to his eyes.

"So, you see, it's all perfectly all right. It's Harriet Jenkins who has gone with Sir Ralph. I gather he proposed before they left and Miss Jenkins's family approved the match, and as they are headed straight back to Gloucestershire, I don't think there's anything to worry about. Oh, and Mr. Minchbury proposed last night and the Crowbridges accepted him, so all's ended well after all and everyone's happy."

"Except for the four of us, who've all aged years in one evening," retorted Max acerbically.

She had the grace to blush. "I came as soon as I found out."

Hugo interrupted. "But they've forgotten one thing. It's all over town that Arabella eloped with Keighly."

"Oh, no. I don't think that can be right," said Caroline, shaking her head. "Anyone who was at the unmasking at the Penbrights' ball would know Arabella was there until the end." Seeing the questioning looks, she explained. "The unmasking was held at one o'clock. And someone suggested there should be a…a competition to see who was the best disguised. People weren't allowed to unmask until someone correctly guessed who they were. Well, no one guessed who Maria Pavlovska was, so Arabella was the toast of the ball."

Max sat back in his chair and grinned tiredly. "So anyone putting about the tale of my ward's elopement will only have the story rebound on them. I'm almost inclined to forgive your sisters their transgression for that one fact."

Caroline looked hopeful, but he did not elaborate. Max stood and the others followed suit. Hugo, still shaking his head in disbelief, took himself off, and Darcy left immediately after. Martin retired for a much needed rest and Caroline found herself alone with her guardian.

Max crossed to where she sat and drew her to her feet and into his arms. His lips found hers in a reassuring kiss. Then, he held her, her head on his shoulder, and laughed wearily. "Sweetheart, if I thought your sisters would be on my hands for much longer, I'd have Whitney around here this morning to instruct him to break that guardianship clause."

"I'm sorry," mumbled Caroline, her hands engrossed in smoothing the folds of his cravat. "I did come as soon as I found out."

"I know you did," acknowledged Max. "And I'm very thankful you did, what's more! Can you imagine how Hugo and I would have looked if we *had* succeeded in overtaking Keighly's carriage and demanded he return the lady to us? God!" He shuddered. "It doesn't bear thinking about." He hugged her, then released her. "Now you should go home and rest. And I'm going to get some sleep."

"One moment," she said, staying within his slackened hold, her eyes still on his cravat. "Remember I said I'd tell you whether there were any gentlemen who we'd like to consider seriously, should they apply to you for permission to address us?"

Max nodded. "Yes. I remember." Surely she was not going to mention Willoughby? What had gone on last night, after he had left? He suddenly felt cold.

But she was speaking again. "Well, if Lord Darcy should happen to ask, then you know about that, don't you?"

Max nodded. "Yes. Darcy would make Sarah a fine husband. One who would keep her sufficiently occupied so she wouldn't have time for scheming." He grinned at Caroline's blush. "And you're right. I'm expecting him to ask at any time. So that's Sarah dealt with."

"And I'd rather thought Lord Denbigh for Arabella, though I didn't know then about Maria Pavlovska."

"Oh, I wouldn't deal Hugo short. Maria Pavlovska might be a bit hard to bear but I'm sure he'll come about. And, as I'm sure Aunt Augusta has told you, he's perfectly acceptable as long as he can be brought to pop the question."

"And," said Caroline, keeping her eyes down, "I'm not perfectly sure, but..."

"You think Martin might ask for Lizzie," supplied Max, conscious of his own tiredness. It was sapping his will. All sorts of fantasies were surfacing in his brain and the devil of it was they were all perfectly achievable. But he had already made other plans, better plans. "I foresee no problems there. Martin's got more money than is good for him. I'm sure Lizzie will keep him on his toes, hauling her out of the scrapes her innocence will doubtless land her in. And I'd much rather it was him than me." He tried to look into Caroline's face but she kept her eyes—were they greyish-green or greenish-grey? He had never decided—firmly fixed on his cravat.

"I'm thrilled that you approve of my cravat, sweetheart, but is there anything more? I'm dead on my feet," he acknowledged with a rueful grin, praying that she did not have anything more to tell him.

Caroline's eyes flew to his, an expression he could not read in their depths. "Oh, of course you are! No. There's nothing more."

Max caught the odd wistfulness in her tone and correctly divined its cause. His grin widened. As he walked her to the door, he said, "Once I'm myself again, and have recovered from your sisters' exploits, I'll call on you—say at three this afternoon? I'll take you for a drive. There are some matters I wish to discuss with you." He guided her through the library door and into the hall. In answer to her questioning look, he added. "About your ball."

"Oh. I'd virtually forgotten about it," Caroline said as Max took her cloak from Hillshaw and placed it about her shoulders. They had organized to hold a ball in the Twinnings' honour at Twyford House the following week.

"We'll discuss it at three this afternoon," said Max as he kissed her hand and led her down the steps to her carriage.

## Chapter Twelve

Sarah wrinkled her nose at the piece of cold toast lying on her plate. Pushing it away, she leaned back in her chair and surveyed her elder sister. With her copper curls framing her expressive face, Caroline sat at the other end of the small table in the breakfast-room, a vision of palest cerulean blue. A clearly distracted vision. A slight frown had settled in the greeny eyes, banishing the lively twinkle normally lurking there. She sighed, apparently unconsciously, as she stared at her piece of toast, as cold and untouched as Sarah's, as if concealed in its surface were the answers to all unfathomable questions. Sarah was aware of a guilty twinge. Had Max cut up stiff and Caroline not told them?

They had all risen early, being robust creatures and never having got into the habit of lying abed, and had gathered in the breakfast parlour to examine their success of the night before. That it had been a complete and unqualified success could not have been divined from their faces; all of them had looked drawn and peaked. While Sarah knew the cause of her own unhappiness, and had subsequently learned of her younger sisters' reasons for despondency, she had been and still was at a loss to explain Caroline's similar mood. She had been in high feather at the ball. Then Max had left early, an unusual occurrence which had made Sarah wonder if they had had a falling-out. But her last sight of them together, when he had taken leave of Caroline in the ballroom, had not supported such a fancy. They had looked…well, intimate. Happily so. Thoroughly immersed in each other. Which, thought the knowledgeable Sarah, was not especially like either of them. She sent a sharp glance to the other end of the table.

Caroline's bloom had gradually faded and she had been as silent as the rest of them during the drive home. This morning, on the stairs, she had shared their quiet mood. And then, unfortunately, they had had to make things much worse. They had always agreed that Caroline would have to be told immediately after the event. That had always been their way, ever since they were small children. No matter the outcome, Caroline could be relied on to predict unerringly the potential ramifications and to protect her sisters from any unexpected repercussions. This morning, as they had recounted to her their plan and its execution, she had paled. When they had come to a faltering halt, she had, uncharacteristically, told them in a quiet voice to wait as they were while she communicated their deeds to their guardian forthwith. She had explained nothing. Rising from the table without so much as a sip of her coffee, she had immediately called for the carriage and departed for Delmere House.

She had returned an hour and a half later. They had not left the room; Caroline's orders, spoken in that particular tone, were not to be dismissed lightly. In truth, each sunk in gloomy contemplation of her state, they had not noticed the passage of time. Caroline had re-entered the room, calmly resumed her seat and accepted the cup of coffee Arabella had hastily poured for her. She had fortified herself from this before explaining to them, in quite unequivocal terms, just how close they had come to creating a hellish tangle. It had never occurred to them that someone might see Harriet departing and, drawing the obvious conclusion, inform Max of the fact, especially in such a public manner. They had been aghast at the realization of how close to the edge of scandal they had come and were only too ready to behave as contritely as Caroline wished. However, all she had said was, "I don't really think there's much we should do. Thankfully, Arabella, your gadding about as Maria Pavlovska ensured that everyone knows you did not elope from the ball. I suppose we could go riding." She had paused, then added, "But I really don't feel like it this morning."

They had not disputed this, merely shaken their heads to convey their agreement. After a moment of silence, Caroline had added, "I think Max would expect us to behave as if nothing had happened, other than there being some ridiculous tale about that Bella had eloped. You'll have to admit, I suppose, that you swapped dominos with Harriet Jenkins, but that could have been done in all innocence. And remember to show due interest in the surprising tale that Harriet left the ball with Sir Ralph.'' An unwelcome thought reared its head. ''Will the Crowbridge girls have the sense to keep their mouths shut?''

They had hastened to assure her on this point. ''Why, it was all for Amanda's sake, after all,'' Lizzie had pointed out.

Caroline had not been entirely convinced but had been distracted by Arabella. Surmising from Caroline's use of her shortened name that the worst was over, she had asked, ''Is Max very annoyed with us?''

Caroline had considered the question while they had all hung, unexpectedly nervous, on her answer. ''I think he's resigned, now that it's all over and no real harm done, to turn a blind eye to your misdemeanours. However, if I were you, I would not be going out of my way to bring myself to his notice just at present.''

Their relief had been quite real. Despite his reputation, their acquaintance with the Duke of Twyford had left his younger wards with the definite impression that he would not condone any breach of conduct and was perfectly capable of implementing sufficiently draconian measures in response to any transgression. In years past, they would have ignored the potential threat and relied on Caroline to make all right in the event of any trouble. But, given that the man in question was Max Rotherbridge, none was sure how successful Caroline would be in turning him up sweet. Reassured that their guardian was not intending to descend, in ire, upon them, Lizzie and Arabella, after hugging Caroline and avowing their deepest thanks for her endeavours on their behalf, had left the room. Sarah suspected they would both be found in some particular nook, puzzling out the uncomfortable feeling in their hearts.

Strangely enough, she no longer felt the need to emulate them. In the long watches of a sleepless night, she had finally faced the fact that she could not live without Darcy Hamilton. In the gazebo the previous evening, it had been on the tip of her tongue to beg him to take her from the ball, to some isolated spot where they could pursue their lovemaking in greater privacy. She had had to fight her own nearly overwhelming desire to keep from speaking the words. If she had uttered them, he would have arranged it all in an instant, she knew; his desire for her was every bit as strong as her desire for him. Only her involvement in their scheme and the consternation her sudden disappearance would have caused had tipped the scales. Her desire for marriage, for a home and family, was still as strong as ever. But, if he refused to consider such an arrangement, she was now prepared to listen to whatever alternative suggestions he had to offer. There was Max's opposition to be overcome, but presumably Darcy was aware of that. She felt sure he would seek her company soon enough and then she would make her acquiescence plain. That, at least, she thought with a small, introspective smile, would be very easy to do.

Caroline finally pushed the unhelpful piece of toast aside. She rose and shook her skirts in an unconsciously flustered gesture. In a flash of unaccustomed

insight, Sarah wondered if her elder sister was in a
similar state to the rest of them. After all, they were
all Twinnings. Although their problems were super-
ficially quite different, in reality, they were simply
variations on the same theme. They were all in love
with rakes, all of whom seemed highly resistant to
matrimony. In her case, the rake had won. But surely
Max wouldn't win, too? For a moment, Sarah's mind
boggled at the thought of the two elder Twinnings
falling by the wayside. Then, she gave herself a mental shake. No, of course not. He was their guardian,
after all. Which, Sarah thought, presumably meant
Caroline would even the score. Caroline was undoubtedly the most capable of them all. So why, then, did
she look so troubled?

Caroline was indeed racked by the most uncomfortable thoughts. Leaving Sarah to her contemplation
of the breakfast table, she drifted without purpose into
the drawing-room and thence to the small courtyard
beyond. Ambling about, her delicate fingers examining some of the bountiful blooms, she eventually
came to the hammock, slung under the cherry trees,
protected from the morning sun by their leafy foliage.
Climbing into it, she rested her aching head against
the cushions with relief and prepared to allow the
conflicting emotions inside her to do battle.

Lately, it seemed to her that there were two Caroline Twinnings. One knew the ropes, was thoroughly
acquainted with society's expectations and had no
hesitation in laughing at the idea of a gentlewoman
such as herself sharing a man's bed outside the
bounds of marriage. She had been acquainted with

this Caroline Twinning for as long as she could remember. The other woman, for some mysterious reason, had only surfaced in recent times, since her exposure to the temptations of Max Rotherbridge. There was no denying the increasing control this second persona exerted over her. In truth, it had come to the point where she was seriously considering which Caroline Twinning she preferred.

She was no green girl and could hardly pretend she had not been perfectly aware of Max's intentions when she had heard the lock fall on that bedroom door. Nor could she comfort herself that the situation had been beyond her control—at least, not then. If she had made any real effort to bring the illicit encounter to a halt, as she most certainly should have done, Max would have instantly acquiesced. She could hardly claim he had forced her to remain. But it had been that other Caroline Twinning who had welcomed him into her arms and had proceeded to enjoy, all too wantonly, the delights to be found in his.

She had never succeeded in introducing marriage as an aspect of their relationship. She had always been aware that what Max intended was an illicit affair. What she had underestimated was her own interest in such a scandalous proceeding. But there was no denying the pleasure she had found in his arms, nor the disappointment she had felt when he had cut short their interlude. She knew she could rely on him to ensure that next time there would be no possible impediment to the completion of her education. And she would go to his arms with neither resistance nor regrets. Which, to the original Caroline Twinning, was a very lowering thought.

Swinging gently in the hammock, the itinerant breeze wafting her curls, she tried to drum up all the old arguments against allowing herself to become involved in such an improper relationship. She had been over them all before; they held no power to sway her. Instead, the unbidden memory of Max's mouth on her breast sent a thrill of warm desire through her veins. "Fool!" she said, without heat, to the cherry tree overhead.

Martin Rotherbridge kicked a stone out of his path. He had been walking for nearly twenty minutes in an effort to rid himself of a lingering nervousness over the act he was about to perform. He would rather have raced a charge of Chasseurs than do what he must that day. But there was nothing else for it—the events of the morning had convinced him of that. That dreadful instant when he had thought, for one incredulous and heart-stopping moment, that Lizzie had gone away with Keighly was never to be repeated. And the only way of ensuring that was to marry the chit.

It had certainly not been his intention, and doubtless Max would laugh himself into hysterics, but there it was. Facts had to be faced. Despite his being at her side for much of the time, Lizzie had managed to embroil herself very thoroughly in a madcap plan which, even now, if it ever became known, would see her ostracized by those who mattered in the *ton*. She was a damned sight too innocent to see the outcome of her actions; either that, or too naïve in her belief in her abilities to come about. She needed a husband to keep a firm hand on her reins, to steer her clear of the perils her beauty and innocence would unquestionably lead her into. And, as he desperately wanted the foolish woman, and had every intention of fulfilling the role anyway, he might as well officially be it.

He squared his shoulders. No sense in putting off the evil moment any longer. He might as well speak to Max.

He turned his steps toward Delmere House. Rounding a corner, some blocks from his destination, he saw the impressive form of Lord Denbigh striding along on the opposite side of the street, headed in the same direction. On impulse, Martin crossed the street.

"Hugo!"

Lord Denbigh halted in his purposeful stride and turned to see who had hailed him. Although a few years separated them, he and Martin Rotherbridge had many interests in common and had been acquainted even before the advent of the Twinnings. His lordship's usual sleepy grin surfaced. "Hello, Martin. On your way home?"

Martin nodded and fell into step beside him. At sight of Hugo, his curiosity over Maria Pavlovska had returned. He experimented in his head with a number of suitable openings before settling for, "Dashed nuisances, the Twinning girls!"

"Very!" The curt tone in Hugo's deep voice was not very encouraging.

Nothing loath, Martin plunged on. "Waltz around, tying us all in knots. What exactly happened when Arabella masqueraded as that Polish countess?"

To his amazement, Hugo coloured. "Never you mind," he said, then, at the hopeful look in Martin's eyes, relented. "If you must know, she behaved in a manner which…well, in short, it was difficult to tell who was seducing whom."

Martin gave a burst of laughter, which he quickly controlled at Hugo's scowl. By way of returning the confidence, he said, "Well, I suppose I may as well tell you, as it's bound to be all over town all too soon. I'm on my way to beg Max's permission to pay my addresses to Lizzie Twinning."

Hugo's mild eyes went to Martin's face in surprise. He murmured all the usual condolences, adding, "Didn't really think you'd be wanting to get leg-shackled just yet."

Martin shrugged. "Nothing else for it. Aside from making all else blessedly easy, it's only as her husband I'd have the authority to make certain she didn't get herself involved in any more hare-brained schemes."

"There is that," agreed Hugo ruminatively. They continued for a space in silence before Martin realized they were nearing Delmere House.

"Where are you headed?" he enquired of the giant by his side.

For the second time, Hugo coloured. Looking distinctly annoyed by this fact, he stopped. Martin, puzzled, stopped by his side, but before he could frame any question, Hugo spoke. "I may as well confess, I suppose. I'm on my way to see Max, too."

Martin howled with laughter and this time made no effort to subdue it. When he could speak again, he clapped Hugo on the back. "Welcome to the family!" As they turned and fell into step once more, Martin's eyes lifted. "And lord, what a family it's going to be! Unless I miss my guess, that's Darcy Hamilton's curricle."

Hugo looked up and saw, ahead of them, Lord Darcy's curricle drawn up outside Delmere House. Hamilton himself, elegantly attired, descended and turned to give instructions to his groom, before strolling towards the steps leading up to the door. He was joined by Martin and Hugo.

Martin grinned. "Do you want to see Max, too?"

Darcy Hamilton's face remained inscrutable. "As it happens, I do," he answered equably. As his glance flickered over the unusually precise picture both Martin and Hugo presented, he added, "Am I to take it there's a queue?"

"Afraid so," confirmed Hugo, grinning in spite of himself. "Maybe we should draw lots?"

"Just a moment," said Martin, studying the carriage waiting by the pavement in front of Darcy's curricle. "That's Max's travelling chaise. Is he going somewhere?

This question was addressed to Darcy Hamilton, who shook his head. "He's said nothing to me."

"Maybe the Twinnings have proved too much for him and he's going on a repairing lease?" suggested Hugo.

"Entirely understandable, but I don't somehow think that's it," mused Darcy. Uncertain, they stood on the pavement, and gazed at the carriage. Behind them the door of Delmere House opened. Masterton hurried down the steps and climbed into the chaise. As soon as the door had shut, the coachman flicked his whip and the carriage pulled away. Almost immediately, the vacated position was filled with Max's curricle, the bays stamping and tossing their heads.

Martin's brows had risen. "Masterton and baggage," he said. "Now why?"

"Whatever the reason," said Darcy succinctly, "I suspect we'd better catch your brother now or he'll merrily leave us to our frustrations for a week or more."

The looks of horror which passed over the two faces before him brought a gleam of amusement to his eyes.

"Lord, yes!" said Hugo.

Without further discussion, they turned *en masse* and started up the steps. At that moment, the door at the top opened and their prey emerged. They stopped.

Max, eyeing them as he paused to draw on his driving gloves, grinned. The breeze lifted the capes of his greatcoat as he descended the steps.

"Max, we need to talk to you."

"Where are you going?"

"You can't leave yet."

With a laugh, Max held up his hand to stem the tide. When silence had fallen, he said, "I'm so glad to see you all." His hand once more quelled the surge of explanation his drawling comment drew forth. "No! I find I have neither the time nor the inclination to discuss the matters. My answers to your questions are yes, yes and yes. All right?"

Darcy Hamilton laughed. "Fine by me."

Hugo nodded bemusedly.

"Are you going away?" asked Martin.

Max nodded. "I need a rest. Somewhere tranquil."

His exhausted tone brought a grin to his brother's face. "With or without company?"

Max's wide grin showed fleetingly. "Never you mind, brother dear. Just channel your energies into keeping Lizzie from engaging in any further crusades to help the needy and I'll be satisfied." His gaze took in the two curricles beside the pavement, the horses fretting impatiently. "In fact, I'll make life easy for you. For all of you. I suggest we repair to Twyford House. I'll engage to remove Miss Twinning. Aunt Augusta and Mrs. Alford rest all afternoon. And the house is a large one. If you can't manage to wrest agreement to your proposals from the Misses Twinning under such circumstances, I wash my hands of you."

They all agreed very readily. Together, they set off immediately, Max and his brother in his curricle, Lord Darcy and Hugo Denbigh following in Darcy's carriage.

The sound of male voices in the front hall drifted to Caroline's ears as she sat with her sisters in the back parlour. With a sigh, she picked up her bonnet and bade the three despondent figures scattered through the room goodbye. They all looked distracted. She felt much the same. Worn out by her difficult morning and from tossing and turning half the night, tormented by a longing she had tried valiantly to ignore, she had fallen asleep in the hammock under the cherry trees. Her sisters had found her but had left her to recover, only waking her for a late lunch before her scheduled drive with their guardian.

As she walked down the corridor to the front hall, she was aware of the leaping excitement the prospect of seeing Max Rotherbridge always brought her. At the mere thought of being alone with him, albeit on the box seat of a curricle in broad daylight in the middle of fashionable London, she could feel that other Caroline Twinning taking over.

Her sisters had taken her words of the morning to heart and had wisely refrained from joining her in greeting their guardian. Alone, she emerged into the hallway. In astonishment, she beheld, not one elegantly turned out gentleman, but four.

Max, his eyes immediately drawn as if by some magic to her, smiled and came forward to take her hand. His comprehensive glance swept her face, then dropped to her bonnet, dangling loosely by its ribbons from one hand. His smile broadened, bringing a delicate colour to her cheeks. "I'm glad you're ready, my dear. But where are your sisters?"

Caroline blinked. "They're in the back parlour," she answered, turning to greet Darcy Hamilton.

Max turned. "Millwade, escort these gentlemen to the back parlour."

Millwade, not in Hillshaw's class, looked slightly scandalized. But an order from his employer was not to be disobeyed. Caroline, engaged in exchanging courtesies with the gentlemen involved, was staggered. But before she could remonstrate, her cloak appeared about her shoulders and she was firmly propelled out the door. She was constrained to hold her fire until Max had dismissed the urchin holding the bays and climbed up beside her.

"You're supposed to be our guardian! Don't you think it's a little unconventional to leave three gentlemen with your wards unchaperoned?"

Giving his horses the office, Max chuckled. "I don't think any of them need chaperoning at present. They'd hardly welcome company when trying to propose."

"Oh! You mean they've asked?"

Max nodded, then glanced down. "I take it you're still happy with their suits?"

"Oh, yes! It's just that...well, the others didn't seem to hold out much hope." After a pause, she asked, "Weren't you surprised?"

He shook his head. "Darcy I've been expecting for weeks. After this morning, Hugo was a certainty. And Martin's been more sternly silent than I've ever seen him before. So, no, I can't say I was surprised." He turned to grin at her. "Still, I hope your sisters have suffered as much as their swains—it's only fair."

She was unable to repress her answering grin, the dimple by her mouth coming delightfully into being. A subtle comment of Max's had the effect of turning the conversation into general fields. They laughed and discussed, occasionally with mock seriousness, a number of tonnish topics, then settled to determined consideration of the Twyford House ball.

This event had been fixed for the following Tuesday, five days distant. More than four hundred guests were expected. Thankfully, the ballroom was huge and the house would easily cater for this number. Under Lady Benborough's guidance, the Twinning sisters had coped with all the arrangements, a fact known to Max. He had a bewildering array of questions for Caroline. Absorbed with answering these, she paid little attention to her surroundings.

"You don't think," she said, airing a point she and her sisters had spent much time pondering, "that, as it's not really a proper come-out, in that we've been about for the entire Season and none of us is truly a débutante, the whole thing might fall a little flat?"

Max grinned. "I think I can assure you that it will very definitely not be flat. In fact," he continued, as if pondering a new thought, "I should think it'll be one of the highlights of the Season."

Caroline looked her question but he declined to explain.

As usual when with her guardian, time flew and it was only when a chill in the breeze penetrated her thin cloak that Caroline glanced up and found the afternoon gone. The curricle was travelling smoothly down a well surfaced road, lined with low hedges set back a little from the carriageway. Beyond these, neat fields stretched sleepily under the waning sun, a few scattered sheep and cattle attesting to the fact that they were deep in the country. From the direction of the sun, they were travelling south, away from the capital. With a puzzled frown, she turned to the man beside her. "Shouldn't we be heading back?"

Max glanced down at her, his devilish grin in evidence. "We aren't going back."

Caroline's brain flatly refused to accept the implications of that statement. Instead, after a pause, she asked conversationally, "Where are we?"

"A little past Twickenham."

"Oh." If they were that far out of town, then it was difficult to see how they could return that evening even if he was only joking about not going back. But he had to be joking, surely?

The curricle slowed and Max checked his team for the turn into a beech-lined drive. As they whisked through the gateway, Caroline caught a glimpse of a coat of arms worked into the impressive iron gates. The Delmere arms, Max's own. She looked about her with interest, refusing to give credence to the suspicion growing in her mind. The drive led deep into the beechwood, then opened out to run along a ridge bordered by cleared land, close-clipped grass dropping away on one side to run down to a distant river. On the other side, the beechwood fell back as the curricle continued towards a rise. Cresting this, the road descended in a broad sweep to end in a gravel courtyard before an old stone house. It nestled into an unexpected curve of a small stream, presumably a tributary of the larger river which Caroline rather thought must be the Thames. The roof sported many gables. Almost as many chimneys, intricate pots capping them, soared high above the tiles. In the setting sun, the house glowed mellow and warm. Along one wall, a rambling white rose nodded its blooms and released its perfume to the freshening breeze. Caroline thought she had seen few more appealing houses.

They were expected, that much was clear. A groom came running at the sound of the wheels on the

gravel. Max lifted her down and led her to the door.
It opened at his touch. He escorted her in and closed
the door behind them.

Caroline found herself in a small hall, neatly pan-
elled in oak, a small round table standing in the middle of the tiled floor. Max's hand at her elbow steered
her to a corridor giving off the back of the hall. It
terminated in a beautifully carved oak door. As Max
reached around her to open it, Caroline asked,
"Where are the servants?"

"Oh, they're about. But they're too well trained to
show themselves."

Her suspicions developing in leaps and bounds,
Caroline entered a large room, furnished in a fashion
she had never before encountered.

The floor was covered in thick, silky rugs, executed
in the most glorious hues. Low tables were scattered
amid piles of cushions in silks and satins of every
conceivable shade. There was a bureau against one
wall, but the room was dominated by a dais covered
with silks and piled with cushions, more silks draping
down from above to swirl about it in semi-concealing
mystery. Large glass doors gave on to a paved courtyard. The doors stood slightly ajar, admitting the
comforting gurgle of the stream as it passed by on
the other side of the courtyard wall. As she crossed
to peer out, she noticed the ornate brass lamps which
hung from the ceiling. The courtyard was empty and,
surprisingly, entirely enclosed. A wooden gate was set
in one side-wall and another in the wall opposite the
house presumably gave on to the stream. As she
turned back into the room, Caroline thought it had a

strangely relaxing effect on the senses—the silks, the glowing but not overbright colours, the soothing murmur of the stream. Then, her eyes lit on the silk-covered dais. And grew round. Seen from this angle, it was clearly a bed, heavily disguised beneath the jumble of cushions and silks, but a bed nevertheless. Her suspicions confirmed, her gaze flew to her guardian's face.

What she saw there tied her stomach in knots. "Max…" she began uncertainly, the conservative Miss Twinning hanging on grimly.

But then he was standing before her, his eyes glinting devilishly and that slow smile wreaking havoc with her good intentions. "Mmm?" he asked.

"What are we doing here?" she managed, her pulse racing, her breath coming more and more shallowly, her nerves stretching in anticipation.

"Finishing your education," the deep voice drawled.

Well, what had she expected? asked that other Miss Twinning, ousting her competitor and taking total possession as Max bent his head to kiss her. Her mouth opened welcomingly under his and he took what she offered, gradually drawing her into his embrace until she was crushed against his chest. Caroline did not mind; breathing seemed unimportant just at that moment.

When Max finally raised his head, his eyes were bright under their hooded lids and, she noticed with smug satisfaction, his breathing was almost as ragged as hers. His eyes searched her face, then his slow smile appeared. "I notice you've ceased reminding me I'm your guardian."

Caroline, finding her arms twined around his neck, ran her fingers through his dark hair. "I've given up," she said in resignation. "You never paid the slightest attention, anyway."

Max chuckled and bent to kiss her again, then pulled back and turned her about. "Even if I were your guardian, I'd still have seduced you, sweetheart."

Caroline obligingly stood still while his long fingers unlaced her gown. She dropped her head forward to move her curls, which he had loosed, out of his way. Then, the oddity of his words struck her. Her head came up abruptly. "*Even?* Max..." She tried to turn around but his hand pushed her back.

"Stand still," he commanded. "I have no intention of making love to you with your clothes on."

Having no wish to argue that particular point, Caroline, seething with impatience, stood still until she felt the last ribbon freed. Then, she turned. "What do you mean, *even* if you were my guardian? You are my guardian. You told me so yourself." Her voice tapered away as one part of her mind tried to concentrate on her questions while the rest was more interested in the fact that Max had slipped her dress from her shoulders and it had slid, in a softly sensuous way, down to her feet. In seconds, her petticoats followed.

"Yes, I know I did," Max agreed helpfully, his fingers busy with the laces of the light stays which restrained her ample charms. "I lied. Most unwisely, as it turned out."

"Wh…what?" Caroline was having a terrible time trying to focus her mind. It kept wandering. She supposed she really ought to feel shy about Max undressing her. The thought that there were not so many pieces of her clothing left for him to remove, spurred her to ask, "What do you mean, you lied? And why unwisely?"

Max dispensed with her stays and turned his attention to the tiny buttons of her chemise. "You were never my ward. You ceased to be a ward of the Duke of Twyford when you turned twenty-five. But I arranged to let you believe I was still your guardian, thinking that if you knew I wasn't you would never let me near you." He grinned wolfishly at her as his hands slipped over her shoulders and her chemise joined the rest of her clothes at her feet. "I didn't then know that the Twinnings are…susceptible to rakes."

His smug grin drove Caroline to shake her head. "We're not…susceptible."

"Oh?" One dark brow rose.

Caroline closed her eyes and her head fell back as his hands closed over her breasts. She heard his deep chuckle and smiled to herself. Then, as his hands drifted, and his lips turned to hers, her mind went obligingly blank, allowing her senses free rein. As her bones turned to jelly and her knees buckled, Max's arm helpfully supported her. Then, her lips were free and she was swung up into his arms. A moment later, she was deposited in the midst of the cushions and silks on the dais.

Feeling excitement tingling along every nerve, Caroline stretched sensuously, smiling at the light that glowed in Max's eyes as they watched her while he dispensed with his clothes. But when he stretched out beside her, and her hands drifted across the hard muscles of his chest, she felt him hold back. In unconscious entreaty, she turned towards him, her body arching against his. His response was immediate and the next instant his lips had returned to hers, his arms gathering her to him. With a satisfied sigh, Caroline gave her full concentration to her last lesson.

# Chapter Thirteen

"Sarah?" Darcy tried to squint down at the face under the dark hair covering his chest.

"Mmm," Sarah replied sleepily, snuggling comfortably against him.

Darcy grinned and gave up trying to rouse her. His eyes drifted to the ceiling as he gently stroked her back. Serve her right if she was exhausted.

Together with Martin and Hugo, he had followed the strongly disapproving Millwade to the back parlour. He had announced them, to the obvious consternation of the three occupants. Darcy's grin broadened as he recalled the scene. Arabella had looked positively stricken with guilt, Lizzie had not known what to think and Sarah had simply stood, her back to the windows, and watched him. At his sign, she had come to his side and they had left the crowded room together.

At his murmured request to see her privately, she had led the way to the morning-room. He had intended to speak to her then, but she had stood so silently in the middle of the room, her face quite unreadable, that before he had known it he was kissing her. Accomplished rake that he was, her response had been staggering. He had always known her for a sensual woman but previously her reactions had been dragged unwillingly from her. Now that they came freely, their potency was enhanced a thousand-fold. After five minutes, he had forcibly disengaged to return to the door and lock it. After that, neither of them had spared a thought for anything save the quenching of their raging desires.

Much later, when they had recovered somewhat, he had managed to find the time, in between other occupations, to ask her to marry him. She had clearly been stunned and it was only then that he realized she had not expected his proposal. He had been oddly touched. Her answer, given without the benefit of speech, had been nevertheless comprehensive and had left him in no doubt of her desire to fill the position he was offering. His wife. The idea made him laugh. Would he survive?

The rumble in his chest disturbed Sarah but she merely burrowed her head into his shoulder and returned to her bliss-filled dreams. Darcy moved slightly, settling her more comfortably.

Her eagerness rang all sorts of warning bells in his mind. Used to taking advantage of the boredom of sensual married women, he made a resolution to ensure that his Sarah never came within arm's reach of any rakes. It would doubtless be wise to establish her as his wife as soon as possible, now he had whetted her appetite for hitherto unknown pleasures. Getting her settled in Hamilton House and introducing her to his country residences, and perhaps giving her a child or two, would no doubt keep her occupied. At least, he amended, sufficiently occupied to have no desire left over for any other than himself.

The light was fading. He glanced at the window to find the afternoon far advanced. With a sigh, he shook Sarah's white shoulder gently.

"Mmm," she murmured protestingly, sleepily trying to shake off his hand.

Darcy chuckled. "I'm afraid, my love, that you'll have to awaken. The day is spent and doubtless someone will come looking for us. I rather think we should be dressed when they do."

With a long-drawn-out sigh, Sarah struggled to lift her head, propping her elbows on his chest to look into his face. Then, her gaze wandered to take in the scene about them. They were lying on the accommodatingly large sofa before the empty fireplace, their clothes strewn about the room. She dropped her head into her hands. "Oh, God. I suppose you're right."

"Undoubtedly," confirmed Darcy, smiling. "And allow me to add, sweetheart, that, as your future husband, I'll always be right."

"Oh?" Sarah enquired innocently. She sat up slightly, her hair in chaos around her face, straggling down her back to cover his hands where they lay, still gently stroking her satin skin.

Darcy viewed her serene face with misgiving. Thinking to distract her, he asked, "Incidentally, when should we marry? I'm sure Max won't care what we decide."

Sarah's attention was drawn from tracing her finger

along the curve of his collarbone. She frowned in concentration. "I rather think," she eventually said, "that it had better be soon."

Having no wish to disagree with this eminently sensible conclusion, Darcy said, "A wise decision. Do you want a big wedding? Or shall we leave that to Max and Caroline?"

Sarah grinned. "A very good idea. I think our guardian should be forced to undergo that pleasure, don't you?"

As this sentiment exactly tallied with his own, Darcy merely grinned in reply. But Sarah's next question made him think a great deal harder.

"How soon is it possible to marry?"

It took a few minutes to check all the possible pros and cons. Then he said, uncertain of her response, "Well, theoretically speaking, it would be possible to get married tomorrow."

"Truly? Well, let's do that," replied his prospective bride, a decidedly wicked expression on her face.

Seeing it, Darcy grinned. And postponed their emergence from the morning-room for a further half-hour.

The first thought that sprang to Arabella's mind on seeing Hugo Denbigh enter the back parlour was how annoyed he must have been to learn of her deception. Caroline had told her of the circumstances; they would have improved his temper. Oblivious to all else save the object of her thoughts, she did not see Sarah leave the room, nor Martin take Lizzie through the long windows into the garden. Consequently, she was a little perturbed to suddenly find herself alone with Hugo Denbigh.

"Maria Pavlovska, I presume?" His tone was perfectly equable but Arabella did not place any reliance on that. He came to stand before her, dwarfing her by his height and the breadth of his magnificent chest.

Arabella was conscious of a devastating desire to throw herself on that broad expanse and beg forgiveness for her sins. Then she remembered how he had responded to Maria Pavlovska. Her chin went up enough to look his lordship in the eye. "I'm so glad you found my little…charade entertaining."

Despite having started the conversation, Hugo abruptly found himself at a loss for words. He had not intended to bring up the subject of Maria Pavlovska, at least not until Arabella had agreed to marry him. But seeing her standing there, obviously knowing he knew and how he found out, memory of the desire Arabella-Maria so readily provoked had stirred disquietingly and he had temporarily lost his head. But now was not the time to indulge in a verbal brawl with a woman who, he had learned to his cost, could match his quick tongue in repartee. So, he smiled lazily down at her, totally confusing her instead, and rapidly sought to bring the discussion to a field where he knew he possessed few defences. "Mouthy baggage," he drawled, taking her in his arms and preventing any riposte by the simple expedient of placing his mouth over hers.

Arabella was initially too stunned by this unexpected manoeuvre to protest. And by the time she realized what had happened, she did not want to protest. Instead, she twined her arms about Hugo's neck and kissed him back with all the fervour she possessed. Unbeknownst to her, this was a considerable amount, and Hugo suddenly found himself desperately searching for a control he had somehow misplaced.

Not being as hardened a rake as Max or Darcy, he struggled with himself until he won some small measure of rectitude; enough, at least, to draw back and sit in a large armchair, drawing Arabella onto his lap. She snuggled against his chest, drawing comfort from his warmth and solidity.

"Well, baggage, will you marry me?"

Arabella sat bolt upright, her hands braced against his chest, and stared at him. "Marry you? Me?"

Hugo chuckled, delighted to have reduced her to dithering idiocy.

But Arabella was frowning. "Why do you want to marry me?"

The frown transferred itself to Hugo's countenance. "I should have thought the answer to that was a mite obvious, m'dear."

Arabella brushed that answer aside. "I mean, besides the obvious."

Hugo sighed and, closing his eyes, let his head fall back against the chair. He had asked himself the same question and knew the answer perfectly well. But he had not shaped his arguments into any coherent form, not contemplating being called on to recite them. He opened his eyes and fixed his disobliging love with a grim look. "I'm marrying you because the idea of you flirting with every Tom, Dick and Harry drives me insane. I'll tear anyone you flirt with limb from limb. So, unless you wish to be responsible for murder, you'd better stop flirting." A giggle, quickly suppressed, greeted this threat. "Incidentally," Hugo continued, "you don't go around kissing men like that all the time, do you?"

Arabella had no idea of what he meant by "like that" but as she had never kissed any other man, except in a perfectly chaste manner, she could reply with perfect truthfulness, "No, of course not! That was only you."

"Thank God for that!" said a relieved Lord Denbigh. "Kindly confine all such activities to your betrothed in future. Me," he added, in case this was not yet plain.

Arabella lifted one fine brow but said nothing. She was conscious of his hands gently stroking her hips and wondered if it would be acceptable to simply blurt out "yes". Then, she felt Hugo's hand tighten about her waist.

"And one thing more," he said, his eyes kindling. "No more Maria Pavlovska. Ever."

Arabella grinned. "No?" she asked wistfully, her voice dropping into the huskily seductive Polish accent.

Hugo stopped and considered this plea. "Well," he temporized, inclined to be lenient, "Only with me. I dare say I could handle closer acquaintance with Madame Pavlovska."

Arabella giggled and Hugo took the opportunity to kiss her again. This time, he let the kiss develop as he had on other occasions, keeping one eye on the door, the other on the windows and his mind solely on her responses. Eventually, he drew back and, retrieving his hands from where they had wandered, bringing a blush to his love's cheeks, he gripped her about her waist and gently shook her. "You haven't given me your answer yet."

"Yes, please," said Arabella, her eyes alight. "I couldn't bear not to be able to be Maria Pavlovska every now and again."

Laughing, Hugo drew her back into his arms. "When shall we wed?"

Tracing the strong line of his jaw with one small finger, Arabella thought for a minute, then replied, "Need we wait very long?"

The undisguised longing in her tone brought her a swift response. "Only as long as you wish."

Arabella chuckled. "Well, I doubt we could be married tomorrow."

"Why not?" asked Hugo, his eyes dancing.

His love looked puzzled. "Is it possible? I thought all those sorts of things took forever to arrange."

"Only if you want a big wedding. If you do, I warn you it'll take months. My family's big and distributed all about. Just getting in touch with half of them will be bad enough."

But the idea of waiting for months did not appeal to Arabella. "If it can be done, can we really be married tomorrow? It would be a lovely surprise—stealing a march on the others."

Hugo grinned. "For a baggage, you do have some good ideas sometimes."

"Really?" asked Maria Pavlovska.

\* \* \*

For Martin Rotherbridge, the look on Lizzie's face as he walked into the back parlour was easy to read. Total confusion. On Lizzie, it was a particularly attractive attitude and one with which he was thoroughly conversant. With a grin, he went to her and took her hand, kissed it and tucked it into his arm. "Let's go into the garden. I want to talk to you."

As talking to Martin in gardens had become something of a habit, Lizzie went with him, curious to know what it was he wished to say and wondering why her heart was leaping about so uncomfortably.

Martin led her down the path that bordered the large main lawn until they reached an archway formed by a rambling rose. This gave access to the rose gardens. Here, they came to a stone bench bathed in softly dappled sunshine. At Martin's nod, Lizzie seated herself with a swish of her muslin skirts. After a moment's consideration, Martin sat beside her. Their view was filled with ancient rosebushes, the spaces beneath crammed with early summer flowers. Bees buzzed sleepily and the occasional dragonfly darted by, on its way from the shrubbery to the pond at the bottom of the main lawn. The sun shone warmly and all was peace and tranquillity.

All through the morning, Lizzie had been fighting the fear that in helping Amanda Crowbridge she had unwittingly earned Martin's disapproval. She had no idea why his approval mattered so much to her, but with the single-mindedness of youth, was only aware that it did. "Wh...what did you wish to tell me?"

Martin schooled his face into stern lines, much as he would when bawling out a young lieutenant for some silly but understandable folly. He took Lizzie's hand in his, his strong fingers moving comfortingly over her slight ones. "Lizzie, this scheme of yours, m'dear. It really was most unwise." Martin kept his eyes on her slim fingers. "I suppose Caroline told you how close-run the thing was. If she hadn't arrived in the nick of time, Max and Hugo would have been off and there would have been no way to catch them. And the devil to pay when they came up with Keighly."

A stifled sob brought his eyes to her, but she had averted her face. "Lizzie?" No lieutenant he had ever had to speak to had sobbed. Martin abruptly dropped his stance of stern mentor and gathered Lizzie into his arms. "Oh, sweetheart. Don't cry. I didn't mean to upset you. Well, yes, I did. Just a bit. You upset me the devil of a lot when I thought you had run off with Keighly."

Lizzie had muffled her face in his coat but she looked up at that. "You thought... But whyever did you think such a silly thing?"

Martin flushed slightly. "Well, yes. I know it was silly. But it was just the way it all came out. At one stage, we weren't sure who had gone in that blasted coach." He paused for a moment, then continued in more serious vein. "But, really, sweetheart, you mustn't start up these schemes to help people. Not when they involve sailing so close to the wind. You'll set all sorts of people's backs up, if ever they knew."

Rather better acquainted with Lizzie than his brother was, Martin had no doubt at all whose impulse had started the whole affair. It might have been Arabella who had carried out most of the actions and

Sarah who had worked out the details, but it was his own sweet Lizzie who had set the ball rolling.

Lizzie was hanging her head in contrition, her fingers idly playing with his coat buttons. Martin tightened his arms about her until she looked up. "Lizzie, I want you to promise me that if you ever get any more of these helpful ideas you'll immediately come and tell me about them, before you do anything at all. Promise?"

Lizzie's downcast face cleared and a smile like the sun lit her eyes. "Oh, yes. That will be safer." Then, a thought struck her and her face clouded again. "But you might not be about. You'll...well, now your wound is healed, you'll be getting about more. Meeting lots of l-ladies and...things."

"Things?" said Martin, struggling to keep a straight face. "What things?"

"Well, you know. The sort of things you do. With l-ladies." At Martin's hoot of laughter, she set her lips firmly and doggedly went on. "Besides, you might marry and your wife wouldn't like it if I was hanging on your sleeve." There, she had said it. Her worst fear had been brought into the light.

But, instead of reassuring her that all would, somehow, be well, Martin was in stitches. She glared at him. When that had no effect, she thumped him hard on his chest.

Gasping for breath, Martin caught her small fists and then a slow grin, very like his brother's, broke across his face as he looked into her delightfully enraged countenance. He waited to see the confusion show in her fine eyes before drawing her hands up, pulling her hard against him and kissing her.

Lizzie had thought he had taught her all about kissing, but this was something quite different. She felt his arms lock like a vice about her waist, not that she had any intention of struggling. And the kiss went on and on. When she finally emerged, flushed, her eyes sparkling, all she could do was gasp and stare at him.

Martin uttered a laugh that was halfway to a groan. "Oh, Lizzie! Sweet Lizzie. For God's sake, say you'll marry me and put me out of my misery."

Her eyes grew round. "Marry you?" The words came out as a squeak.

Martin's grin grew broader. "Mmm. I thought it might be a good idea." His eyes dropped from her face to the lace edging that lay over her breasts. "Aside from ensuring I'll always be there for you to discuss your hare-brained schemes with," he continued conversationally, "I could also teach you about all the things I do with l-ladies."

Lizzie's eyes widened as far as they possibly could.

Martin grinned devilishly. "Would you like that Lizzie?"

Mutely, Lizzie nodded. Then, quite suddenly, she found her voice. "Oh, yes!" She flung her arms about Martin's neck and kissed him ferociously. Emerging from her wild embrace, Martin threw back his head and laughed. Lizzie did not, however, confuse this with rejection. She waited patiently for him to recover.

But, "Lizzie, oh Lizzie. What a delight you are!" was all Martin Rotherbridge said, before gathering her more firmly into his arms to explore her delights more thoroughly.

A considerable time later, when Martin had called a halt to their mutual exploration on the grounds that there were probably gardeners about, Lizzie sat comfortably in the circle of his arms, blissfully happy, and turned her thought to the future. "When shall we marry?" she asked.

Martin, adrift in another world, came back to earth and gave the matter due consideration. If he had been asked the same question two hours ago, he would have considered a few months sufficiently soon. Now, having spent those two hours with Lizzie in unfortunately restrictive surroundings, he rather thought a few days would be too long to wait. But presumably she would want a big wedding, with all the trimmings.

However, when questioned, Lizzie disclaimed all interest in wedding breakfasts and the like. Hesitantly, not sure how he would take the suggestion, she toyed with the pin in his cravat and said, "Actually, I wonder if it would be possible to be married quite soon. Tomorrow, even?"

Martin stared at her.

"I mean," Lizzie went on, "that there's bound to be quite a few weddings in the family—what with Arabella and Sarah."

"And Caroline," said Martin.

Lizzie looked her question.

"Max has taken Caroline off somewhere. I don't know where, but I'm quite sure why."

"Oh." Their recent occupation in mind, Lizzie

could certainly see how he had come to that conclusion. It was on the tip of her tongue to ask for further clarification of the possibilities Caroline might encounter, but her tenacious disposition suggested she settle the question of her own wedding first. "Yes, well, there you are. With all the fuss and bother, I suspect we'll be at the end of the list."

Martin looked much struck by her argument.

"But," Lizzie continued, sitting up as she warmed to her theme, "if we get married tomorrow, without any of the others knowing, then it'll be done and we shan't have to wait." In triumph, she turned to Martin.

Finding her eyes fixed on him enquiringly, Martin grinned. "Sweetheart, you put together a very convincing argument. So let's agree to be married tomorrow. Now that's settled, it seems to me you're in far too composed a state. From what I've learned, it would be safest for everyone if you were kept in a perpetual state of confusion. So come here, my sweet, and let me confuse you a little."

Lizzie giggled and, quite happily, gave herself up to delighted confusion.

The clink of crockery woke Caroline. She stretched languorously amid the soft cushions, the sensuous drift of the silken covers over her still tingling skin bringing back clear memories of the past hours. She was alone in the bed. Peering through the concealing silk canopy, she spied Max, tastefully clad in a long silk robe, watching a small dapper servant laying out dishes on the low tables on the other side of the room.

The light from the brass lamps suffused the scene with a soft glow. She wondered what the time was.

Lying back in the luxurious cushions, she pondered her state. Her final lesson had been in two parts. The first was concluded fairly soon after Max had joined her in the huge bed; the second, a much more lingering affair, had spun out the hours of the evening. In between, Max had, to her lasting shock, asked her to marry him. She had asked him to repeat his request three times, after which he had refused to do it again, saying she had no choice in the matter anyway as she was hopelessly compromised. He had then turned his attention to compromising her even further. As she had no wish to argue the point, she had meekly gone along with his evident desire to examine her responses to him in even greater depth than he had hitherto, a proceeding which had greatly contributed to their mutual content. She was, she feared, fast becoming addicted to Max's particular expertise; there were, she had discovered, certain benefits attached to going to bed with rakes.

She heard the door shut and Max's tread cross the floor. The silk curtains were drawn back and he stood by the bed. His eyes found her pale body, covered only by the diaphanous silks, and travelled slowly from her legs all the way up until, finally, they reached her face, and he saw she was awake and distinctly amused. He grinned and held out a hand. "Come and eat. I'm ravenous."

It was on the tip of Caroline's tongue to ask what his appetite craved, but the look in his eyes suggested that might not be wise if she wished for any dinner.

She struggled to sit up and looked wildly around for her clothes. They had disappeared. She looked enquiringly at Max. He merely raised one black brow.

"I draw the line at sitting down to dinner with you clad only in silk gauze," Caroline stated.

With a laugh, Max reached behind him and lifted a pale blue silk wrap from a chair and handed it to her. She struggled into it and accepted his hand to help her from the depths of the cushioned dais.

The meal was well cooked and delicious. Max contrived to turn eating into a sensual experience of a different sort and Caroline eagerly followed his lead. At the end of the repast, she was lying, relaxed and content, against his chest, surrounded by the inevitable cushions and sipping a glass of very fine chilled wine.

Max, equally content, settled one arm around her comfortably, then turned to a subject they had yet to broach. "When shall we be married?"

Caroline raised her brows. "I hadn't really thought that far ahead."

"Well, I suggest you do, for there are certain cavils to be met."

"Oh?"

"Yes," said Max. "Given that I left my brother, Darcy Hamilton and Hugo Denbigh about to pay their addresses to my three wards, I suspect we had better return to London tomorrow afternoon. Then, if you want a big wedding, I should warn you that the Rotherbridge family is huge and, as I am its head, will all expect to be invited."

Caroline was shaking her head. "Oh, I don't think

a big wedding would be at all wise. I mean, it looks as though the Twinning family will have a surfeit of weddings. But," she paused, "maybe your family will expect it?"

"I dare say they will, but they're quite used to me doing outrageous things. I should think they'll be happy enough that I'm marrying at all, let alone to someone as suitable as yourself, my love."

Suddenly, Caroline sat bolt upright. "Max! I just remembered. What's the time? They'll all be in a flurry because I haven't returned...."

But Max drew her back against his chest. "Hush. It's all taken care of. I left a note for Aunt Augusta. She knows you're with me and will not be returning until tomorrow."

"But...won't she be upset?"

"I should think she'll be dancing a jig." He grinned as she turned a puzzled face to him. "Haven't you worked out Aunt Augusta's grand plan yet?" Bemused, Caroline shook her head. "I suspect she had it in mind that I should marry you from the moment she first met you. That was why she was so insistent that I keep my wards. Initially, I rather think she hoped that by her throwing us forever together I would notice you." He chuckled. "Mind you, a man would have to be blind not to notice your charms at first sight, m'dear. By that first night at Almack's, I think she realized she didn't need to do anything further, just give me plenty of opportunity. She knows me rather well, you see, and knew that, despite my reputation, you were in no danger of being offered a *carte blanche* by me."

"I did wonder why she never warned me about you," admitted Caroline.

"But to return to the question of our marriage. If you wish to fight shy of a full society occasion, then it still remains to fix the date."

Caroline bent her mind to the task. Once they returned to London, she would doubtless be caught up in all the plans for her sisters' weddings, and, she supposed, her own would have to come first. But it would all take time. And meanwhile, she would be living in Twyford House, not Delmere House. The idea of returning to sleeping alone in her own bed did not appeal. The end of one slim finger tapping her lower lip, she asked, "How soon could we be married?"

"Tomorrow, if you wish." As she turned to stare at him again, Max continued. "Somewhere about here," he waved his arm to indicate the room, "lies a special licence. And our neighbour happens to be a retired bishop, a long-time friend of my late father's, who will be only too thrilled to officiate at my wedding. If you truly wish it, I'll ride over tomorrow morning and we can be married before luncheon, after which we had better get back to London. Does that programme meet with your approval?"

Caroline leaned forward and placed her glass on the table. Then she turned to Max, letting her hands slide under the edge of his robe. "Oh, yes," she purred. "Most definitely."

Max looked down at her, a glint in his eyes. "You, madam, are proving to be every bit as much a houri as I suspected."

Caroline smiled slowly. "And do you approve, my lord?"

"Most definitely," drawled Max as his lips found hers.

The Duke of Twyford returned to London the next afternoon, accompanied by his Duchess. They went directly to Twyford House, to find the entire household at sixes and sevens. They found Lady Benborough in the back parlour, reclining on the chaise, her wig askew, an expression of smug satisfaction on her face. At sight of them, she abruptly sat up, struggling to control the wig. "There you are! And about time, too!" Her shrewd blue eyes scanned their faces, noting the inner glow that lit Caroline's features and the contented satisfaction in her nephew's dark face. "What have you been up to?"

Max grinned wickedly and bent to kiss her cheek. "Securing my Duchess, as you correctly imagined."

"You've tied the knot already?" she asked in disbelief.

Caroline nodded. "It seemed most appropriate. That way, our wedding won't get in the way of the others."

"Humph!" snorted Augusta, disgruntled at missing the sight of her reprehensible nephew getting legshackled. She glared at Max.

His smile broadened. "Strange, I had thought you would be pleased to see us wed. Particularly considering your odd behaviour. Why, even Caro had begun to wonder why you never warned her about me, de-

spite the lengths to which I went to distract her mind
from such concerns.''

Augusta blushed. ''Yes, well,'' she began, slightly
flustered, then saw the twinkle in Max's eye. ''You
know very well I'm *aux anges* to see you married at
last, but I would have given my best wig to have seen
it!''

Caroline laughed. ''I do assure you we are truly
married. But where are the others?''

''And that's another thing!'' said Augusta, turning
to Max. ''The next time you set about creating a bor-
dello in a household I'm managing, at least have the
goodness to warn me beforehand! I come down after
my nap to find Arabella in Hugo Denbigh's lap. That
was bad enough, but the door to the morning-room
was locked. Sarah and Darcy Hamilton *eventually*
emerged, but only much later.'' She glared at Max
but was obviously having difficulty keeping her face
straight. ''Worst of all,'' she continued in a voice of
long suffering, ''Miriam went to look at the roses just
before sunset. Martin had apparently chosen the rose
garden to further his affair with Lizzie, don't ask me
why. It was an hour before Miriam's palpitations had
died down enough for her to go to bed. I've packed
her off to her sister's to recuperate. Really, Max,
you've had enough experience to have foreseen what
would happen.''

Both Max and Caroline were convulsed with laughter.

''Oh, dear,'' said Caroline when she could speak,
''I wonder what would have happened if she had

woken up on the way back from the Richardsons' ball?''

Augusta looked interested but, before she could request further information, the door opened and Sarah entered, followed by Darcy Hamilton. From their faces it was clear that all their troubles were behind them—Sarah looked radiant, Darcy simply looked besotted. The sisters greeted each other affectionately, then Sarah drew back and surveyed the heavy gold ring on Caroline's left hand. "Married already?"

"We thought to do you the favour of getting our marriage out of the way forthwith," drawled Max, releasing Darcy's hand. "So there's no impediment to your own nuptials."

Darcy and Sarah exchanged an odd look, then burst out laughing. "I'm afraid, dear boy," said Darcy, "that we've jumped the gun, too."

Sarah held out her left hand, on which glowed a slim gold band.

While the Duke and Duchess of Twyford and Lord and Lady Darcy exchanged congratulations all around, Lady Benborough looked on in disgust. "What I want to know," she said, when she could make herself heard once more, "is if I'm to be entirely done out of weddings, even after all my efforts to see you all in parson's mouse-trap?"

"Oh, there are still two Twinnings to go, so I wouldn't give up hope," returned her nephew, smiling down at her with transparent goodwill. "Apropos of which, has anyone seen the other two lately?"

No one had. When applied to, Millwade imparted the information that Lord Denbigh had called for Miss

Arabella just before two. They had departed in Lord Denbigh's carriage. Mr. Martin had dropped by for Miss Lizzie at closer to three. They had left in a hack.

"A hack?" queried Max.

Millwade merely nodded. Dismissed, he withdrew. Max was puzzled. "Where on earth could they have gone?"

As if in answer, voices were heard in the hall. But it was Arabella and Hugo who had returned. Arabella danced in, her curls bouncing, her big eyes alight with happiness. Hugo ambled in her wake, his grin suggesting that he suspected his good fortune was merely a dream and he would doubtless wake soon enough. Meanwhile, he was perfectly content with the way this particular dream was developing. Arabella flew to embrace Caroline and Sarah, then turned to the company at large and announced, "Guess what!"

A pregnant silence greeted her words, the Duke and his Duchess, the Lord and his Lady, all struck dumb by a sneaking suspicion. Almost unwillingly, Max voiced it. "You're married already?"

Arabella's face fell a little. "How did you guess?" she demanded.

"No!" moaned Augusta. "Max, see what happens when you leave town? I won't have it!"

But her words fell on deaf ears. Too blissfully happy themselves to deny their friends the same pleasures, the Duke and his Duchess were fully engaged in wishing the new Lady Denbigh and her Lord all manner of felicitations. And then, of course, there was their own news to hear, and that of the Hamiltons. The next ten minutes were filled with congratulations and good wishes.

Left much to herself, Lady Benborough sat in a corner of the chaise and watched the group with an indulgent eye. Truth to tell, she was not overly concerned with the absence of weddings. At her age, they constituted a definite trial. She smiled at the thought of the stories she would tell of the rapidity with which the three rakes before her had rushed their brides to the altar. Between them, they had nearly forty years of experience in evading parson's mouse-trap, yet, when the right lady had loomed on their horizon, they had found it expedient to wed her with all speed. She wondered whether that fact owed more to their frustrations or their experience.

Having been assured by Arabella that Martin had indeed proposed and been accepted, the Duke and Duchess allowed themselves to be distracted by the question of the immediate housing arrangements. Eventually, it was decided that, in the circumstances, it was perfectly appropriate that Sarah should move into Hamilton House immediately, and Arabella likewise to Denbigh House. Caroline, of course, would henceforth be found at Delmere House. Relieved to find their ex-guardian so accommodating, Sarah and Arabella were about to leave to attend to their necessary packing, when the door to the drawing-room opened.

Martin and Lizzie entered.

It was Max, his sharp eyes taking in the glow in Lizzie's face and the ridiculously proud look stamped across Martin's features, who correctly guessed their secret.

"Don't tell me!" he said, in a voice of long suffering. "You've got married, too?"

Needless to say, the Twyford House ball four days later was hardly flat. In fact, with four blushing brides, sternly watched over by their four handsome husbands, it was, as Max had prophesied, one of the highlights of the Season.

* * * * * *

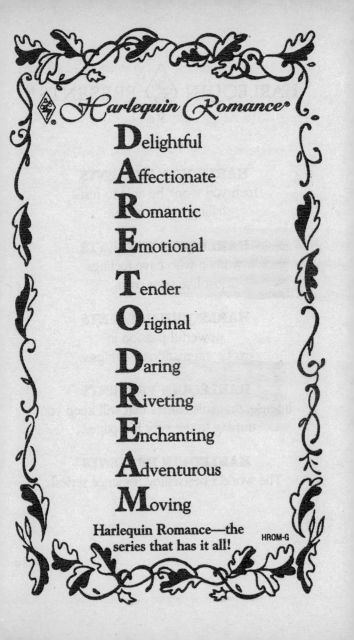

# *Harlequin Romance*®

**D**elightful

**A**ffectionate

**R**omantic

**E**motional

**T**ender

**O**riginal

**D**aring

**R**iveting

**E**nchanting

**A**dventurous

**M**oving

**Harlequin Romance—the
series that has it all!**

HROM-G

# HARLEQUIN  PRESENTS®

**HARLEQUIN PRESENTS**
men you won't be able to resist
falling in love with...

**HARLEQUIN PRESENTS**
women who have feelings
just like your own...

**HARLEQUIN PRESENTS**
powerful passion in
exotic international settings...

**HARLEQUIN PRESENTS**
intense, dramatic stories that will keep you
turning to the very last page...

**HARLEQUIN PRESENTS**
The world's bestselling romance series!

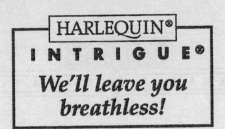

# INTRIGUE®

## *We'll leave you breathless!*

If you've been looking for thrilling tales of
contemporary passion and sensuous love stories
with taut, edge-of-the-seat suspense—
then you'll *love* Harlequin Intrigue!

Every month, you'll meet four new heroes
who are guaranteed to make your spine tingle
and your pulse pound. With them you'll enter
into the exciting world of Harlequin Intrigue—
where your life is on the line
and so is your heart!

## THAT'S INTRIGUE—DYNAMIC ROMANCE AT ITS BEST!

HARLEQUIN®

# INTRIGUE®

# HARLEQUIN®
# AMERICAN ◆ ROMANCE®

## LOOK FOR OUR FOUR FABULOUS MEN!

Each month some of today's bestselling authors bring
four new fabulous men to Harlequin American Romance.
Whether they're rebel ranchers, millionaire power brokers
or sexy single dads, they're all gallant princes—and
they're all ready to sweep you into lighthearted fantasies
and contemporary fairy tales where anything is possible
and where all your dreams come true!

You don't even have to make a wish...
Harlequin American Romance will grant your every desire!

Look for Harlequin American Romance
wherever Harlequin books are sold!

# S HARLEQUIN SUPERROMANCE®

## ...there's more to the story!

Superromance. A *big* satisfying read about unforget-
table characters. Each month we offer
*four* very different stories that range from family
drama to adventure and mystery, from highly emotional stories to romantic comedies—and
much more! Stories about people you'll
believe in and care about. Stories too
compelling to put down....

Our authors are among today's *best* romance writ-
ers. You'll find familiar names and
talented newcomers. Many of them are
award winners—and you'll see why!

If you want the biggest and best
in romance fiction, you'll get it
from Superromance!

Available wherever Harlequin books are sold.